THE SILENCE OF SEVERANCE

A DCI YORKE THRILLER

WES MARKIN

ALSO BY WES MARKIN

A Lesson in Crime

One Last Prayer for the Rays

The Repenting Serpent

Details of how to claim your **FREE**

DCI Michael Yorke quick read, ***A Lesson in Crime***,

can be found at the end of the book.

Text copyright © 2019 Wes Markin

First published 2019

ISBN: 9781687529435

Imprint: Independently published

Edited by Jenny Cook and Jo Fletcher

Cover design by The Cover Collection

For Marjorie

11:02 A.M.

HANDSOME, HE THOUGHT as he looked in the mirror.

Or so he'd always been told. First, by his mother, and then by the many men, and women, he'd shared himself with over the years.

'Dashing like Robert Pattinson,' a previous lover had said.

But that was long ago, he thought, drawing a horizontal line under his nose in the reflection, and separating his face into two halves.

Top and bottom ... before and after ... then and now ... handsome and ugly.

He leaned in and pressed his forehead against the cold glass.

You shouldn't be doing this. Not now. The time of acceptance has long passed. Dwelling can be compelling but depressing.

Dwelling can be compelling but depressing, he repeated in his mind.

Then, he lifted his head from the glass, and looked at his face again.

You've worked so hard to heal and you've found some satisfaction. You should be proud of what you have achieved.

He looked at his watch and saw that it was almost time. An important day lay ahead. An important time. He wondered if he would ever return to this mirror. After all, anything could go wrong from this point on.

Before he left, he turned to look at the room.

He could see: the damp on the walls; the rust on the old bikes with bent wheels; the flies jigging around the spluttering light bulb; the shit-stained rat holes; and the young woman sealed in the plastic coffin at his feet.

ST AGATHA'S CHURCH, SALISBURY.
1:05 P.M.

THROUGH THE STAINED-GLASS window, the light was diced and then blended, forming a simmering stew of colour around Marie Holt. As they turned to face the aisle, she looked at her father.

He smiled and said, 'I love you.'

She smiled back and repeated his words.

'Shall we?' He said, offering his arm.

Despite the wedding music, Marie could hear her father's cane banging against the stone flags. She didn't mind it. He'd used it for as long as she could remember, and she associated it with a calm and reassuring presence that had nurtured her into the woman she now was.

And this is what you've always wanted, she thought, *ever since you were five and you married off all of your dolls and teddies in one explosive ceremony...*

Facing down the aisle, she quickly became aware that something was wrong.

She couldn't see Ryan. Her eyes darted between the best man, Andy, and the two groomsmen.

Where was he?

She squeezed her father's arm so tightly that he gasped. She looked at her guests, who seemed oblivious to the missing groom. She noted that they were split into two brain-like hemispheres, throbbing, and ready to explode with joy. Her eyes rose to a life-sized model of *Jesus Christ* staring down from above the altar. Blood oozed from His wounded hands.

'It's fine,' her father whispered into her ear. 'You're beautiful.'

But it wasn't fine was it?

As she moved further down the aisle, her eyes scanned the east wall. Saint Agatha, to whom the church was dedicated, was portrayed in a stained-glass window. She sat in a brothel, praying and *giving* herself to God despite the barbaric acts she endured. Breathing more quickly now, Marie's eyes flew to a mural in the church's South Chapel depicting Agatha carrying her severed breasts on a plate.

Halfway down the aisle, she stopped and said, 'He's not here.'

'I'm sure there's a reason,' her father said.

Andy was staring at her from the front. He looked confused, apologetic even. Ryan wasn't here then ... had she been jilted?

Here was her shame. Her breasts on a platter.

The music stopped and she stared at the organ pipes above the altar, suddenly severed from the whole. The guests, who'd accompanied them so far on their magical journey, began a nervous chatter. This was not the happy ending they'd expected.

'Where's Ryan?' Marie said. Tears stung her eyes,

making the murals around the room melt. 'Where's Ryan?' This time louder so everyone in the church could hear.

The church door opened, and she turned quickly, silently praying that Ryan was there, flying in with his shirt untucked, his hair dishevelled, wearing a look of desperate apology.

Nothing. Just a heavy burst of wind, spearing the church. She felt all the warmth, and her last dregs of hope seep out of the punctured building.

She heard the clatter of her father's cane against the stone flags as he dropped it to draw her in close.

She felt the congregation's eyes on her.

Breasts on a platter.

'I don't believe it,' she said and tasted the tears running into the corners of her mouth.

Andy jogged up towards her. His buttonhole, a red fabric rose, came loose and fluttered to the ground.

'Where's Ryan?' she said again, pulling away from her father.

'I haven't seen him for ten minutes,' Andy said.

Whispers came from her family on the left. She identified her imposing uncle's growl and a hiss from her blunt, high-flying lawyer sister. The blame game had started. They'd be looking across to the groom's family right now — sizing them up.

She stared down at the purple orchids gripping the carved-wooden ends of the pews. They didn't look as fresh as they had done when she chose them. 'Where did he go?'

'I really don't know,' Andy said.

She then noticed something peculiar at the pulpit. *Very peculiar.* 'Look at the priest.'

Andy turned to observe the priest, and then turned back.

'Yes, that's odd. It's not the one from the rehearsal yesterday.'

'No,' Marie said, shaking her head. 'Where's Father Simon?'

'Maybe he's sick?'

A thud shook the church.

Her father grabbed her arm. 'What the—'

Another thud.

Marie put her hand to her mouth. Andy turned again to look for the source of the alien sound.

Thud-thud-thud.

It was coming from the door of the South Chapel, located just in front of the altar and the Chancel.

Thud-thud-thud.

Someone desperately wanted to be out of there.

'Ryan?' Marie said, launching forward. Her father yanked her back by her arm, almost taking her off her feet, but instead taking her into the side of a pew. An orchid was crushed under her weight. The congregation gasped as one.

Thud-thud-thud.

'Let me go!' Marie said, wrenching her arm free. Ahead, she saw that Andy had almost reached the South Chapel door.

Racing down the aisle, she noticed the mysterious priest staring at her from the pulpit. Why was he not rushing to the chapel with Andy and some of the other guests? Her blood ran cold when she saw a large smile spread across his face.

She sensed movement all around her now that the thudding had become more desperate. Guests had exited the pews and gathered in the aisle. She ignored the priest, keeping her eyes firmly on the chapel. Andy was pulling at the door while the person continued to assault it from the inside.

Then, from the corner of her eye, she noticed a glimmer. The priest leaned over and presented her with an antique skeleton key. He nodded when she took it. He was much younger than Father Simon, and his small eyes seemed sad, despite the smile.

Hoisting up her wedding dress, she marched to the chapel, brushed aside Andy, whose face was red and sweating from his desperate tugs, and thrust the key into the lock. It was stiff, but eventually the key turned. The knocking immediately ceased. She took a step back as the church grew silent.

Marie held her breath, listening for sounds in the silence. *Nothing.* She reached out for the handle—

The door swung open and Ryan burst from the chapel. Everyone gasped.

He was hunched over, out of breath from trying to break his way out.

Andy darted forward and grabbed his best friend's shoulder. 'Ryan, thank God, thank God, what happened?'

Ryan reached up to grip Andy's shoulder with a blood-stained hand.

Marie looked back at the priest, who watched with his sad eyes. *'What have you done?'*

She turned back to see Ryan standing upright now and looking towards her. At least, he *seemed* to be looking at her; there was a vacancy in the eyes of her intended. She stifled a scream when she noticed that his beard and cravat were covered in blood. Beside her, Andy stumbled back with his hand to his mouth.

Ryan staggered towards Marie. Despite her fear, she forced herself to stand before him. Whatever the reason for the vacancy on his face, the blood on his cravat, she would not abandon him. She would not fail him. She felt her father's arm loop around her, and it helped keep her steady.

'Ryan, I'm here. Talk to me,' she said.

His suit was scuffed all over. His hair was dishevelled. He moved listlessly, as if there was now more blood in his beard and down his front than there actually was in his veins.

'For Christ's sake, get an ambulance!' her father called to the crowd.

Ryan stepped forward, opened his bloody palms and pressed them against her chest. She put her hands against his elbows to steady him, but he slumped forward, and slid down her body, until his hands rested on her thighs. She stared down at the two long red lines he'd drawn down her wedding dress.

She glanced at her father, trembling, feeling like a child now, in need of his guidance, but he didn't have the answer. From the corner of her eye, she again saw the smirking priest.

She looked down at Ryan. Tears ran down her face and dripped onto his forehead.

He tilted his head back to look at her, but that same empty expression persisted. Blood oozed from the corners of his mouth and dripped from his beard.

His mouth fell open and more blood gushed out onto her dress. She stared into the liquid blackness and saw something wriggle. It reminded her of a sandworm trying to burrow itself to the surface before—

What was left of Ryan's tongue burst free and swayed in the air. She backed away, gagging and, when the remains of his tongue fell back into his throat, she vomited.

Then, Detective Constable Ryan Simmonds began to moan.

And it echoed in the silence.

1

D ETECTIVE CHIEF INSPECTOR Michael Yorke was now a married man, and he was desperately happy.

Yet, as the confetti tumbled down around him, breaking the world up into a colourful kaleidoscope, he couldn't help but think of his mother and his sister; two people he had loved and hated in equal measure, and so desperately missed. They would have enjoyed today. They *deserved* to be here today.

Then, the cheers and a burst of intense sunlight brought him back to the moment, and he pulled Patricia Yorke close to his side. She looked striking in her unconventional wedding dress, a gorgeous emerald green, which worked perfectly with her red hair. He kissed her. A long kiss in public. Perfectly acceptable on your wedding day.

His hand fell to her stomach and he let the back of his fingers brush against their unborn child. Seven months. Gender unknown.

Best man, Detective Sergeant Jake Pettman, a big,

hulking figure, cut them off. 'Didn't think you were getting away that easy did you, Mike?' He emptied a bucket of confetti over Yorke's head.

'Good job that there isn't much hair left for it to stick to!' He heard Detective Inspector Emma Gardener say at his side. He also heard DI Mark Topham's raucous laugh.

The crowd cheered and Yorke kissed Patricia again.

AFTER DINNER, Yorke delivered his well-rehearsed speech. He reeled off a few jokes that had been lifted from a website dedicated to first-time public speakers. Yorke was anything but a first-time public speaker. He'd proven very efficient at it, as his high rank would suggest, but then, this was a very different context. Making people laugh had never really been his forte. Encouragement, reassurance, and just plain, old-fashioned man management, were more his thing. He glanced at Patricia on numerous occasions who nodded him along. She'd heard the speech a multitude of times, and although he sounded wooden, at least he didn't put a foot wrong. After praising Patricia for several minutes on her intelligence, beauty and drive to succeed in her role as a Divisional Surgeon, he said, 'And now we get to the part of the speech which hasn't been checked and edited by my beloved wife...'

Cue laughter. Yorke wondered if it was real or alcohol-induced, and then wondered if this really mattered. Weddings were all about conventions, weren't they?

'I just wanted to say a *hello* to my mother, Paige, and my older sister, Danielle. Neither of whom could be here today but are forever in our thoughts.' He paused, forcing back the tears. He held up his champagne glass. 'So, join me in a toast to absent friends...'

As they drank, Yorke noticed that Topham's boyfriend, Neil, was sitting alone. He realised that he'd not seen Topham in a while. Yorke glanced over at Gardner, who was also watching Neil drink alone, clearly with the same curiosity as him.

'So,' Jake said, rising to his feet, 'it seems Mike has treated us to quite a lavish event today which does beggar belief as I've never seen him open his wallet; in fact, I never even knew he had one until I saw it being fumigated by pest control for a moth infestation...'

More laughter. Yorke joined in this time.

Jake's speech continued just as savagely as it'd begun. 'And when he ran that marathon, we all marvelled at that wonderful time. Little did we realise that Mike was simply chasing the man in front of him because he had a Morrison's 10% off voucher stuck to the sole of his shoe...'

The laughter became more raucous. Yorke wondered why he had decided to make Jake his best man. He smiled at Patricia, and she smiled back, no doubt thinking the same thing.

While the speech continued, he became more and more concerned about Topham's absence. He glanced over at Gardner and saw that she was looking anxious too. She kept checking her phone under the table and clearly wasn't paying attention to the speeches.

'And then, finally, someone who could stomach the domi-nating workaholic emerged from the darkness...'

Darkness being the appropriate word, thought Yorke. Yorke had met Patricia while she was poring over a murder victim.

'Myself and Sheila, the light of my life,' Jake looked down at his long-suffering wife, and they both shared a rare tender moment. 'Have now got the perfect couple to spend an evening with. It wouldn't be New Year without them anymore. I even get to see Mike with a couple of drinks in him – which is interesting. As I'm sure you'll find out later ... did you know we have a keg of *Summer Lightning* behind the bar?'

'We know, Jake, it's all you've been talking about all week!' heckled one of the guests from the back.

After reeling off Patricia's qualities, of which they were many, Jake paused for a moment before turning back to Yorke.

'And now it's time to get serious for a moment. Through ten years of being friends, we've seen some tough times and, although Mike isn't always the first one to crack a joke, he's always the first one to put an arm around your shoulder and pick you up when you are down, and I'm sure it's the same for many people around this table. I have never met a man so driven for justice, and with such a desire to make things right. There is no one else you would rather have on your side. He has a heart of gold ... he keeps it in a safe under his bed, but he does have one.'

Waiting for the laughter to subside, Jake paused to take a mouthful from his pint.

'Finally, I would also like to raise a toast to our absent friends, Iain and Jessica Brookes, who will forever be in all of our hearts and will certainly be looking down on us at this point.'

Yorke released a few tears. He felt Patricia's grip on his hand tighten. He looked to the front table where their adopted son, Ewan Brookes, sat alongside Gardner and her family. He too had tears in his eyes but he offered Yorke and Patricia a smile despite the anguish. It'd only been seven months since he'd lost his parents in so savage a manner.

What a brave boy, thought Yorke. *What a brave, wonderful boy.*

'And remember,' Jake continued, 'Iron Mike will shake off his rugged, icy veneer this evening and take to the stage with his guitar with some of his University mates. What was the band called, Mike?'

'Heist.'

'Well, see Mike as you've never seen him before, and never will again, playing indie classics with Heist later this evening. So all that remains is to ask you to be upstanding for the toast, wishing them a life together filled with laughter and happiness, to the bride and groom...'

As Yorke drank his champagne, he surveyed his guests again.

Topham was still nowhere to be seen.

DI Mark Topham parked on double-yellow lines, threw a police-business sign on the dashboard and exited his vehicle. At a steady pace, on a day topping thirty-five degrees, he sweated his way past an ambulance and the black major incidents van which was only just parking up. He looked at the ambulance again and acknowledged it was on standby for emergencies. DC Ryan Simmonds, the victim, had already been rushed to hospital almost an hour ago.

With most of his tongue missing.

At least that is what he'd learned from DC Collette Willows' emergency call-to-arms. She'd apologised for hitting him up for early response on his day off. He'd told her not to worry about it; there was no such thing as a 'day off' when the victim was one of your own.

He nodded at two uniforms. They nodded back, keeping their fingers hooked in their duty belts, looking official. They were trying to tame the restless wedding guests.

Shirts hung loose from the men around him, while hats became crushed beyond recognition in clenched female fists. Under the hot sun, steam warped the air above the small crowd and reminded Topham of a summer-cooked audience at a festival gig.

While weaving through the throbbing crowd, he stared up at the simple, stone church. Above the western door, in a niche, was a statue of St Agatha. A woman tortured by man, but also a woman who found comfort in her unwavering faith. Her face was sculpted to show the two contrasting emotions. It wasn't the most popular church in Salisbury, and Topham wondered if it was down to Agatha's conflicted expression and the sense of unease you felt in her presence.

At the open door of St Agatha's, he realised that he too had sweated excessively. He peeled off the jacket of the new black suit he'd purchased especially for Yorke's wedding.

As he crossed the threshold to confront whatever monstrosity had taken place this day, an old Shakespearian quotation memorised during his school days reared in his consciousness.

For now, these hot days, is the mad blood stirring.

Inside, he was surprised by the sudden drop in temperature. As a gay man, he'd not had much cause to go to church these last few years. He was sure, in this modern age, he would be more than welcome, but still, historically, to say that the church had never really been supportive of homosexuality would be an understatement. Even today, Yorke's wedding had been conducted by a registrar in a cosy country club, and so Topham had no immediate experience of these stone, archaic dominions.

PC Sean Tyler emerged from the shadows and immediately started scribbling his superior's name in the logbook. 'Hello sir, how's DCI Yorke's wedding?'

'Well, I wouldn't really know, Sean, as I'm here.'

'Oh yeah ... sorry.'

'It started well, anyway,' Topham said, taking the overshoes and bagged-up suit from Tyler's outstretched hand. He covered himself to protect the fresh crime scene for the SOCOs who were waiting outside like hawks in the treetops.

'Always cold in churches,' Willows said, approaching.

Topham nodded, thinking that he would just have to take her word on that.

She patted his stomach. 'Sir! Not up to your usual standard!'

Topham, usually complimented on his enviable physique and good looks, glanced down at his waistline. His shirt buttons did, indeed, look strained. He didn't appreciate the joke, but ran with it anyway. 'Been too busy for sit-ups.'

She smiled. She was trying to keep the conversation light but was obviously shaken up. She and Tyler were first responders at a crime scene. Their responsibilities were huge, and not just with logging. They had to assess and protect the scene without interference.

Additionally, she knew the victim, Ryan Simmonds - not incredibly well because they were based in different stations around Wiltshire - but well enough.

She looked down. 'I just heard from the hospital, Ryan is not out of the woods yet. He's lost a lot of blood.'

'Can they reattach it? His tongue?'

'Sorry ... sir, I thought I'd explained that to you. It's not been recovered. There's a lot of blood, but no tongue.'

'Shit,' Topham said. 'This is far too surreal for me to make any sense of at the moment.'

She gestured with a flick of her head at an elderly man and a younger woman on the back pew just behind her.

'Marie Holt who was about to become Marie Simmonds. She is with her father, Jason Holt.'

Topham looked over again. Marie was burying her head into her father's chest and sobbing.

'I was going to give her a couple more minutes with her father and then take her out to the ambulance,' Willows said. 'She needs to be treated for shock. I was hoping the uniforms could clear the masses before she left.'

'No such luck at the moment,' Topham said. 'They're lingering. Probably think they can do some good. As soon as you've run me through everything, you should head back out and instruct them all to return home. The press will be here shortly, no doubt, so the last thing we want is a crowd.'

'Okay,' Willows said and led him to the police tape strung up between the final two pews, explaining what Marie had witnessed as she walked down the aisle. Along the way, Topham glanced up at the sculpture of *Jesus Christ* hanging from a concentric arch; he wondered what the messiah would think of the events that had recently transpired here.

Willows explained the incident with the smiling priest and Topham stopped in his tracks. 'So, you are telling me that the person responsible for all this depravity was here?'

Willows nodded.

'Standing right *there*?' Topham pointed at a pulpit draped in purple velvet.

'Yes. Exactly as Marie and Jason Holt described it to me.' She threw open her notebook and scanned her scribblings. 'Much younger than the priest that was going to marry them ... Father Simon was in his sixties ... this one was in his late twenties ... do they start that young? ... anyway, he was rather handsome ... Marie said he had a smile that seemed to pierce you, although she didn't specify whether that was in a good or a bad—'

'And he was standing right there?'

'Yes, and—'

'*So where is he?*'

Willows shrugged. 'Marie and Jason don't know. They were tending to Ryan while they waited for the ambulance. They assumed he'd upped and left.'

Another two officers were being logged in at the door by Tyler. Topham summoned them over. 'Listen, carefully.'

They immediately threw their shoulders back and stood up straight, looking purposeful. Being tasked by superior officers at a crime scene was obviously still new and exciting.

'I want you to escort Marie and Jason Holt outside. Tell them they need some fresh air. I want you to ask them if the priest who was going to marry them today is present in that wedding crowd, plain clothed or otherwise. Not the original priest ...' he looked over at Willows.

'Father Simon,' Willows said.

'Not Father Simon ... the stand-in priest.'

'And if we see him?' One of the young officers said.

Topham paused to consider and then went with his gut. 'Arrest him.'

'Okay sir,' the other officer said. Her eyes widened; the assignment had given her day a real purpose.

Topham and Willows watched the officers escort father and daughter out of the church past a growing group of white-suited SOCOs; then, they continued their journey down the aisle to the pulpit.

Willows looked at her notes again. 'It was here that the smiling priest handed Marie a key.'

Topham flashed her a confused look. Willows pointed at a chapel several metres away.

'Where Simmonds came out?' Topham said.

'Yes. After she unlocked it for him. Before that, Jason Holt said it sounded like there was a small elephant in there.'

'I'm not surprised,' Topham said, feeling his heart flutter in his chest, 'after being mutilated in that way.'

Willows nodded, keeping her head held high, and eyes wide, desperate to deliver a carefree attitude. The tremble in her eyelids and lips betrayed her veneer.

Topham's eyes fell on the flagstones ahead. There had been enough bloodshed to turn the cracks in the stones to blackened veins. For a moment, in his mind's eye, he saw the groom on his knees displaying the inside of his destroyed mouth to his bride-to-be. This time his heart beat like the wings of a raven.

'Let's not go any further. Let forensics work the immediate area. Around the chapel, this pulpit,' he gestured down at the floor. 'There's so much fucking blood. Is he going to be okay?'

'I don't know, sir.'

'Did you try the rectory for the priest? Either of them?'

'Yes. Neither were there.'

Topham surveyed the scene and his eyes fell to a small

door to the left at him, adjacent to the end of the front pew. *A convenient exit,* Topham thought, *merely strides from the pulpit.* He pointed it out to Willows and asked where it went.

'I haven't been here that much longer than you, sir. The church garden, perhaps? The graveyard?'

'Wait here,' Topham said and headed for the door.

Along the way, he glanced down at the order of service. A little pink booklet with a picture of Ryan and Marie preparing to commit their lives to one another. He thought of Neil for a moment and considered the civil service they'd been giving a lot of air time to in their conversations of late. Admittedly, it was an inappropriate time for him to be considering this, but given the context of this evolving situation, he could probably be forgiven for being reminded of it.

He stood at the door which had been left ajar and trembled slightly in a breeze. On exiting, he felt the sudden transition from cold to hot again. He felt as if he was stepping into something burning. Now that he was buried in his white over suit, he would have to wilt for a few moments.

Willows had called it right. A graveyard. An orderly, well-dressed graveyard. Mowed grass and unbroken gravestones in parallel lines. Interlocking yew trees shaded the eternal sleepers. It seemed strange to renovate graveyards, but that surely must have been the case. He thought of the graveyard attached to his Church of England primary school as a kid – a terrifying place with smashed gravestones, balding ground and dead animals.

Earlier, it had rained briefly, so when he left the flagged path to wander through the graveyard, he slowed down to avoid slipping. He welcomed the shade offered by the yew trees, and turned around the furthest one to face the other side of the graveyard.

There was a man, dressed in white, kneeling on a grave.

A *young* priest.

YORKE SHOWED many of his colleagues something they didn't yet know about him. That he knew how to rock and roll.

At least that's what Patricia had assured him would be the effect of his band's revival. Now, he wasn't so sure. Do people really enjoy watching a man in his forties sweat over a string instrument? At least he wasn't singing. He'd left that unforgiving chore to Nigel, an old friend from his university days, who was currently staging his best Liam Gallagher impression over *Rock n Roll Star*.

Fortunately, when he descended from the stage, re-tucking his sodden white shirt, Jake was waiting for him with a pint of his favourite beer.

'Extra cold, how you like it,' Jake said. 'I had it put in the freezer just before you went on stage. Special, that was, by the way. Well done for having the guts.'

'Did you like it then?' Yorke said, taking the pint off his best man.

'I said it was *special*. Let's leave it there.'

'You're a dickhead, do you know that?'

Jake laughed and said, 'Yes, I am, but out of all the dick-heads you know, I am the only one who is nice to you.'

'Bloody hell. Where does that leave me then?' He said and took a large mouthful of beer.

'Needing that drink,' Jake said, smiling.

Gardner came up alongside them and said, 'Nice one, Mike. I even managed a dance when you played the *Stone Roses*.'

'It was good then?' Yorke asked her with an eyebrow raised.

'Well ... it was better than I could do.'

'Don't you bloody start!'

He noticed Patricia was in the distance, talking to a group of friends, so it was a good opportunity to raise his concerns over Topham. 'Now, I want the truth. No bullshit. I'm still the boss, even on a day off.'

Yorke and Gardner nodded.

'Where did Mark go?'

They both spoke at the same time. Jake said, 'Family emergency.' Gardner said, 'Felt unwell.'

Yorke rolled his eyes. 'So, we opted for bullshit then?' He watched his colleagues exchange glances. 'Emma, speak.'

Gardner threw back the remainder of her wine, cleared her throat, and said, 'Operation Autumn. That's why we didn't want to say anything. You're on your honeymoon tomorrow.'

'You found her?' Yorke said, unable to force back a slight tremble in his voice.

'No,' Gardner said, 'just acting on a lead—'

'Which we are not going to be telling you about,' Jake said. 'Two weeks in South Africa. That is all you should be thinking about.'

'It's hard not to think about a missing seventeen-year-old girl.'

'Susie Long is our concern now, Mike,' Gardner said, '*ours*. You need this time off. You have done a fantastic job of delegating it out over the last 48 hours. You cannot keep cancelling holidays ... and especially not this one.'

'Give me a clue as to what the lead is?'

'No,' Gardner said.

Yorke noticed Patricia coming his way. 'Yes, you're right. Not now.'

Minutes later, Yorke was back on stage with an acoustic guitar, providing the rhythm for Radiohead's *Fake Plastic Trees*. During the final verse, while he struck the strings, and Nigel's voice reached an incredible crescendo despite his forty years, Yorke realised something.

So often, before now, it had always been about others.

But his time was right now. And he deserved it. And it felt good.

‘HELLO?' Topham said, approaching the kneeling priest. There was no reply. So, he tried again. Louder. This time, he wouldn't just be heard back in the graveyard, he would also be heard back in the church.

Still no response.

He wiped sweat from his forehead and moved closer to the priest. 'Excuse me father?'

The furthest reaches of the graveyard were older and deteriorating. Gravestones were weathered and inscriptions were becoming unreadable. Grass was yellowing; dandelions crested stones steps, while weeds fractured the foundations.

Clouds started to thicken overhead.

With his pulse racing, he paused and glanced over his shoulder. No Collette. No back-up. He looked back at the kneeling priest. *What if he was dangerous? What if he had a weapon?*

He thought of his partner, Neil, who, the previous evening, had started to make noises about the risk involved in Topham's job. Noises he'd never made before. However, he guessed that three years into a relationship, such noises were to be expected.

A metre from the priest, Topham asked again. 'Excuse me father?'

The priest tilted his head back and moaned. The long moan fluctuated in pitch, suggesting that he was opening and closing his mouth at the same time.

Concerned for his well-being, he stepped forward and put a hand on the priest's shoulder. The priest stopped the horrendous noise, lowered his head and turned the top half of his body around so he could look up at Topham.

He was early twenties at a push. His lank, sweaty hair was pasted to his forehead.

'My name is Detective Inspector Topham. Are you aware of what has happened in the church today?'

The priest held out a hand. Topham took it and helped him to his feet. The priest turned as he rose and so was able to take Topham's other hand.

Topham felt something squishy and wet being forced into his palm. He backed away, gagging, looking down at a lump of bloodied flesh in his hand.

Ryan's tongue...

Topham let it tumble to the ground and stumbled away from the smiling priest.

2

CHOOSING TO IGNORE the modern convention of waving a smartphone in the air to film the entire moment, Jake and Gardner were content to simply watch and enjoy their boss slow-dance with Patricia to *Angels* by Robbie Williams.

Jake leaned over and whispered in Gardner's ear, 'Actually, maybe we should film it? You know, he *almost* looks happy. We may need it as evidence in the future—'

Gardner elbowed him in the side. 'I'm missing it.'

Jake smiled.

After the dance ended, and the DJ turned the sentimental atmosphere on its head with *A-ha*, Jake and Gardner wandered over to the bar. Along the way, Ewan Brookes, Yorke's adopted son, strayed across their path. Jake ruffled his hair, and put him into a gentle headlock.

'Uncle Jake!' Ewan said.

'I caught you looking,' Jake said, releasing him and pointing out a girl, no older than thirteen, swaying alone at the edge of the dance floor. 'Go and ask her to dance.'

'I wasn't looking!'

'Go and ask her what she's drinking, and then come and tell me.'

Ewan went bright red.

'Leave him alone, Jake!' Gardner pulled him back by the shoulder.

Jake winked at Ewan as they continued to the bar. 'Seriously! Coke or Lemonade? Come and let Uncle Jake know.'

Ewan skulked off, glowing.

At the bar, both Jake and Gardner ordered a *Summer Lightning*. As they waited, they surveyed the crowd.

'What a turnout. Glad for him really. Been a tough couple of years,' Jake said and took a huge mouthful of his pint when it landed. He sighed as the cold ale tingled on its descent. Then, he noticed that Gardner was almost a third of her way through her pint. 'Whoa! Easy tiger!'

'It's been a stressful week.'

She wasn't far wrong.

Two days ago, seventeen-year-old college student Susie Long, had disappeared. The young lady with pigtails, torn jeans and a new set of braces had been glass collecting on Wednesday night at *The Cloisters,* a popular public house opposite Salisbury cathedral. She had last been seen by her colleagues at 11:31 p.m. leaving via the back door of the pub. Then, she was caught by the electronic eyes of CCTV in the carpark where her walk home started.

But it never did start because a balaclava-wearing abductor had seized her while she was engrossed in a text message. He'd then bundled her into the back of a transit van. Despite the assailant camouflaging himself head-to-toe in black, the footage was clear enough to suggest that he was male, tall and rather slight in build. Unfortunately, the black van had worn a fake REG plate, but a SOCO had managed to recover Susie's phone which she'd dropped during the ambush.

She had been texting a seventeen-year-old boy called Johnny West. Or rather, *sexting*. Johnny, Susie's first sexual partner, had then been grilled within an inch of his life, yet the consensus was that he'd not been involved. Other bullets of information had come thick and fast. There was the recreational use of marijuana. Although this was common enough, and not necessarily a huge issue, they had still tracked down and shaken up a recreational teenage dealer. As expected, this lead had fizzed out like a faulty firework. Susie's bank statements showed an addiction to budget fashion. Again, as common as ever. Mourning neighbours and relatives didn't have a bad word; they clearly didn't know about the drug use. She had a small social grouping which revelled in excessive emotion; they were practically drowning in it now that she'd gone missing. Co-workers at the *The Cloisters* public house claimed that she brought a much-needed sparkle to a place experiencing waning trade. She had excellent grades and was a bright young thing.

So far, a very regular teenager.

A ransom, or any form of contact from the abductor, failed to materialise. The team had continued to dig and had leaned on Angela Long, her mother. Reasonably well-off, but not well-off enough to make her a target for kidnappers. Divorcee. Two children which included a fourteen-year old boy called Francis. Also, a bright young thing.

It was with the father that things had started to become interesting. Marcus Long was an ex-teacher who was now serving time for attempted murder. They'd interviewed him a few times, but their excitement was short-lived, as he maintained that the connection to his daughter was long dead and they hadn't discovered anything to suggest otherwise.

Still, they'd persevered. They'd interviewed anybody Long had annoyed, or was loosely connected with. Yet, the person they really needed to talk to, the man Long had attempted to kill, had disappeared six months ago. Suspects did not come any firmer, but a lot of manpower had gone into tracking him down. As yet, there was no sign of this individual.

All motes. Dust in the air. Nothing sticking.

They'd be back at it first thing, and Jake had promised himself that he would stop at four pints today. He needed to remain sharp, just in case anything broke today, or tomorrow, in Operation Autumn. If Susie Long was still alive, her life might depend on his sharpness.

'Do you think Mike knows that we just lied to him?' Gardner said.

'Yes,' Jake said, 'when was the last time you bluffed him?'

'Do you think he appreciates it?'

'No, but I think he knows that it is good for him. Imagine if we'd told him an officer had been assaulted? He'd have left already.'

'Have you heard anything else?' Gardner said.

'No,' Jake said. 'Same as you. Topham got the call to come and investigate an assault at Simmonds' wedding. He didn't elaborate. Hopefully, it will come to nothing. Perhaps it was just a punch-up with his fiancés' bitter ex, desperate to derail the wedding?'

Gardner shook her head. 'Your mind? What the hell goes on in there?'

Jake shrugged. 'Good question.' He felt his phone

buzzing in his pocket. He stepped to one side. It was one of the officers on Operation Autumn.

'Sir, I tried contacting DI Gardner, but she's not answering.'

'We are at a wedding, Tom, she did the sensible thing and turned it off.' *Unlike me*, he thought.

Tom said, 'I just finished a follow-up interview with one of Susie's teachers, Mary Stradling. What is it with teachers these days? Always so defensive! She kept thinking I was questioning her ability to look after children—'

'To the point, please Tom. It's my day off.'

'Sorry, sir. She let slip something that Susie had told her in confidence. Susie has been writing letters to her father.'

Marcus Long had claimed his connection to his daughter was long dead.

'Two years,' Jake said, 'Two bloody years. That's how long he'd said it'd been since they last spoke. Why lie? When your daughter has been bundled into a fucking transit van and no one knows where she is?'

'Don't know, sir, you want me to go and visit him now?'

He looked over at Yorke and several of his friends and relatives dancing to *Wham!*

Shit, Jake thought. *What should he do?*

What would Mike do?

'Phone the prison, Tom. I'll meet you there within the hour.'

He wandered back over to Gardner. The expression on his face spoke volumes.

'Shit, really, now?' Gardner said.

'It was a good idea to switch your phone off, Emma; unfortunately, I left mine on.'

'Go on.'

'That bullshit lead we just reported to Mike? It came in. Marcus Long has been in touch with Susie. The bastard lied. I'll go and talk to him now. But you, Emma, are going nowhere. I was going for at least another pint, so you'll have to have it now. And you will also have to pacify Sheila. She's going to be pissed off.' He could hear his two-year-old son, Frank, starting to cry in the distance. 'Even more pissed off than usual.'

THE PRIEST WAS STILL SMILING, but not quite as broadly as before.

Maybe he was losing his enthusiasm? Topham thought. Almost an hour of being grilled in a poky hot interview room would do that to their prisoners, even the most strong-willed of candidates. However, this boy was proving impressively resistant and continued to exercise his right to remain silent in the face of rapid-fire questioning.

At this point, the only real thing that they knew for sure was that he wasn't a priest. They'd had that confirmed via a photograph of him. The Catholic Church was unable to identify him as one of theirs.

The DNA, fingerprints, facial recognition software had all yielded nothing. He wasn't in the system.

Topham grew impatient. He leaned over to Willows and said, quietly, in her ear, 'Go and check on Simmonds. Find out if they could reattach his tongue.'

It had been packed in ice and rushed off to the hospital less than a minute after it had slipped from Topham's palm. He looked down at the hand he'd scrubbed raw.

After Willows had left the room, Topham rose to his feet and wandered to the side of the room.

From the wall, he observed the fake priest. He looked far too smooth. He'd glued his hair into a tight side-parting. His face was pale, clean-shaven and unblemished. All the time, he stared ahead, occasionally blinking, but always maintaining a contented expression. Every now and again, he paused to scratch the inside of his forearm.

'Something bite you?' Topham said.

No response.

'Well, it is the time of year for it. Midges and tics and whatnot,' Topham continued. 'We found the priest you know? An old disused toilet at the back of the church. He's at hospital with a large bump on his head. Was that you by any chance?'

He still didn't reply.

Topham tried to control his anger over this man's dogged determination to exercise his right to silence. 'We will find out who you are, you must know that?'

No movement. Fifty minutes and he was yet to even nod a response.

Topham pressed on. 'A wedding day? The happiest day of their lives? Someone must have done something to really piss you off.'

Nothing.

Topham looked up at the camera on the ceiling – tracking his, and the young man's every move. He could see why many of his predecessors, pre-camera days, had stopped a rolling audio tape and succumbed to madness. He could feel this same madness rising through him now. The Shakespearian quotation rolled through his mind again: *For now, these hot days, is the mad blood stirring.*

'And how did you do it? Cut such a huge chunk of some-one's tongue out? You must have knocked him unconscious first, surely?'

The boy's expression remained unaltered.

Topham looked at his watch. *Five more minutes*, he thought. *That is all you have left you bastard.*

'You must be twenty? Twenty-one? A good-looking young man. Your whole life ahead of you, *or at least it was ...* why did you just go and ruin it?'

Topham noticed movement. In his eyes. Ever so slight, but it was certainly there.

'I don't know anything about who you are, but why are you not studying? Preparing yourself for life? Chasing girls?'

The young man's eyes moved again. They darted towards Topham and back again. All in less than a second. The grin seemed to be fading too.

Topham felt his anger shift to excitement, retook his seat, stared at him and said, 'Yes, you are handsome. I really strug-gled at your age. I had bad skin and I was overweight.'

The young man's eyes widened. A bolt of adrenaline ricocheted through Topham. 'You've been called that before, haven't you? *Handsome?*'

The boy's grin fell away. He looked at Topham and—

There was a knock at the door. The young man flinched and looked away.

Shit, Topham thought, *I almost had him!*

Topham saw it was Willows at the door, so he went outside to talk to her. She was standing there looking deathly pale. 'Sir?'

He placed a hand on her shoulder to try and calm her. She gave him the news.

He went back into the interview room, and sat down

opposite the young man again. He wondered if he now looked as deathly pale as Willow had looked. He certainly felt it.

The young man was smiling again.

'There's nothing for you to be smiling about, young man. You've no longer got your whole life ahead of you.'

THEIR UNION WAS as passionate as always, and the aftermath as affectionate. They lay on tangled sheets in their wedding suite.

'Divisional Surgeon Patricia Yorke,' he said, running his fingers through her hair.

She looked up at him from where she rested her head on his chest. 'That'll take some getting used to...'

'But it's better, no?'

Patricia smiled. 'There's a ring to it. People will like it, especially now that they know I'm married to a rock and roll star.'

'Don't...'

'Some of those moves, my God, I didn't know you were that flexible.'

'I'm not, and tomorrow I will pay.'

'Speaking of tomorrow ... will we be doing this every night during our ten days away?'

'What? Discussing my dance moves?'

Patricia gripped his side and he writhed underneath her. 'No, stop it...'

'And the correct answer is?'

'Yes ... I will make love to you every night!'

'And morning?'

'Yes, if you remove your pincer from my side!'

Patricia stopped and slipped free of Yorke. She emerged naked from the bed. Lit by the moonlight breaking in through a net curtain, she looked particularly ravishing, especially with her seven-month-old bump. His first child. Or, technically, his first biological child. He cast a smile over an earlier memory of Ewan chatting to a girl by the dancefloor. After a while, the young couple had sat together, silently, twiddling with their phones for over an hour. Lost together in a social media wilderness. A brave new world.

'Where are you rushing off too?' Yorke said.

'Where do you think?'

'Well, it's too late now, we're already married.'

'Annulment?'

'You're cold!'

'How do you think I'm able to spend so much of my time hovering over dead people?'

Yorke smiled. 'Now, you're taking it too far.'

Patricia waved and disappeared into the toilet.

Yorke reached over for his smart phone. He'd made a pact with himself not to switch it on today for two reasons. He didn't want to be tempted to look at how Southampton were doing in a pre-season friendly. The second reason was, of course, work. He'd deliberately steered clear of Operation Autumn despite his obvious devastation over the case of a missing girl. Over the last 48 hours he'd offered advice, checked the right people were in the right jobs, but he'd made a conscious effort to keep himself emotionally distant.

Never an easy task, but one he'd managed to accomplish.

This was the most important day of his life, and the next ten days were *his*. Sorry. *His and Patricia's*.

But he needed to check them in for the flight, so he

switched his phoned on, silently vowing not to check his emails or the Southampton football result – he would do that on the plane tomorrow...

He'd started to check in when BBC News decided to send him a breaking news notification. His eyes widened.

Patricia emerged from the bathroom.

'You checking-in?'

Yorke looked up.

'What's wrong, Mike?'

He struggled to find the composure to answer the question. Instead, he held his phone out and she came forward to read the notification. She read it out loud. '*Assaulted Salisbury police officer dies in hospital.*'

Her hand flew to her mouth. At that point, Yorke realised that he wouldn't be going to South Africa tomorrow.

3

MARCUS LONG'S HAIR looked like moss festering on a historic ruin. The prison shirt he wore was stretched tight; hair burst free from between the buttons like weeds breaking through concrete.

It wasn't unusual for a police officer to feel uncomfortable when visiting a jail; after all, most of the clientele were in residency there as a direct result of their work, but that wasn't the real reason Jake felt uncomfortable right now.

He felt uncomfortable because the man in front of him had committed, in Jake's opinion, the most heinous of sins. A crime against a minor.

A guard stood at one side of the poky room, staring longingly at an old fan which was extremely good at producing noise, but not so good at cooling people down.

'You lied to us,' Jake said, rolling up the sleeves of his shirt.

Opposite him, Long slumped back in his chair; the chains that held him to the table rattled. 'I don't know what you mean?'

'Your daughter, Susie, has been missing for two days. *Your daughter.*' Jake stopped there. He felt there was little need for any more emphasis. If that didn't have an impact on the cold-hearted dickhead, nothing would.

'*I know that.* Do you think I've slept?' A large birthmark, connecting his nostrils to his top lip, quivered as he spoke – it presented the appearance that he had a bloody nose.

'She wrote to you. Her teacher told us. She wrote to you, Marcus, and you decided not to tell us – even though her life could be in danger.'

'There's nothing in any of those letters that will help you.'

'How can you be so sure?'

Clearly agitated, Long turned to look at the guard, probably wondering if he should just ask to leave. Of course, this wasn't an option. 'I'm sure. Trust me.'

'Trust you? You've lied once. How can you expect me to trust you again?'

'Because there's nothing in those letters about what has happened to her.'

'What are you hiding? Is this to do with him? With Christian Severance?'

Long lifted his hands and slammed them down on the table. The noise of the chains hitting the wood made Jake flinch. The guard took a step forward. Jake halted him by raising his palm in the air.

'How many times are you going to ask me that? Why would it have anything to do with *him?* He's got his justice. He's watching me rot in here. That will suit Christian just fine. And anyway, have you not asked him yourselves yet?'

No, Jake thought, *because we can't find him.*

'We need those letters, Marcus.'

Long shrugged. 'Fine, it's not like I have any privacy left anyway.'

'Your concern for your daughter is overwhelming.'

Long rattled the chains again. 'You have no idea, Detective.'

———

WENDY, the Management Support Assistant, raised an eyebrow at Yorke as he entered the incident room. He raised one back at her. It was a clear instruction from him not to ask why he'd forsaken his wedding night to shoot straight down to Wiltshire HQ in a taxi. She acknowledged the instruction with a nod and said, 'It looks like you need a cup of tea, sir.'

'No,' Yorke said, watching Topham scribble over the incident room whiteboard in preparation for the briefing, 'this is a cup-of-coffee situation.'

'Cafetière or a frothy one from the machine?'

'Cafetière with two spoons worth.'

She paused to look him up and down.

He looked for a stain on his T-shirt. 'Have you seen a toothpaste mark or something, Wendy?'

'No, sir, I've just never seen you—'

'—out of a suit before?'

She nodded.

'Do I not look good in casual wear?'

'You've never looked better, sir,' Topham said, turning from the board. 'You're wearing it for the airport I assume?'

Yorke knew that a raised eyebrow would not be enough to shut Topham up so he opted to just say it instead, 'You know why I'm here Mark, Let's not—'

'It's your wedding night!'

'It was supposed to be Simmonds' wedding night too.'

'Sometimes I think you don't trust us to do a good job, sir,' Topham said and turned back to the board. Wendy retreated to get the coffee.

Yorke looked up at the black web Topham was spinning with a marker and photos over the whiteboard. *I trust you all,* Yorke thought, *you're the best people I've ever worked with. But—*

He thought back to the awkward wedding speeches and his attempt to reclaim his teenage years playing guitar.

This is where I really belong.

While he waited for the team to arrive, Yorke wandered among the wooden desks, letting his fingers brush against them. With surprise, he looked at the dust on his fingertips. These days, it usually sparkled in here. He was immediately nostalgic for past times when incident rooms were mired in grime.

It was late, so only core team members were called away from an evening with their loved ones. DI Emma Gardner was Senior Investigating Officer on *Operation Autumn,* the investigation into the disappearance of Susie Long, so she was a big miss from the room. Gardner was the most conscientious and driven officer Yorke had ever worked with, and mother to his goddaughter, so he always wanted her close. Jake was also on Operation Autumn and was currently interviewing Susie's father, Marcus Long, in prison. A man with a history that would probably prove to be tangled up with his only daughter's disappearance.

Despite these great losses, Yorke had no concerns about the team filing into the room because they all looked devastated. *Absolutely devastated.*

Not only had DC Ryan Simmonds been one of them, but

he'd also been one of the most popular members. He'd been diligent, thoughtful of others, and the centre of most office banter. He'd just lost his life on his wedding day. These officers would venture to the ends of the earth, and then some, to seek justice for Simmonds.

Yorke waited for Jeremy Dawson from HOLMES to set up his laptop so he could document every second of the unfolding drama. Then, he addressed the crowd. 'There isn't an easy way to begin this except to say I'm sorry. Sorry for your loss.'

He scanned the glum faces. Some nodded their appreciation for Yorke's words.

'Ryan was an excellent officer, and a solid friend to many of us in this room. You can all be sure that we will celebrate his life, *thoroughly*, just as soon as we attend to one piece of business. Find out what happened today, on what should have been the happiest day of his life. And then we'll do what we do best, we will get justice.'

DC Luke Parkinson thrust his hand up. 'Sir, justice? The bastard who did this is in the room next door. So could we not hurry this along?'

This invigorated several slouching officers; they sat upright in their chairs and nodded.

Despite being stunned by Parkinson's abrasive tone, Yorke tempered his response to it and kept the surprise out of his facial expression. He was dealing with raw emotions here. These were good men. And they were dealing with loss. 'In a moment, DI Topham, our SIO, will address all of us on the particulars of the case so far. One of those particulars is the unidentified man sitting in this building. Yes, I agree, it looks like we have got our man. CROWN have informed us we have enough to charge. But until he's identified, and motive established, it is sensible to keep our options open.'

A few officers shook their heads while several others nodded in agreement.

Yorke took a seat under the air-conditioning unit. He welcomed the steady stream of cold air. He was red hot and not just because of the heat wave; he was hot because that was a particularly difficult speech to deliver - even harder than the one earlier to his wedding guests. This was a broken room. It was going to take a hell of a lot to put it back together again. But they could at least make a start by establishing the events of the day.

Topham, still wearing his suit from Yorke's wedding, addressed the officers. He pointed out the randomly generated operation name: Operation Coldtown. *The complete opposite to how it currently feels*, Yorke felt like saying, but he kept his poor attempt at humour away from an unreceptive audience.

Topham went through the particulars of the case. Everything he'd experienced in the church with Willows and Tyler, who were both in attendance now. He relayed the frustrating interview with the young man who continued to exercise his right to remain silent.

'We've yet to get any kind of hit. Fingerprints, DNA, facial recognition software have all turned up nothing,' Topham said. 'We have no idea who this man is. We suspect he arrived early at the church when Father Simon was setting up. He managed to knock him unconscious, gag, and tie him.' He pointed at a photo on the whiteboard. 'He was left incarcerated in an old, disused toilet at the back of the church.'

Topham took everyone on a journey from picture to

picture over his whiteboard. Jeremy Dawson typed fast. Everyone would be able to access all of this data on the file-sharing system. There wasn't a great deal yet, but every morsel would need to be consumed again and again over the coming hours.

'Familiarise yourselves with it as soon as you leave this room,' Topham said. 'As the data grows, we need to grow with it.'

Yorke looked down. It wasn't an expression he would use. It was typical Topham-esque hyperbole. 'We don't have a post-mortem yet, but we know that most of his tongue was cut away by a sharp instrument. This could be a scalpel, but that has yet to be confirmed. They will also probably confirm that he died from a haemorrhage.' Topham paused to check his notes. 'From the branches of the lingual arteries. This was unlucky – the killer may not have anticipated this reaction.'

There was a snort from someone in the crowd. It was Parkinson again. Yorke bit his lip one last time. Parkinson had been allowed two strikes tonight already; Yorke wouldn't allow him a third.

Parkinson immediately threatened a third when he thrust his hand up. 'How can dying from having your tongue cut out be unfortunate? I'd anticipate my victim bleeding to death!'

It wasn't a strike; it was a fair question. Yorke held back.

Topham said, 'The pathologist told me that a similar injury can be caused by accidents such as biting your tongue, or even having a piercing, *but* that the tongue has a good capacity for clotting and bleeding can usually be stopped quickly. Ryan experienced a rare condition called lingual hematoma.'

'If the bastard even knows this!' Parkinson crossed his

arms. 'Anyway, whichever way you look at this, it's still murder.'

'No one disagrees,' Yorke said, looking Parkinson directly in the eyes.

'Focus of the investigation at this stage,' Topham said, 'is to gather all possible information about Ryan. Yes, most of us in this room knew him very well. But everyone in this room understands that you never really know everything about someone until you really look.'

'He was the best of us,' Parkinson said, uncrossing his arms and leaning forward.

Yorke leaned forward too.

'And no one is disputing that,' Topham said, '*no one*. We want to know why someone targeted him. Because without motive, we have little.'

Yes, Mark, that is correct, Yorke thought. Parkinson leaned back.

Topham continued, 'We interview Father Simon. We interview those who know Father Simon. It looks cut and dried that he was ambushed and incapacitated, but it's not gospel. We talk to every person in that church today. Everybody. We want the events through every possible perspective. CCTV footage around that church for the last 48 hours. The comings and goings of every individual. Who does this? On someone's wedding day? There is a severe amount of hate here and we will get the answer soon enough even if the bastard in that other room refuses to open his mouth between now and the day they close that cell door.' He paused for a breath. 'Individual assignments on the noticeboards as usual. Bring everything to me. Immediately. If you can't get hold of me, then head to Willows.'

Topham turned to look at the picture of Ryan Simmonds

at the top of the board. 'However tired and frustrated we feel, just remember how much we owe Ryan.' He turned back and looked at Jeremy Dawson. 'You get everything?'

Dawson nodded.

'And everyone, *please,* before you start, get on the system and digest all of this again.'

As the officers left, Topham stared at the photo of Simmonds. Yorke came and stood beside him.

'What a way to go,' Topham said.

'Different,' Yorke said. 'Creative. There's a purpose here.'

'Remind you of anything?'

'How could it not?' Yorke said. 'It has not even been a year since that slaughtering bastard tore this city apart.'

'And now someone's trying to do it again.'

'Trying ... but we will stop them,' Yorke said.

'Have we got him? Is he really in that room?'

'Let's go and find out.'

JAKE'S PHONE battery had died. So, sitting in the car, with his engine running and his phone connected and charging up, he read carefully through the letters written from Susie Long to her father. There were four in total. After he'd finished reading, he checked his phone, and saw that it had burst back into life. He had several missed calls from Gardner, and several text messages instructing him to call her back.

She answered on the first ring. 'I've been trying to phone you.'

'Yes, I can see—'

'It's awful ... Jake. Just awful.'

She explained to him what had happened to Simmonds. As she did so, he felt like he was suffocating, so he opened the car door to let air into the vehicle.

By the time, she'd started to explain that Yorke had left his own wedding day to assist in the investigation, Jake was outside of the car, pacing around. He didn't say anything and just listened, for fear of breaking out into a series of incomprehensible expletives.

He looked up at the dominating prison fences and wondered if he felt more trapped than the people in there.

Trapped in the knowledge that this was the world he lived in. That these things just kept happening. You stopped one senseless orchestrator of violence, only for another one to start a new symphony.

'But, it's not ours, Jake. Mike and Mark have a suspect in custody. If they can't get to the bottom of it, no one can. We stay focused on Operation Autumn, and I'll see you at briefing tomorrow.'

Jake took a deep breath. *She was right. Back to Susie Long. And only Susie Long.* It was too late for Simmonds – it might not be for her.

'I've got a handful of letters here. She's been writing to her father in prison for the past year. Approximately one every three months,' Jake said.

'Have you read them?'

'Yes.'

'And?'

He sat back in the car, closed the door, ensured the air conditioning was on to fend off the late evening humidity, and switched on the overhead light. He ran his eyes quickly over the first one again.

'It begins obviously enough. She felt isolated and abandoned for a long time … now she just wants to understand … she is willing to write to him a few times but isn't ready to see him yet.'

Jake switched to the second letter, had a quick look again, and then checked Gardner was still on the line before continuing, 'He obviously wrote back with his excuses, and it looks as if she bought them … she understands now that he was a sick man … the third letter is about the power of love and how it can cause tragedy. She, too, has been experiencing the same effects of love.'

'And the final letter?'

'She's going to come and visit him.'

'Correction. *Was* going to come and visit him. In your opinion, does he know more than he is letting on?'

'Yes.'

'How do you know?'

'Hard to explain, I just know.'

'We will have a closer look at those letters tomorrow morning in briefing.'

LYING HERE, during this tiny window of reading time before they killed the lights, Marcus Long was desperate to feel his hand around a cold whisky glass and listen to the ice trembling in the coarse liquid, just before it burnt his mouth, and throat, and mind.

It would be easier to do what had to be done with some of the good stuff in him.

He climbed off his bed and paced the several steps in his tiny cell to the desk in the corner.

He'd spent so many cold, and more recently hot,

evenings at this desk with his daughter's letters laid out before him with his fingers tracing over the lines etched by her pen into the paper. Words of forgiveness and words of acceptance.

And now that fucking detective had them, and he would probably never see them again.

He reached over for a copy of *A Tale of Two cities* by Charles Dickens. He opened to the first page and read the first line. *It was the best of times, it was the worst of times.* It *had* been the best of times – he'd had his daughter back in his life. And she'd not been forced into his life. She had come of her own will.

He shook out the envelope he'd hidden in the book. He slid out the letter, read it again, and sighed. What was demanded of him was ... was ... unthinkable.

It was the worst of times and he longed for a drink.

'WHAT'S WRONG? Cat got your tongue?' Yorke said to the young man sitting across from him at the table. 'At least say *no comment* rather than staring off into space like a bloody zombie.'

Topham said, 'You could even try asking for a solicitor?'

The young man scratched his forearm and continued to ignore them. At least he wasn't smiling any more. Topham had said that the grin had been persistent and eerie.

'Well, as I'm sure DI Topham explained to you earlier, this is about to get very ugly for you. We have enough to charge you. Sitting there with his tongue in the graveyard wasn't the brightest idea. At least tell me one thing: did you mean to kill DC Ryan Simmonds?'

No movement.

Yorke continued, 'I don't think you did, did you? We should have been able to save him. The problem is he haemorrhaged, and they couldn't revive him. That means you are going away for good, Mr ... sorry ... your name?'

Nothing.

Topham leaned forward. 'Earlier, when I was here with you, you were about to tell me something. I'm certain of it.'

The boy didn't even look at Topham.

'I said you were good-looking.'

Yorke looked at Topham. For creativity in interviewing techniques, he'd just scored full marks.

'I think handsome was the word I used,' Topham said.

Yorke looked at the young man, wondering whether he was going to have to step in and stop this peculiar approach, but then caught a flicker of movement on the suspect's face. Feeling a rush of adrenaline, he joined in with the creativity. 'So much wasted potential in such a young, good-looking boy...'

Then the young man lifted a hand and pointed at Yorke's notebook.

Yorke looked down at the book and said, 'Why do you want that?'

The young man pointed again, more forcefully this time.

And then it dawned on Yorke. 'Open your mouth.'

The young man refused with a slow shake of his head.

'You can't talk, can you? You've no tongue.' Yorke said.

He shrugged and again pointed at the notebook.

Yorke pressed him. 'Is that why you took officer Simmond's tongue? Did he have anything to do with why you lost yours?'

No response.

Yorke ripped out a page and slid it over with a pen. He looked up at the camera and said, 'For the record, interviewee has been handed a piece of paper and is now writing a response.'

Yorke took it back. 'Interviewee has written: *someone else called me good-looking once.*'

Yorke paused and considered the strange words. *His mother? His father? Why has this bothered him? Why has a reference to his appearance woken him up from his inane stupor?*

'Who?' Yorke said.

The boy wrote quickly, but in clear, printed letters. *That doesn't matter.*

'Well, why bring it up then?' Topham said.

Yorke tore out the pages with his notes on it and handed the entire notebook over.

The boy nodded and wrote: *because I want you to know the irrelevance of that man and his words.*

'Ryan Simmonds?' Yorke said.

The boy wrote: *No*

'Who then?' Topham said.

He wrote: *Irrelevant again. What is relevant is that I have been healed.*

'Healed? Are you talking about your mouth?' Yorke said.

The boy wrote: *Just healed.*

And then a thought struck Yorke which made his blood run cold. 'Where is this person who called you good-looking?'

The boy didn't need long to produce the one word.

Yorke spoke for the camera. 'Interviewee has written *dead.*'

*T*HE BEST OF TIMES...

Marcus Long thought about the first time he'd held his baby daughter in his arms. 6.6 lb of innocence swaddled in a cloth. It was the moment in which he'd truly realised that the world was the most wonderful place to be. He'd tried so hard, for so long, to hide from his sexuality and fit in. And this was his reward. A beautiful daughter.

He tucked the envelope back into the Charles Dickens book, and returned it to his small library at the back of his desk.

The worst of times...

But you cannot hide from what you truly are. Temptation had got the better of him, and even though his young daughter, who he so adored, had only just turned five, he'd committed that atrocity.

A small buzzer sounded and a minute later the room lights went off. It wasn't pitch black as there were still lights out in the corridors which would remain on all evening, but it was dim.

He then kneeled in front of the small stool he'd been sitting on.

Since that moment, since the atrocity, his life had been on a downward spiral. Mistakenly, he'd thought that this, his second stint in jail, had been the final nail in his coffin for lying to himself and lying to others. It hadn't been. This was.

The final nail.

After this, it would be over.

He parted his teeth to allow his tongue out into the air. His breathing had quickened now, and his hands were trembling as he clutched the edges of the stool. He pressed his teeth down onto the fleshy centre of his tongue.

He squeezed his eyes shut, and felt the tears running down the sides of his face.

He prayed this was quick. God, he needed this to be quick.

He slammed his chin down onto the stool as hard as he could. With his eyes squeezed shut, he saw only a blinding white light. Before he had chance to truly register the pain, he drove his chin full-force into the wood again...

And again.

Now, the pain was kicking in, and there was a salty taste in his mouth. He reached up, touched the flesh hanging loose from his mouth, forced back the need to scream, grabbed the stool and thrust repeatedly until his teeth were just bashing against one another.

He opened his eyes. His tongue lay on the stool like a slug arching its back under a dose of salt.

He lifted his head up and wailed.

4

T HE YOUNG MAN had finally stopped smiling.

'So,' Yorke said, 'did you kill the man who said you were good-looking in the same way that you killed Ryan Simmonds?'

No response.

'How many people have you killed?' Topham said.

There was a knock at the door. Yorke was grateful for the interruption. A small break from this frustrating inter-rogation.

Outside, Yorke and Topham greeted Willows in the corridor. She'd been tasked with tracking back through Simmond's career and all of his cases. She looked agitated.

'I found something. In fact, I can't quite believe what I found...' She looked down at her notes, shaking her head.

'Go on,' Topham said, edging forward.

Yorke noted the impatience in Topham's voice, and the eager movement. This case had got hold of him. *Really* got hold of him.

'Three years ago, Christian Severance, came to the station to report that he was being followed—'

'—by Marcus Long?' Yorke said.

'Yes, sir.'

Topham looked at Yorke and said, 'Is Christian Severance the man wanted in connection with the disappearance of Susie Long in Operation Autumn?'

'Yes,' Yorke said, 'go on, Collette, what else have you found out?'

'Christian Severance filed a report with DC Ryan Simmonds in which he claimed he was being followed by Marcus Long, two weeks before an attempt on his life was made by the same man. Simmonds had dragged his heels over the investigation which is how I came across the report so quickly – it had been flagged. He was questioned about his approach to the investigation, but no disciplinary charges materialised.'

Topham gripped Yorke's shoulder and said, 'They're connected. The cases are *fucking* connected.'

'Follow me,' Yorke said.

Together they charged down the corridor to the room for Operation Autumn. They opened the door, automatic lights burst into life, and a warm torrent of air speared them. Yorke hit the switch to ignite the air conditioner.

Yorke approached the whiteboard which was covered in information; all quickly accessible due to the neatness of Gardner's handwriting. He scanned the images quickly: Susie Long, her father, Marcus Long, relatives, friends ... then his eyes fell to the two images of Christian Severance. One was taken before, and the other after, his appearance was dramatically altered by Marcus Long.

'Just back me up here.' Yorke pointed at the scarred face

of Severance. 'That is definitely not the boy in the other room?'

'Of course not,' Topham said. 'Not unless he's had extensive plastic surgery?'

'But, even then, he would look more like *this*,' Yorke said, pointing at Severance's *before* photograph, 'than the boy in the interview room?'

'Yes, bar some miracle of surgery, they are not the same person. Even their builds are completely different. Why are you trying to link them, sir?' Willows said.

'Well, Christian Severance was shot in the face, destroying a huge part of his jaw, and his tongue. Now, the man who could have stopped it, DC Ryan Simmonds, is dead, having had his tongue cut out. Add to that, the guy in the other room who is communicating via cards, something you may do if you cannot speak, because you do not have a tongue ... how can I not make links?'

They all paused to reflect. If Topham and Willows felt anything like he did now, Yorke reasoned, their minds would be reeling.

'Now what?' Topham said.

'We find out if that killer in the other room has a tongue or not, and then we find out who the bloody hell he is.'

CHRISTIAN SEVERANCE STARED out of the window at the two young boys who lived in the house opposite, playing football. They passed the ball to each other, several times, before the taller of the two smashed the ball into an inflatable goal. They embraced, and shared the experience.

One of the boys noticed him watching through the window and whispered into the other's ear.

He's spotted the freak, Severance thought. He tried to smile. He couldn't. His face was too damaged.

The other boy turned and looked at the face in the window too. Happy expressions fell off the pair of adolescents like torn clothes. The ball rolled off; neither stooped to pick it up, or give chase. They simply stopped and stared at Severance as if hypnotised.

Boo Radley perhaps? Or worse, something out of a horror movie?

Severance turned from the window, wondering if one day the two boys would dare each other to go into the monster's garden.

Well, you will have to hurry up young men, because one day soon, I will be gone.

This wasn't his house after all.

As he sat himself down on the sofa, he undid a few buttons on his shirt. It was stifling today. As it had been every other day this week. A dry breeze through the open window wasn't cutting it.

He reached over to the coffee table and took hold of one of his old diaries. He flicked through the pages before settling on an entry he hadn't read in a while.

The Conduit's warning hit him. Sharply. *Dwelling can be compelling but depressing.*

Yes, but is it dwelling? I was fourteen then; I'm twenty-nine now. We should not forget who we are and why we are what we are. Memory can be deceitful. Learning about yourself can be an academic pursuit. My diary is a reliable source.

He began to read. He listened to the fourteen-year-old boy talking to him.

Today was finally the day I told Mr Long about my father. He listened too. Most people I have told this story to don't really listen. They nod. They sigh. They smile. But they don't really listen. Listening is complete silence and no movement. A blink or two, maybe, but no more. Mr Long really stared at me when I talked and it made me feel warm and important. I told him the story because Mr Long wants to know why I always come and sit with him at lunch. He asked me why the smell of his tuna sandwiches had not put me off yet! So I told him. Because I have no friends. Not since Jeremy found the DVD at his house. The one of his father having sex with my mother. The one he showed everyone at school. It's okay for Jeremy, because my ex-friends think it's kind of cool for his father to be cheating on his wife. But, my mother, well that's a whole different ball game – she's a whore, apparently. After I'd finished my story, Mr Long acted like he didn't know already, but he probably did. It is common knowledge. Most of the students know, so it's more than likely all the teachers know. Plus I've told the school councillor, and he will certainly have sent out a notification or two. Mr Long observed that I didn't have any lunch today. I told him that my mother always made my sandwiches before everything fell apart, and now I must make them. So, sometimes I forget. He offered me some of his tuna sandwich and I surprised him by having a wedge! He'd clearly thought I'd be repulsed. The thing is with Mr Long he always knows what to say and what to do to make me feel better. We then talked about music. He's always telling me about his record collection. It sounds amazing! He reckons he has signed vinyl from all the masters. The Beatles, The Stones etc. Passed down from his father apparently. I asked him about his wife and his daughter. Just trying to be polite really, but as usual he does not really want to talk about them. So, we talked through lunch, and half-an-hour after school. Before I left this evening, he brushed my fringe over my ear. He apologised and said he was sorry. He said it was what his father used to do to his hair every day when he was younger and now it was a habit. I said I didn't mind. It felt good actually.

Severance placed the diary on the table and reached up to run his hand over his smashed cheek; the rough skin scratched his fingertips.

He looked at his watch and saw it had already passed ten. He wondered if Long had fulfilled his end of the bargain. He suspected he would have done. It was his only chance of him ever seeing his beloved daughter alive again. Not that he would be seeing her again. That had been a lie of course. Severance wanted to smile but his smashed face would not allow it.

With his eyes closed, he thought of Susie Long: pale, still and silent in her plastic coffin.

———

YORKE STILL COULDN'T BELIEVE what he was saying to Gardner down the phone. Unprecedented, to say the least. The collision of two cases.

'So, what, we just roll them into one?' Gardner said.

'Not just yet,' Yorke said. 'Yes, Severance is our prime suspect for the missing girl, but Simmond's murder was committed by someone completely different. Someone sitting in our interview room. But as yet we know only two things about him. He smiles a lot, and he doesn't speak.'

'But he is missing his tongue? Surely, then, he is connected to Severance?'

'The boy's missing tongue has yet to be confirmed. And even if it is, I want his identity first. Emma, get an early night. You took full advantage of my free bar today and must be ready to get your head down. You said before that new evidence has come to light?'

'Yes, the letters sent to Marcus Long from Susie. Jake is scouring them.'

'Good. Get Jake in the loop after this call. Run the briefing tomorrow morning for Operation Autumn. Cover the new discoveries, and then I will bring any new information from Operation Coldtown along and brief your officers.'

'Sounds good. So, if they are connected, sir, what does that say about Susie's chances?'

'I don't want to speculate, but ... not good. There have been no ransom demands. If Severance is taking revenge on people in such a brutal manner, by removing their tongues, then I fear for her. It is difficult to remain optimistic, but that is where you will come in Emma.'

'What do you mean, sir?'

'That you are always more positive than me.'

'Really? Thanks.'

'Goodnight, Emma.'

'Goodnight Mike ... and congratulations for today.'

'Yes, thank you.'

As he hung up, he felt dreadful that his wedding day was not the first thing on his mind.

CHRISTIAN SEVERANCE LOOKED DOWN at the body. Its face was obscured by the thick plastic sheeting that he'd just wrapped tightly around it. Severance rolled his shoulders, heard his spine crack, and felt hot sweat pool in the small of his back.

He saw the splodge of blood spreading out on the interior of the plastic sheet where the victim had been cut.

Before moving the body, he'd need a break. He removed his damp shirt, screwed into a ball and dabbed at his upper body.

He returned to the living room, and the sofa, shirtless. If the boys playing football looked in to see a half-naked, disfigured man, so what? They already considered him out of the ordinary.

As he sat down and picked up the diary again, the words from the Conduit came back: *dwelling is compelling but depressing...*

'Leave me alone,' he said, and began to read:

When I went inside Mr Long's house today, I asked him if he was worried about anyone seeing. He said he wasn't. He said that he often had teenagers around for exam tuition so no one would pay any attention. My mouth fell open when he told me that he gets fifteen pounds an hour for that. Fifteen pounds! I joked that I wouldn't be paying him that much as it takes weeks to earn that on my paper round! He laughed. I like making him laugh. He told me that no one makes him laugh like I do. Not even his own wife. When I asked him where his family were, he told me that they were away. His wife teaches in a different area and their holidays were different so he had his house all to himself. He showed me his huge new television. I made him laugh again by joking about how his tutoring had got him living like a king. Not likely, he said, and he laughed a lot. He took me upstairs to see the record collection, he'd been boasting about all these weeks. Jesus! He'd not been exaggerating. Signed copies of

Beatles and Stones' records. All passed down from his dead father! I touched some of them and ran my fingers over the signatures. Jagger, McCartney, Lennon ... Impressive I said. I can't believe they actually touched these particular records! You didn't believe me, he said. Yes I did, I said. I had believed him. Every word he ever says to me sounds so real. It always has done. More than anyone else's. Then we sat and talked for hours, like we always do in the classroom. About music, about films and about books. He loves books. Why did you become a History teacher and not an English teacher? I asked him. The marking, he told me. Then he talked to me about his job. He said he loves talking to me and he feels he can talk to me about anything. I also love him talking to me, just like I love him teaching me. When he teaches, his every word, movement, gesture, draws an image in your mind. I tell him this. I told him that he brings the American West to life like no other and that his rendition of the Khan legacy once left me speechless. I checked my watch. It was late but I wasn't worried. I'd told my parents I was at Martin's. He moved closer to me and asked me if I was hungry. I could smell the mint on his breath. I didn't mind. It felt good to have him close to me. He put his hand on my leg, and he widened his eyes. I think he was trying to ask me if it was okay. I nodded.

Severance stopped reading and threw the diary at the mantlepiece. An ornamental clock fell and smashed into thousands of pieces on the fake fireplace.

TOPHAM APPROACHED Yorke in the corridor, shaking his head. 'He won't budge, won't let me see inside his mouth.

Can't we just take a look? You hold his arms, sir, and I'll hold his nose. Ten seconds and we'll know...'

'And then we will be under investigation rather than him,' Yorke said. 'No, we do it properly. I'll try again in a moment. If I fail, we will have to get a warrant to force a look. I'm sure we can manage one quick enough with a missing girl on our radar...'

'Sir?'

Both Topham and Yorke turned to face Willows.

'Vice have contacted us. Someone in their department recognised the boy's picture. He's not in the system, hence the reason he was overlooked by the facial recognition software, but one of the officers clocked him from an area he works regularly. His name is David Sturridge.'

Yorke felt his heart beating in his chest. 'Go on.'

'He is a suspected male prostitute, although no charges have yet been brought against him. DC Jeff Powers from Vice, who phoned this in to me, says the area of Tidworth in which he operates is rife with prostitution. Several squats exist within the vicinity, and Sturridge had been sighted and questioned in one of those squats.'

'So, he's homeless? Okay, Collette, can you pull up all the details of David Sturridge? Mark, contact DC Jeff Powers again and get the address of this squat.'

CHRISTIAN SEVERANCE EMPTIED the remains of the clock into the bin and returned the dustpan and brush to the cupboard under the sink. The Conduit would not be best pleased about his outburst.

He didn't like to upset the Conduit. The man had been

particularly kind to him, after all. He also possessed a strength in character and purpose that could dominate your will. So, on the whole, it was best to avoid these situations.

Plus, Severance also craved a few hours of therapy, which would not be forthcoming if the Conduit's mood was sour. That was if he returned this evening. Quite often, he returned very late or stayed over in hotels.

He returned to the sofa and picked up another diary. He looked at the date and saw that it was almost a year after the events in the previous extract he'd read. After looking around for any valuable and breakable objects in case his temper got the better of him again, he opened the diary and began to read:

Today was the worst day of my life. Seeing the man who claims to love me crying as he gave his statement. My mother's hand gripped mine throughout the whole process. He was contrite. He confessed to knowing I was fourteen. He confessed that he had betrayed his duty of care to me as my teacher. He said he understood that this was statutory rape now, and the fact that it was consensual means nothing. He accepted all of these wrongdoings, but he said he would not apologise for loving me. That he would never apologise. I buried my head in my mother's lap. I told her that I'd changed my mind, that I didn't want him punished for what he had done to me. But it was too late. I'd given my statement. I'd exposed him. The evidence had been presented. My mother kept whispering to me that I was doing the right thing. But every time I looked up from her lap, I could see him staring right at me. Worse of all, it was not a look of hatred. It was a look of forgiveness. A look of longing. Now, as I sit here, writing this, I wonder what it is I am feeling. I am sad, not because I have lost someone I loved, because I never really loved Marcus. I feel sad that I've lost the only person in the world I could really talk to. I feel sad that I've lost my only friend.

I also feel sad that this man manipulated me into feeling this way.

Severance wiped a tear away and wished the Conduit was here. He could really do with that therapy right now.

5

YORKE SHOOK DC Jeff Power's hand. The Vice officer had already finished for the day, so had gone beyond the call of duty to meet them in a spot renowned for prostitution and drugs. It wasn't the best place for a copper to knock around.

When Yorke thanked him, repeatedly, Powers said, 'Don't sweat it. They all know me round here. They trust me too. So, there's nothing for us to worry about.'

They stood under a sodium lamp, opposite the Rising Sun pub, and beside the entrance to the dingy street they were about to venture down. It was chucking out time, so several lads emerged from the pub. As the pack crossed the street towards them, they pulled their hidden pint glasses from underneath their jackets and continued drinking. They sneered as they passed. One spat on the floor close to where Topham stood.

Topham looked at Yorke. 'Do you think they know we're police?'

Yorke raised his eyebrows and pointed at Topham's expensive suit. 'What do you think?'

Powers offered Topham and Yorke a rolled-up ciggie. Topham declined immediately. Yorke considered it, and then refused.

Powers was a looming man with a shaved head and big hands. He smoked quickly as he filled them in. 'I've got a soft spot for David Sturridge ... at least I did. Always seemed one of the nicer boys around here. Polite, you know? Most of them sneer and spit – as you've just seen. At least, until they really *know* you. David was never really like that. Always polite. Willing to talk.'

'You mean grass?' Topham said.

'Nah, not like that. It's more of a containment job around here. We try to keep a lid on things before they get out of hand. Last thing we want to do is stitch any of them up. We work closely with the charity *Second Chance*, and we try our best to ensure that the prostitutes are fed, watered and *protected* - if you get my drift. Best to get these prostitutes off drugs, off the game and off the street in that order. Banging them up just slows that process down.'

A group of girls, barely out of their teens, emerged from the Rising Sun. The excessively short skirts, see-through tops, and three-inch high heels told Yorke a story that he never ceased to be disturbed by. They crossed the street and strolled past the small group of officers. This time, one of the girls addressed Powers. 'Good evening, Detective.'

Powers returned the salutation, and then said, 'Evening Cindy. Straight home, now.'

They all nodded and headed down the street Powers was about to take them down.

'We need to know everything about Sturridge,' Yorke said as they followed the girls down the street.

'Unfortunately, there isn't a great deal to know at this point. His story is a familiar one. Father in jail. His mother is an alcoholic who welcomed a new stepdad into the house. The new stepdad didn't take kindly to David, and over a year ago, he flushed himself down the toilet and onto the street.' Powers sighed. 'Well, I guess if he is responsible for what happened today, he's no longer homeless, is he? He'll be better off in jail than out here, I can assure you of that!'

'How long has he been on your radar?' Yorke said.

'Just under a year,' Powers said. 'He's small-fry. We mainly target the pimps and drug-dealers. Many do both jobs. They keep the prostitutes hooked, so they have to keep working and buying. It's a very cyclical, vicious system.'

'Who is Sturridge's pimp?'

Powers sighed. 'Funny you should say that. That's partly the reason you really caught my attention today.'

Yorke recalled the words from the interview earlier. *Someone else called me good-looking once ... he's dead.*

'He's missing, isn't he?' Yorke said.

Powers was taken aback. 'What makes you say that?'

'I just put two and two together based on something that Sturridge said, sorry, *wrote* down earlier. Did you know he doesn't talk?'

Powers looked confused. 'I actually spoke to him a couple of weeks ago. So ... no.'

'Well, things have dramatically changed since then,' Yorke said. 'We think his tongue may have been removed. As you are aware, he may have murdered a police officer, and he *also* claims to have murdered someone else. You didn't answer the question – is the pimp missing?'

'Alex Drake. Yes. Nasty piece of work. Bounced in and out of the station enough times. His days are numbered.'

'*Were*,' Topham said.

'Mark,' Yorke said, 'let's not jump to conclusions just yet. How many people are in this squat you are about to take us to?'

'Seven or eight?'

'Anyone that is particularly close to Sturridge?'

'They're all close, in their own way. Society's rejects tend to find solace in each other.'

'Obviously, we can get a warrant to search and seize, but let's go gentle. Gung-ho will not get us information.'

'Couldn't agree more,' Powers said. 'Round here, it's best to keep relationships strong.'

Powers led them past several run-down Edwardian houses. Lights glowed behind some curtains. Other houses were completely boarded over.

'How many people live down here?' Yorke said.

'Most are occupied, and not, as you would imagine, by down-and-outs. Children set off to school from some of these houses.'

Yorke sighed.

They turned into a driveway of a house which, oddly, was one of the nicest on the street. Yorke looked at Powers. 'The council doesn't want these houses back?'

'Yes, but as I said before, we are running a containment job around here, and things are moving rather slowly. Chucking people out of a squat has never been easy.'

'Even when they are brothels?'

'How can we be expected to catch those behind the brothel if we round up the small fry? We're playing a long game.'

'Well, you may have been playing too long with Alex Drake,' Topham said. 'I think Sturridge may have beat you to him.'

Powers knocked on the door.

A young woman wearing a silver nightie opened the door. Her eyeliner was smudged and she looked as if she'd been crying. 'Detective Powers?'

'Hello, Sylvia,' Powers said, 'we need to talk if that's okay?'

Sylvia's hand was on the edge of the door. As her eyes flicked from one officer to another, again and again, Yorke prepared himself for the door being slammed in their faces.

'No one is in trouble, Sylvia.' Powers offered her a smile. 'We just want to talk.'

'About what?'

'About David Sturridge.'

There was a pause while she looked down at the floor.

'Yes, I know you two are close,' Powers said.

'Come in, but you need to know that some of the rooms are busy.'

Topham looked at Yorke. Yorke knew what he was thinking. *Ignoring crime?*

Yorke stared back at him as if to say: *priorities.*

'That's fine, Sylvia,' Yorke said, 'please take us to the lounge and tell us what you know.'

Yorke expected squalor: pizza boxes and syringes; instead, he was presented with a tidy, clean living room.

As they sat, Yorke heard a knock at the front door. Sylvia was sitting with them now, so someone else was greeting the punter. He heard a muffled male voice and then looked over at Sylvia, who was looking down at her bare feet, clearly concerned that the law was being broken in front of three high-ranking officers.

'Sylvia?' Powers said.

'I haven't seen David in almost a month.' She looked at Yorke as she spoke. 'And I've been worried sick.'

'David is safe,' Yorke said, 'and he will remain safe, Sylvia.'

She looked at Powers and gestured at her mouth. He wandered over to her and handed her a rolled-up cigarette. After popping it into her mouth, she took a lighter from the arm of chair and lit it. Her hand trembled as she took a hungry puff. 'So, he's in jail then?'

'I'm afraid so,' Yorke said, 'but as I said, that makes him safe.'

'What's he done?'

'It is too early for us to comment on that.'

'Is it to do with Alex?'

Alex Drake – the pimp.

'Why do you ask that?' Topham said.

'Because we haven't seen him in weeks either,' Sylvia said.

Topham and Yorke exchanged glances.

'When did you last see him, and what happened?' Yorke said, readying his notepad.

Sylvia ignored the question and gave them a potted history of David Sturridge instead: a kind and sensitive boy who had been badly damaged by the events back in his home city of Southampton. He sounded a far cry from the smiling murderer sitting opposite Yorke in the interview room earlier. Sylvia continued by explaining how the idea of prostitution had repulsed Sturridge, as it did with many of the workers, she added. So, he'd tried his very best to keep it to a minimum and had only turned to it when he'd become too strapped for cash. However, pimp Alex Drake, who was providing the roof over their heads, was forever demanding more money. Several local army barracks ensured that there was never a shortage of business, she explained, and the number of repressed homosexual soldiers was staggering. Alex had wanted him working harder and had been becoming increasingly frustrated with Sturridge's excuses. Sturridge could get by on less because, like her, he never touched drugs. A rarity, she admitted, and one of the reasons they were particularly close. He was like the brother she'd never had. She described how they planned to save what little money they earned and get a place together – away from the drugs and prostitution. 'Sounds like fantasy, doesn't it?'

'No,' Powers said. 'It sounds like a good idea.'

She smiled. 'Well, it isn't going to happen now. I've lost him, haven't I? What did he do anyway? Did he kill Alex?'

Yorke flicked to a fresh page of his notebook. 'We don't know that, Sylvia. You are really helping us though. When was the last time you saw David?'

'Three weeks ago. He'd been struggling for a month or so before that. He wouldn't tell me why – just spent a lot of time online, quiet and alone. Didn't really want to speak to me that much anymore. Thought I'd done something to offend him.'

'You have the internet?' Topham said.

'Some of the legally owned houses on the street do. We just tag along on their wi-fi, for a small cost. Not much.'

'What was he doing online?' Yorke said.

'I don't know. Again, we kind of drifted apart.'

'Did he have a laptop to surf the internet?' Yorke said.

'He had a smashed-up old tablet which he could get online with.'

'And what happened the day he disappeared?'

'Not much. He just went out and didn't come back.'

'And what did Alex Drake have to say about that?' Topham said.

'What you'd expect. Shouting and swearing. Demanding to know where he was. Threatening to evict him if he ever came back. It was irrelevant. No one knew where he'd gone, and that was that.'

'Does Alex Drake come around often?' Yorke said.

'Daily. But not anymore. That's why I thought he might be dead. It's David, isn't it? He killed the bastard. He probably deserved it. Used to knock some of us around.'

'Did David leave any of his belongings?' Topham said.

'Yes – but there's not much. Like most of us, he literally lived out of a backpack.'

'Can you get his belongings please?' Yorke said.

Five minutes later, Sylvia returned with a *Lidl* bag-for-life.

Yorke asked Topham and Powers to log the items as he took them from the bag and laid them out. Yorke then pulled a pair of plastic gloves from an inside pocket of his suit. Just as he was about to start laying the items out, his phone rang. He took the phone out of his pocket and read the name on the screen.

Harry Butler.

Yorke's heart thrashed against his chest. He jumped up as a collection of images turned over in his mind: standing with his best friend, Harry, as they graduated as officers together; sitting at the dinner table with Harry and his new wife; dragging Harry away from his wife who was lying dead on the ground after being shot by a deranged farmer; watching Harry lose his job after planting evidence on an innocent man suspected of killing Yorke's sister ...

Yorke steadied himself against the wall as he stared at the name on the phone screen.

It'd been years. What does he want?

He felt Topham's hand on his shoulder. 'Sir?'

Yorke sent Harry to Voicemail, and put the phone in his pocket. 'Let's continue.'

Trying to steady his gloved hand, Yorke took out the items one by one and laid them on the coffee table. 'Item one - a Stephen King novel. Item two – a photograph of a younger boy, potentially him with his family.'

He continued to pull out the items, most of which were pieces of clothing before reaching, 'Item 11, a 10-inch tablet with a smashed screen.' He looked up at Sylvia. 'Do you know how to get onto this?'

'Yes,' she said.

JAKE HAD BEEN WAITING over an hour to speak to Marcus Long. That was how long the medical staff had needed to check everything was in order following the operation, and to talk Long through his life-changing injuries.

His self-inflicted life-changing injuries. They couldn't reattach his tongue because he'd flushed it down the toilet.

Jake took a seat beside Long's bed and watched him run his fingers over the gauze covering his mouth.

'Why Marcus? God, *why?*' Jake said.

Long shrugged. He was pale and weary. This interview would not be lasting long. Jake pulled the food table attached to the bed by an arm over his lap. He lay a notepad and pen down so Marcus could write.

He wrote: *No choice.*

'Explain.'

Severance wrote letter. Told me to do this or Susie dies.

'Where is this letter?'

Cell.

'You should have told me.'

Then what? Susie dead? Long stared at him.

'But why your tongue?'

Obvious? I took his and now he's taken mine.

After Marcus Long had served his sentence for sexually abusing Christian Severance, he had returned to a broken life. A jobless, *and* loveless, life. A decade elapsed in which he sank further and further into misery, while the young man, Severance, grew more successful in his chosen scientific field. One day, Long decided to go and see Severance again. It wasn't well received by his former student, but it still rekindled old feelings in Long. Feelings that contributed to his every waking thought for months on end. Eventually, he succumbed to his feelings, and initiated a campaign which saw him stalking, and trying to weave himself, like a spider, into every aspect of Severance's life. It was nothing short of obsession and mania. It had ended in Severance's kitchen with a gun that Long had acquired from the dark web. The solution, Long had told the jury, was one that was clouded with love and fatalism – if he couldn't have Severance, no one could. The bullet entered Severance's cheek, smashed his jaw, and destroyed his tongue.

'We cannot find Severance, Marcus, not for the want of trying. Are you even sure it was him that wrote the letter?'

Long scribbled. *Yes. It's him. I know his words.* Jake

noticed a tear in his eyes. Did he still love him? After all of this pain and misery?

Long flipped to another page of the notebook and continued writing. *I destroyed him. He destroyed me. Fairness?*

There is nothing fair in mutilation, thought Jake. He kept his thoughts to himself.

Jake leaned nearer to Long. 'Does he say anything else in that letter? Any indication of where he might be? What else he wants?'

No. This was what he wanted. Maybe Susie will be released now?

'I hope so. You know that I need to see that letter?'

Yes. Charles Dickens. A tale of two cities.

Jake gave him a puzzled look.

On my bookshelf in the cell.

'Thank you.' Jake made a note in his own book to have the guards retrieve the letter from his cell.

I thought this was for the best.

Jake nodded, and thought, *how could you possibly think that this would be for the best?* 'You need to rest now.'

The next message that Long scribbled was longer. Jake waited patiently, observing the man crumbling under the heavy weight of a failed life.

I've made mistakes. A lot of them. I'll apologise for them. Suffer and die for them. But she doesn't deserve it.

'No, she doesn't, and we are trying to find her.'

Long had the energy for one last message.

Please Detective. Help her. I beg you.

Jake nodded.

THERE WAS ONLY one file on the home screen for them to open. Yorke, Powers, Topham and Sylvia gathered around the cracked tablet.

They played a video file of a room which was barely furnished. A mattress on the floor. A small pile of magazines beside it acting as a bedside table. Lights were dim, although this could have been the quality of the tablet's camera.

'It's the room he was staying in ... upstairs,' Sylvia said. 'There is a television opposite the bed. This is where he must have positioned the tablet.'

'To film what?' Powers said.

The room was briefly illuminated by a brighter light, presumably from the landing outside as someone opened the door to come in.

A voice grew louder as it neared the tablet. 'How many times do we have to have this fucking conversation? You have to provide for me, or I won't provide for you.'

'That's Alex, charming as ever,' Sylvia said.

Alex and Sturridge moved in front the camera. The size difference was vast. Alex was a large, looming man, not unlike Powers. Sturridge was a boy barely out of his teens; skinny and fresh-faced.

'I provided for you last time you were here. I did exactly what you asked,' Sturridge said.

Sturridge was yet to open his mouth in Yorke's presence, so to see him talking here was disorientating.

Alex turned around and moved away from the camera. The room dimmed again, indicating that the door had been closed. When he came back into view, he pointed a finger in Sturridge's face. 'Any louder and you may have been heard. How do you think that would have gone down?'

'Sorry...' Sturridge said.

'Do you think I'm *like* you?'

'No ... of course not.'

'Good. Do I look desperate? Queer?'

'No.'

'I think you need to think about leaving. You've been here a long time now.'

'No ... please. You know I'll do whatever you want. *Right* now.' He reached out a hand and placed it on Alex's crotch. 'I need this place.'

Alex shook his head. 'So, you won't suck a punter's dick, but you'll suck mine? What's that all about?'

'I don't want to be like the others. I don't want it to be everything.'

Alex laughed. 'Or, you could just admit it? You like me, don't you?'

Sturridge didn't reply.

'Say you like me.'

'I like you.' Sturridge looked down. He was shaking.

'Look me in the fucking eyes as you say it.'

Sturridge looked up. 'I like you.'

Alex stroked his face. 'You're good-looking, do you know that?'

Sturridge nodded.

'Very handsome.' Alex kissed him on the lips. 'Now, say you like me again.'

'I like you.'

'Again. Convince me.'

'*I like you.*'

'Good.' Alex continued to stroke his face for a moment until Sturridge started to shake less. 'Relax, David.'

Sturridge nodded.

Alex slapped him hard across the face. 'Fucking faggot.'

Yorke heard Sylvia gasp beside him. Yorke paused the video file and looked at Powers, who read his cue.

'Come with me Sylvia. Let's go outside,' Powers said.

Once Powers and Sylvia were outside, Yorke and Topham watched the end of the recording.

Alex grabbed Sturridge by his shoulder and threw him onto the bed. Before the young boy was able to turn over, Alex had straddled him.

'Jesus,' Topham said. 'The man is about twice his size. What chance did he have?'

At first, Sturridge struggled, but it was futile under the crushing weight of the huge man. Alex pulled up Sturridge's arms and pinned them down with one hand, while he used his other hand to pull down the boy's jeans and underwear.

'You are good-looking, David, that's the problem really,' Alex said as he fumbled with his own belt. 'Fuck you for being so good-looking.'

Sturridge struggled for a couple of seconds more before submitting; then, he screamed out loud when Alex forced himself inside.

Yorke put a hand to his mouth.

Topham ran a hand through his hair. 'Sick bastard.'

6

I T WAS VERY late, but Yorke needed to follow up on what he'd just seen. He also knew that as soon as he finished his shift, he had his old friend, Harry Butler, to contend with. Harry was a widowed, disgraced copper who needed to stay as far away from his old life in law-enforcement as possible. Contacting Yorke certainly did not fulfil that criteria. He'd felt his phone buzz several times on the journey back into the station with Topham, but he'd sensibly kept it in his pocket.

In the car, he'd offered Topham the opportunity to go home and get some rest, but it had been declined. Yorke could see a familiar fire in his colleague's eyes. A fire that burned regularly in the eyes of the people he so often worked with.

Before they went into the interview room with Sturridge, Yorke turned to face his colleague. 'What that boy endured is horrific, and indescribable. But he's still responsible for destroying the lives of other people.'

Topham said, 'I was one of the first at the scene this

morning. *I held that tongue.* Don't worry about me, sir, sympathy is in short supply.'

Yorke looked through the glass door at the prisoner staring into space. *A monster, yes. But a monster that had been created by another monster. How many times had he seen this in his career?*

Sturridge knew that they knew. Yorke could tell this as he took a seat opposite him. Completely gone were the confidence and the sneers. He now actually looked like the person he really was.

A shattered boy.

Yorke looked at Topham, gave the date and time for the recording, emphasising the name *David Sturridge*, and then said, 'You're a clever young man, David, you knew we'd find out who you were eventually.'

Sturridge shrugged.

Good, thought Yorke. *He's responding. He knows it is time.*

Yorke pushed a notepad and pen over.

'Why did you kill DC Ryan Simmonds?'

He wrote something down and then passed it back to Yorke.

Yorke read it out for the recording, 'David Sturridge has written: *I didn't mean for him to die.*'

'But he's dead, isn't he? So, it's murder, David,' Topham said.

'We have your identity, the evidence that you committed the crime, we do not need your confession,' Yorke said, 'but if you help us to understand and explain it all to us, it could help you in the days to come.'

Sturridge stared at Yorke long and hard. The look

seemed to say to Yorke: *Do you really not get it? Is it not obvious?*

Yorke touched the notepad and Sturridge wrote.

'David Sturridge has written: *Do you ever feel alone?*'

Instinctively, Yorke answered the question in his head, but he sensibly refrained from saying it out loud. He felt pricked by his own response though.

Sturridge grabbed the notepad back again and Yorke watched him write the words: *Do you ever feel the need to strike back?*

Again, Yorke's mind automatically sought an answer, and his thoughts immediately flew to his dead sister, Danielle, and Harry Butler's phone call.

Topham must have noticed that his boss had been caught off-guard because he read the message out for the recording and then continued the interview. 'David, we know what happened to you. We went to the squat. The place you *rent* from Alex Drake by prostituting yourself. We met Sylvia – and she loves you. At least she loved the David Sturridge that she knew – I do not think she knows this one sitting in front of us. She opened the tablet, and we watched the film of you and Alex. I can't imagine how you must feel—'

Sturridge slammed his fist on the table. He reached over, grabbed the notepad and scribbled.

Topham took it back and said, 'David Sturridge has written: *see above*. And has drawn an arrow up to the previous two questions which have been recorded in this interview.'

Yorke brought himself back in. 'David, why did you make that film?'

Sturridge wrote his reply.

'David Sturridge has written: *exposure*,' Yorke said. 'So, David, you wanted to expose Alex Drake as homosexual?'

Sturridge wrote: a*mong other things.*

'A rapist too?' Yorke said.

Didn't expect him to do that.

'What did you hope to achieve by exposing him?'

I wanted to destroy his reputation.

'So, why didn't you move forward with the plan? You *had* the ammunition.'

Found another option.

'To actually kill him?'

Sturridge did not write an answer.

'Look,' Yorke said, 'despite what you've done, I cannot help but feel sympathetic over what has happened to you, but with the truth out on the table, we can close this off. Things will be so much better for it.'

Sturridge wrote: *the truth isn't simple.*

'It rarely is, but we have to start somewhere. David, did you kill Alex Drake?'

Sturridge considered and wrote: *No, but I am part of the experience.*

Now what the hell does that mean? Yorke thought. He looked at Topham. His colleague's eyes sent over a similar thought.

'So, you were there?'

No.

'But you know he's dead?'

Yes.

'Who did it then?'

Sturridge didn't write a response.

Yorke felt his frustration grow. He glanced up at the busted air con, wishing for a blast of refreshing cool air. He decided it was time to take the interview up a notch. 'Christian Severance?'

Sturridge flinched. He hadn't expected that. *Got him.*

'How do you know this man?' Yorke said.

Sturridge stood firm and remained still.

'Severance had motive to kill Ryan Simmonds. Have you done this for him?'

No response.

'One last time, I will ask you about this man. After that, this well of goodwill towards you runs dry. Where is Christian Severance? How do you know him? And did he kill Alex Drake?'

Sturridge considered and then wrote: *It is not my place to talk about Christian Severance.*

Yorke bit his bottom lip and narrowed his eyes.

Sturridge wrote: *I will not be pushed on this.*

Topham jumped in. 'Have you got a little deal between yourselves? You kill this man for me, and I'll kill this one for you?'

I told you already – Simmonds was not supposed to die.

'Why didn't you just deal with your own problems? Wouldn't it be more satisfying that way?' Topham said.

You do not understand.

'Well, help us to,' Yorke said.

No point.

'Then we can help you.'

No need. I am healed.

'Healed?' Topham said, raising his eyebrows. 'Look at yourself David. Have you still got your tongue?'

Sturridge opened his mouth to show them that he hadn't.

Yorke pressed on. 'You've been mutilated and you are going to be found guilty of murder ... at what point are you going to give yourself a bloody break?'

I've accepted what I have become.

'Did Christian Severance take your tongue?' Yorke said.

Sturridge paused to look Yorke in the eyes for a few moments and then wrote: *I've shared and I'm no longer alone.*

Yorke looked away.

Topham pointed at Sturridge. 'You sound brainwashed!'

And I've displaced my pain onto others.

Yorke gently pushed down Topham's finger which was too close to Sturridge's face for comfort. He nodded to the guard in the corner and called the interview to a close.

TOPHAM THREW down his bag and collapsed onto his sofa. He reached over to the vacant side of it, wishing desperately that it wasn't empty right now, and grabbed a cushion. He lodged it under his head and closed his eyes.

The sleep he entered was fitful, and the dreams were relentless. Colleagues, people he knew and loved, stared at him as blood ran from the corners of their mouths. In front of them, Alex Drake, pointed at him, and called him a faggot over and over again, breaking the repetition every now and again with the words, 'I am not like you.'

He woke with tears in his eyes, and Neil was sitting beside him on the sofa now, dabbing his forehead with a towel.

'It looked like you were having a nightmare, thought I'd wake you gently.'

Topham reached up and stroked Neil's face. 'I appreciate it. You wouldn't believe the things that happened today.'

'Want to talk about it?'

Topham shook his head, and then brushed the back of his

hand over Neil's new goatee. 'Still not sure about this new look.'

'Does that mean I don't get a kiss?' Neil raised his eyebrows.

Topham reached up, looped his arm around the back of Neil's head, and pulled him in for a kiss.

They broke away and Neil said, 'Does that help you get used to it?'

'It's a start,' Topham said, and winked.

They took a few moments to stare at each other, before Neil said, 'You've been crying, haven't you?'

'In my sleep, I think.'

Neil stroked his face. 'What did happen today?'

Topham sighed. 'I shouldn't really talk about it. Besides, you really don't want to know.'

'It's about that dead policeman, isn't it?'

Topham nodded. 'Please ... let's talk about your night first. How did it go with Martin Adams?'

'Well, it wasn't easy going for dinner after the wedding meal, but I forced it down anyway. Didn't want to look ungrateful!'

Topham smiled. 'And?'

'And?' Neil said, smiling back.

'It's in the bag, isn't it?'

Neil beamed.

Topham sat up. '*Really?*'

'Yes!'

'Part of *his* team?'

'He loved my my second book. The one about PTSD. He just went on and on about it.'

'Boom!' Topham said, giving Neil a knuckle bump.

'That's my boy. It's all those interview questions I gave you yesterday. Got to be some credit in this for me?'

Neil laughed. 'Sorry to break this to you, Mark, but it wasn't really an interview. Martin said that the meal was just a formality. He just needed to know that I wasn't as socially awkward as most of his team.'

'Well, you're definitely not socially awkward.'

'Thanks.'

'I mean, did he even get a word in edgeways?'

'One or two.'

Topham narrowed his eyebrows, feigning suspicion. 'He's not gay is he?'

'Wasn't the first question I asked, believe it or not!'

Topham sat up and put his arms around Neil. He whispered in his ear. 'I'm so proud of you.' They then placed their foreheads together.

After another brief kiss, Topham said, 'So when do you start?'

'Tomorrow.'

'Bloody hell! He is keen. You really have made an impression.'

'I think it's going to be a test of some kind.'

'What do you mean?'

'Well, he only wants me to see one patient. A long-standing patient, and a notoriously tricky one. I suspect Martin wants to see how I handle it.'

'Well, if it is a test, you'll fly through it. God, Neil, I'm so proud of you.'

They embraced.

'So, there is absolutely no chance that I'm hearing about your day?' Neil said.

Topham rose to his feet. 'Work another time. Champagne, sex, sleep; in that order.'

'If you insist.'

'Yes, I *fucking* insist.'

───────

THANKFULLY, Patricia was asleep. If she hadn't been, he would have unloaded the toxic stew in his brain onto her, and that wouldn't have been kind.

Not on their wedding day.

It was stifling, even with the windows open. He lay there, naked, next to his new wife, also naked, and listened to the cars outside.

He turned onto his side and reached around to stroke her stomach, trying to feel for some movement from his unborn child. Then he moved around to stroke the scars on her back. Skiing, apparently.

A lie. Every time they discussed it, she looked away. Then, after the discussion ended, sadness always lingered in her eyes. The truth was close though. He felt it. Every time he mentioned it, she seemed to move that little bit closer to him. Trust him that little bit more.

He kissed her shoulder blades and said, 'I'm sorry.'

And he genuinely was. He'd ruined her wedding day.

Was this a sign of things to come? The life that he was offering her?

He rolled onto his back and thought of David Sturridge's question written on that notepad. *Do you ever feel alone?*

He ran his hand through Patricia's hair. *I wish so much, so very much, that I didn't. I owe you more than that.*

He thought of Harry Butler and the three messages on Voicemail. All demanding that Yorke phone him immediately because the news was urgent. He'd not rang back because that man didn't deserve a phone call. A text message would have to suffice. *What do you want?* He was yet to hear back.

He thought of Sturridge's second question: *do you ever feel the need to strike back?*

The answer to that was very simple.

Danielle had been everything to Yorke growing up. While their mother sought out drugs and men, only communicating with her children in a stoned haze, Danielle remained *focused* on Yorke, feeding him, and walking him to school. As Yorke grew, becoming more introverted and awkward, she became more protective and took him everywhere. A fourteen-year-old girl had no business being trailed by a prepubescent boy. Her friends weren't so sure either. It wasn't long before she didn't have many left. All because of her commitment to raise a child that no one else could be bothered raising.

Yes. Danielle always *sacrificed* for him.

But then she became an eighteen-year-old girl, crumbling under the pressure of not only loving and supporting one boy, but their mother's other two boys as well; both of whom eventually ended up in care. One memorable night, Danielle told Yorke that she'd failed his brothers.

But why was it her failure? Simply because their mother would never have allowed it to be her failure. She had been too busy with drugs and men to take any responsibility.

When Danielle turned twenty, she found relief in the same addictions as their mother.

Leaving Yorke alone.

Danielle quickly became consumed by the dark world

she'd thrown herself into. Tom Davies, a selfish and spiteful young man, helped nurture her heroin addiction. He got her pregnant twice, but never came to the hospital to hold her hand after she miscarried. Davies was with her the night she died. In a dingy hole somewhere with a drug dealer called William Proud. A man who took too much from the world and left it cold in his wake.

Proud tried to rape Yorke's sister in the kitchen. When Danielle resisted, he held her face against a hot stove until she died. Maybe he hadn't expected her to die? Cause of death was a heart attack. Proud ran, leaving Davies to hold the body, because deep down, beneath the spite, he loved her. He cried with her for hours, until the police arrived and arrested him for a murder he hadn't committed.

Yorke, then a detective constable, was supposed to be kept in the dark regarding the murder. Identifying her body was meant to be his only involvement. On that slab, they turned the burned side of her face away from him – which allowed his imagination to work its grisly spell, and the preserved memories of her beautiful face crumbled.

Looking back now, his memories were clouded and hazy. Unsurprising. It had been a time drowning in alcohol.

Detective Inspector Harry Butler, his best friend, had been nominated SIO. Capable hands.

Yorke sneered.

The only thing Harry had been capable of in that investigation was keeping Yorke informed on the details around the developing case. Something he really shouldn't have been doing.

Maybe that was the reason? Maybe Yorke's secret involvement in the case had pushed Harry too far? Those clandestine meetings and phone calls – in which Yorke had cried and demanded that Harry find justice.

Harry was no stranger to loss, having lost his own wife to the hands of a murderous recluse, so he had moved swiftly.

Davies became the victim of that swiftness. When William Proud was nowhere to be found, Harry coerced a confession from Davies. Away from the tape recorder, Davies was lied to. Harry told him that the DNA pointed to the fact that Proud was never present; that it was his, Davies' DNA, that was going to ensure a life sentence. Harry also told Davies that he would prosecute his mother for dealing heroin, having found a large supply in her house when they searched it. This, of course, would never have washed – the drugs belonged to Davies and no one in their right mind would have ever believed them to belong to his mother. But, for all his failings, Davies loved his mother a great deal, so he agreed to confess, and went to jail for the murder of Danielle Yorke. It seems, in his desperation for swiftness, and a desperate need to support his best friend, Harry really had started to believe in his own fabrications.

When Davies committed suicide in jail, leaving a note in which he disgraced Harry for coercing confessions, and named Proud as the rightful heir to this prison sentence, Harry not only lost his job, he also suffered a nervous breakdown.

Proud, wanted in connection with the murder of Danielle Yorke, had never been seen since.

And Yorke blamed Harry.

And his anger, and resentment, burned deep.

To see this man, desperate for his forgiveness, desperate to atone for his sins, made him sick, so staring at the phone now, made him angry.

As he'd thought through these traumatic events from years ago, he'd thrown on a dressing gown and headed out into his back garden with his mobile phone. The walls on his garden were low and the neighbouring terraced houses loomed over him – the occasional window burst into light, taking away the feeling of isolation he'd journeyed outside to find.

He looked at his mobile phone again. Still no response.

His dressing gown flopped open, but he had underwear on, and it was another hot evening, so he didn't bother to close it. He saw the flashing green eyes of a cat as it swept past him and disappeared into the darkness at the end of his garden.

A run. That's what he wanted right now.

He'd found a solace in running that was indescribable. It wasn't just that sense of freedom, but rather that *headspace*, that he was failing to find right now.

To be left alone. To stop thinking. Just to feel.

But it was too late for a run, so he reached into his pocket for a cigarette.

He thought of Gardner's eyes on him. Not just a close colleague, but one of his closest friends, and mother to his godchild. She disapproved of his smoking. *Vehemently.* Which could be rather irritating, especially when standing outside a crime scene with the adrenaline riding high.

Before he lit his cigarette, his phone beeped.

Tomorrow, 1 p.m. Wyndam. Be there Mike. It's about Proud.

His sister's murderer. Yorke dropped his cigarette to ring him back. His heart thumped and his hands shook. He was sent through to voicemail.

He tried five more times, but the bastard had switched off his mobile phone.

GARDNER SAT IN THE KITCHEN, alone, writing down her thoughts. Then, she challenged these thoughts with evidence to the contrary, before adapting them to new, more palatable ones.

CBT was going well, but she still wasn't sleeping properly.

She drank an entire pint of water, swallowed an Ibuprofen to help with the period pains, and wrote down a stream of consciousness born from her new thoughts.

Despite having an intense job, I am a good mother. Many people have intense jobs and are still good parents. I help people every day. That's what I always wanted to do. So, by working long hours, I am not sacrificing my life and happiness. This is something important that I always wanted to do. My daughter is happy, and she loves me. She tells me and Barry that every day.

But then her thoughts settled on Barry again. He was the stay-at-home husband, the trend-breaker. He spent so much time with her daughter. He'd sacrificed the job he'd loved. Why hadn't she? Was she the selfish one?

She kept writing.

Because your job pays more. It is not selfish to want to support your family. It is not selfish to want the very best for everyone...

A car backfired outside and she flinched.

She thought of the gunshot.

She thought of the dead man lying on the floor in front of her.

She thought of the gun in her hand.

And she thought of the real reason her mind had started to unravel all those months ago.

IT WAS LATE, but Jake decided to shave his head.

It had really started to thin these last months, and maintaining a style, no matter how simple, was beginning to feel rather pointless. Over the bath, he gave it a Number One all over, and smiled to himself over the thirty seconds he would be saving every morning in front of the bathroom mirror.

As he examined his new look in the mirror, he thought of the raised eyebrows at work tomorrow. *Hopefully*, he thought, *if that sociopath, Lacey, ever returns, she won't be able to recognise me.*

Despite his attempts to distract himself, his mind wandered back to the nod he'd given to Marcus Long.

Please Detective. Help her. I beg you.

Jake's nod. An affirmation that he would help her.

He sighed and ran his hand over his stubbly head.

Why did you promise to help someone who is probably already dead?

His son, Frank, started to cry, and for once, Jake was happy for it.

It offered a welcome distraction from Lacey Ray, Susie Long and his ridiculous new haircut.

7

YORKE HADN'T SLEPT, and Ewan, ever observant, pointed it out immediately. 'Are you alright, Mike? You look sick.'

Yorke swallowed a mouthful of cornflakes and said, 'It was a long night.'

'And will it be a long day?'

'Probably.'

'When you should be going to South Africa?'

Yorke put his spoon in the bowl and raised his eyebrows. 'Don't you start! Anyway, at least we'll have time to plan that birthday party to end all birthday parties.'

'Nah,' Ewan said, sitting down at the kitchen table with Yorke. 'Changed my mind. Getting a bit old for all that.'

'Bloody hell. You don't actually have to *become* a stereotypical teenager the day you turn thirteen, you know.'

'Okay, maybe something quiet, then? Last year, Dad took me to Alton Towers, and then Mum took me to the cinema after. Think I got my fair share then!'

Yorke nodded. 'Okay, agreed. Whatever you want, Ewan. It's the least we can do.'

Ewan reached over for the bran flakes.

'There's Coco Pops in the cupboard,' Yorke said.

'No thanks. I'm getting back into the running, I need to try and slim down.'

Yorke smiled. 'Two things: One, that's amazing! Two, there's nothing of you to slim down!'

Ewan stood up, turned to his side and flattened his pyjama top to try and show Yorke his gut.

'I rest my case,' Yorke said. 'Now get some food down you.'

As they ate, something occurred to Yorke. 'This slimming down and running has nothing to do with that young lady at our wedding yesterday, does it?'

Ewan glowed red.

'Okay,' Yorke said, 'don't answer that.'

Patricia walked into the kitchen. 'Leave him alone, Mike.'

Yorke smiled and opened his hands in a gesture to suggest confusion. 'What?'

'You know what?'

'I was thirteen once you know?'

'Right now, I'm starting to wonder if you still are.'

Ewan and Yorke laughed. Patricia walked over and kissed Ewan on the top of his head. 'You all packed for your grandad's?'

'Yes,' Ewan said and sighed.

Patricia and Yorke exchanged a glance, and she said, 'You are usually over the moon about going to your grandad's...'

'Yeah,' Ewan said. 'I guess. Just wanted to get out running, you know?'

'I'm sure you can do that up in Harrogate!' Patricia said.

'Yes, but it's not the same there.'

Yorke couldn't help himself. 'You mean that young lady isn't there?'

'Mike!' Patricia said. She wasn't smiling.

'Sorry. Well, I suppose you could stay now that South Africa is postponed?' Yorke said.

'Nonsense,' Patricia said. 'You are going to see your grandad. You'll love it when you're there. You always do.'

Ewan nodded. 'I suppose we can go to that massive pet shop and look at snakes.'

Yorke and Patricia exchanged another look. It had been seven months since he'd lost his pet corn snake, Freddy, and unfortunately, it now sounded like he was ready for another one.

'Just looking mind,' Yorke said.

Ewan smiled. 'You said before – *whatever you want?*'

Yorke opened his mouth to reply, but Patricia jumped in. 'We will discuss it when you come back, Ewan.'

Minutes later, after Ewan had gone upstairs to check his packing, Patricia sat opposite Yorke. 'Have you looked in the mirror this morning?'

Yorke smirked. 'You always know how to make me feel special.'

'You were out in the garden for God knows how long, and then you tossed and turned all night.'

Yorke looked down. 'Sorry. I know it wasn't the wedding night you envisaged.'

She reached over and took his hand. 'It's not that. It's just I'm worried about you. I don't want you riding a wave of nervous exhaustion like ... like—'

'—last time?'

Patricia sighed. 'Yes, like last time.'

'I won't do,' Yorke said. 'The wedding yesterday was wonderful, and the events after just got to me. They reminded me of last year, and what happened with Iain. I'll make it up to you, Patricia. I promise—'

'Don't even say it, Mike. You don't have to make anything up to me. I know who you are, who I married. You don't have to pretend to me or hide away. You tell me everything, and I'll *accept* everything.'

But are you telling me everything? Yorke thought. *That scar on your back? The fabled skiing accident?*

He inwardly cursed himself for his moment of mistrust, but knew that it had legs, and knew the thoughts would return.

She held his hand tightly now. 'Just phone me today. Just a couple of times to let me know you're okay.'

'I will do,' Yorke said.

'Promise?'

Yorke paused, knowing he was really committing himself here, but knowing he had no room to manoeuvre. 'Promise ... but promise me that we won't be bringing a snake into this house!'

***

JAKE WOKE up when his two-year-old boy Frank started to stroke his head. After yanking his boy up onto his chest, Jake tickled his tummy. Frank arched his back and giggled hysterically.

Then, Jake flipped him over so he could hold him up and look at his handsome little face.

'Dadda ... hair?'

Remembering his interaction with the electric shaver last

night, he laid his son gently to one side, and reached up to touch his stubbly head. 'Cut it all off, Frankie.'

Frank accepted it with a smile.

Water off a duck's back to Frank! He doubted Sheila would respond in quite the same way.

He looked around the spare room. It was barely furnished. Jake had been *permanently* busy with promotions since they'd bought the house. Sheila wasn't best pleased about this busyness, and his neglect of the DIY. His argument that if he hadn't gone for promotion then they wouldn't have been able to afford the house in the first place fell on deaf ears.

Most things fell on deaf ears these days, hence the reason he was in the spare room again. He'd spent that many nights in here now, Frank knew where to come and find him in the morning.

He carried his son downstairs and found Sheila in the kitchen. She was dressed in a thin, yellow nightie and smoked a menthol cigarette out of the window.

She looked at Jake, and then looked away. It was a warning to prepare for the silent treatment. Jake didn't believe it. She could never hold out. He ran into the lounge, deposited Frank in a den loaded with shape sorters, his ultimate pastime, and then approached his wife.

'Don't,' she said, flicking the menthol out of the window and closing it.

'Best we talk now, I've got to go—'

'—to work soon?'

'Yes. Funnily enough, I do.'

'It's all work and no play for Jake these days, isn't it?'

Well, thought Jake, *it has been for a very long time to be honest.*

'We do have responsibilities. We have a mortgage.'

'No one else I know seems to work sixty-hour weeks.' Her tone was anything but calm, but she did keep the volume out of her voice. She'd never let Frank hear them arguing.

'Are we really going to do this now?'

'Well, there never seems to be any other time to do it! Yesterday at the wedding was just ridiculous. Upping and leaving us like that.'

Jake sighed. 'I know it's not the best, Sheila, I do. But it was important. A young girl is missing, and I'd like to think that if that ever happened to us, somebody could help us.'

'Don't give me that, Jake! Making yourself out to be a hero! You don't do these things for anyone else but yourself.'

'That's not fair, Sheila, and you know it's not true.'

'Do I? It's always about you and your ego. Your next success. What about me, and your son? What about your best friend, Mike? You walked out of his fucking wedding!'

'And you don't think he would have done the same thing?'

She didn't answer.

'He's not even going on his honeymoon!' Jake said.

'Well, if someone else wants to ruin their lives, that's up to them, but you don't have to follow them over the cliff like a fucking lemming!'

'What's the point?' Jake said. 'You don't listen. You never have done.'

'Dada?' Frank said.

Jake turned around and his son was in the kitchen door-way. 'Frankie, are you okay?' He scooped him up in his arms and kissed him on his head. 'Go to Mummy now, Daddy has to get ready.'

He handed Frank over to Sheila. She cuddled and kissed him, put him down and he ran off back to his shape sorters.

Jake turned and left the room.

Behind him, Sheila said, 'And your hair looks bloody ridiculous.'

Sprawled naked on the bed, Topham watched Neil get dressed. 'This is why I always get up second.'

Neil smiled. 'That just sounds odd.'

'Why? I love watching you move.'

'Odder still.'

'Could watch it all day...'

'Okay, pack it in now.'

They both laughed.

After Neil was dressed, he turned to face Topham. 'How do I look?'

'Good. Do doctors wear suits?'

'Some do, some don't.'

'Well, I guess it's your first day.'

'Precisely. So ... does this tie work with this shirt?'

Topham nodded, swung out of bed and came over to hug him. Following their embrace, Topham tried to pull him back towards the bed.

'You are joking?' Neil said. 'I've just got dressed!'

'I'll help you put them back on! What time do you have to be there, anyway?'

Neil pushed him away, laughing. 'Soon!'

Topham did a commando roll on the bed and then disappeared under the sheets.

'Attractive,' Neil said.

'Well, I might have to entertain myself if...'

Neil charged over and straddled Topham. Then, he playfully held his arms above his head. 'I don't think so.' He leaned over and kissed him slowly.

After they had made love, they lay facing each other, catching their breaths. Neil stroked Topham's face. 'I was worried about you last night.'

'No need.'

'Go easy on yourself today, Mark; you do a great job as it is, but sometimes you get that look in your eyes.'

Topham crossed his eyes. 'Like this?'

Neil hit him gently on the forehead. 'No! You know what I mean. It's like ... you've been consumed.'

'Well, I've never heard it described in so dramatic a fashion before, but I guess I know what you mean. Perils of the job, I'm afraid.'

'So, you'll take it easier, today?'

'Well, I always plan to take it easy, to be honest. But something always gets in the way. I promise to try. Now, can we just talk about you for a minute...'

'Okay, what do you want to ask me?'

'Are you nervous about today?'

'A little. But Martin, well, he has this way. He spoke so highly of my book, and then just put me at ease. That patient I mentioned last night though ... I'm expecting him to be really difficult.'

'How so?'

'Well ... this guy has had some really traumatic experiences. I really hope I can help him.'

'If anyone can help him, Neil, you can.'

'Yes, but I'm just worried it might be a test.'

'If it's a test, you'll smash it. I'm so proud of you.'

'I am proud of you too. Just take it easy today as you promised.'

'Yes, sir.'

GARDNER REACHED into the fridge and pulled out a jar of strawberry jam. She opened the lid and looked inside. *Good, no thin layer of mould. Not like last time.*

As she closed the fridge door with her other hand, she was suddenly seized by an image of the man she'd shot in the line of duty seven months earlier. He was clutching the bullet wound on his neck while blood squirted out from the cracks between his fingers.

The jam jar smashed on the ground at her feet and she stumbled backwards into someone's arms.

'Are you okay, Emma?' Barry said.

Gardner looked down at her trembling hand and then closed it into a fist. 'Yes, it just slipped.'

'Go and sit down. I'll handle this.'

She turned in his arms and kissed him. 'Thanks, I appreciate that.'

'I noticed that you were up late last night and, when you did make it to bed, you were restless.'

'Just a bad day with what happened to Simmonds.'

'Yes, I can imagine, but are you sure nothing else is bothering you?'

She widened her eyes to fake surprise. 'Like what?'

'You know what, Emma.'

'That's all behind me now, Barry, the CBT is working. Like I said, it's just the fact that we lost one of ours yesterday, it's just left me a little shaken.'

'Why don't you take a day off just to clear your head?'

Gardner slipped from her husband's grip and headed over to the kitchen table. 'There's a lot going on at the moment. I'll be absolutely fine. Thanks for looking out for me though.'

She heard Barry sighing behind her. She scooped up her dry toast and said, 'I might just eat this on the way, honey, if that's okay? Running a little late.'

She turned around, went over and kissed him again. 'Thanks for tidying up after me, I'll see you later.'

He nodded. 'I love you.'

'I love you too,' she said, and left as quickly as she could, before he tried to convince her to stay again.

———

FUELLED with the adrenaline that comes with desperation, Susie Long pushed one last time against the roof of her plastic prison, watched the locking mechanism strain, threatening, but not quite giving, and then slumped back into a puddle of her own sweat, gasping for air.

She could feel the tears welling up again, but she fought them back and closed her eyes. Crying was useless. She'd given enough of the last two days to despair, and it had not shifted the lid on this box.

She took a deep breath and opened her eyes. *Did he mean to kill her? But if he meant to kill her, wouldn't she be dead already?*

She wondered, as she had done a thousand times, if she'd been kidnapped. *But if it was down to ransom, then why had it not been paid yet?*

Her mother adored her. She'd have paid in a heartbeat.

Unless – and this really did make her blood run cold – he had been paid but had now decided to keep her forever like a pet.

There were many possibilities, and this uncertainty was not helped by the fact that he just didn't speak. Not ever.

I wish, just once, she thought, *he'd open his mouth and tell me why he was here.*

At least he'd left the light on, so she could see the hell hole he'd stored her in. A cellar strewn with broken things and old boxes. It also allowed her to see the junk food he passed through a slot in the box. Burgers and pizza.

He wished she would let her out to go to the toilet. Just once. She'd lost control of her bladder a few times, but she'd managed not to shit herself. She prayed to God she could hold on. She'd lost enough of her dignity already.

Susie thought of Mrs Stradling at school, and those long-winded conversations about life, and its meaning that took them to the lofty heights of four, or even five in the evening. Mrs Straddling had experienced a lot of loss in her life, which included her husband, and she had a cool motto: *In this world, you must be ready for anything.*

So Susie, why weren't you ready for that bastard in the carpark at the Cloisters?

Three years of Tae-Kwon-Do at an early age should have seen her right. She could have struck his shins, knees or even his bollocks, but she'd failed. The thought of his strong arms looped around her from behind made her tremble. She flinched at the sound of her smartphone hitting the floor - God, how she wished she had that now. Her mouth ran dry over the thought of that rag clamped over her mouth that sent the lights out.

If she hadn't been a claustrophobic person before, she

certainly was now. She was in a plastic coffin about half-a-metre high and a metre wide. She kicked out at the lid again. It barely moved. *Was the box handmade? How long had he planned to contain her like this?* There were three locks along the side that kept the lid down. They were buried deep into the plastic, but she kept kicking and straining against it nonetheless. *What other option did she have? And if, by some miracle, it came loose, then what?*

She didn't know where she was, what time it was or who she was with.

Planning, reasoning, thinking ... it was all completely pointless when you have no knowledge of context.

Who are you? Susie Long thought again.

Who? Who? Who?

Are you the man my dad hurt?

Are you Christian Severance?

THE THUDDING SOUND woke Christian Severance. He sat up and listened. It was most certainly Susie kicking the lid of her plastic coffin.

Despite having pushed aside the sheets during another stifling night, Severance's t-shirt was damp. The heatwave was really starting to tighten its grip on Salisbury. He peeled it off and cast it aside.

The kicking continued.

He took a deep breath. The pounding was incessant, but it was a detached house, so he wasn't too concerned about anyone overhearing. He fought the irritation, and let his mind wander back to the events of yesterday.

Detective Constable Ryan Simmonds.

His death had been a side-effect of the *displacement*. Not unfortunate, because it did not detract from the success of the *displacement,* but it had been unforeseen. It shouldn't affect how the plan unravelled. Dead or alive, an assault like that on an officer would have brought significant heat regardless.

David Sturridge. In custody. But, again, this was how Severance had planned it. Sturridge would carefully drip feed them the information, at just the right tempo, so the rest of the plan could take effect. The police would be focused on him while *displacement* continued.

Susie Long was unrelenting. He didn't fear her escape. She could not break free. Yet the sound, and its repetition, was really starting to annoy him. He returned to his train of thoughts.

Marcus Long.

Severance *still* did not know if this *displacement* had been successful. Had he done what he'd been asked to do in his letter? This information was unlikely to find its way into the news in a great hurry. He would have to wait on this one; he had a friend within the prison community who would be informing him by phone later. If Marcus had responded to the threat, and *displacement* had been successful, he would no longer need his insurance policy. Susie. He'd be rid of that incessant kicking.

He swung his feet out of the bed and thought of yesterday's late night with the Conduit. The meditation and visualisations had been particularly gratifying. He had relived the moment when he had cried, uncontrollably, on the other side of that table in front of Ryan Simmonds as he'd explained his fear that Marcus Long was seeking retribution. He had begged Simmonds for support.

'He's *watching* me. Every time I leave the house. Everywhere I go – he's watching.'

'Have you *actually* seen him?'

'I know, he's there. I can sense him. He can't have me and he can't accept it. I don't think he will ever go away. Please help me.'

'Of course. Of course, we will.'

But that had been a lie, hadn't it, Simmonds? Where was the help? Days had turned to weeks, and weeks to months, and still no help. Yes, Simmonds, you helped after he'd blown a hole in my face, and I could no longer talk. But wasn't that a case of too little too late?

Accepting these moments of trauma, of intense pain, while meditating and visualising, offered small bursts of relief, and he'd slept well.

The kicking below continued. It was unbearable. He rose to his feet.

Yes, he needed her alive, for now. At least until the phone call confirmed that *displacement* onto Long had been successful. However, he could certainly do something this second about that kicking, something that would ensure she would stop.

And never do it again.

8

Operation Autumn and Operation Coldtown were linked. *Firmly.* Eyebrows were raised, and chatter within the heavy investigation team was at record levels. Gone was the broken and eerie shakiness of yesterday. A strong sense of purpose had come with the recent revelations, and solidity was rightfully returning to a crew who had a long history of success behind them.

Jeremy Dawson, the HOLMES database operator, was no longer running solo. His female counterpart, who had been assigned Operation Autumn, was busy tapping away beside him, making those links between the cases which could prove invaluable in the journey ahead.

Yorke stood in front of them as the SIO of this new umbrella operation. Flanked on one side by Gardner, originally SIO of Operation Autumn; and, on the other by Topham, originally SIO of Operation Coldtown.

There was a sudden moment of silence when Jake walked in.

'Nice trim, sir,' one of the officers said.

Jake blushed, and there was laughter among the officers. Yorke appreciated the moment. Banter helped build comradery.

Yorke began by talking the twenty-plus team through everything. It was necessary because every officer would be hazy on the details of one of the two operations. He did his best to create a timeline and was happy to see many of his officers scribbling down notes.

He began with the abduction of Susie Long from outside of *The Cloisters*. He ran through the particulars: the CCTV footage which showed the abduction; the dropped mobile phone; the interviews with the boyfriend and the family; and the *supposed* estrangement from Marcus Long, her imprisoned father. He allowed Gardner to interject frequently with details regarding this investigation and, on several occasions, Jake filled in some gaps. Most notably that Susie and her father had *actually* been in correspondence.

Then, Yorke took them through the events surrounding the murder of Simmonds again. The room was more upbeat than yesterday because Sturridge had been charged with the murder, so Yorke went through the facts concisely and formally without euphemisms.

At this point, Yorke noticed Parkinson fidgeting in his chair. Yorke hoped that he wasn't about to experience a repeat of last night when Parkinson had continually voiced his frustration.

'We know that Ryan conducted an interview with Christian Severance.' He'd already decided to refer to Simmonds by his first name, because many of the occupants of the room had been so close to him. 'Severance and Marcus Long bumped into each other in a supermarket almost fifteen years after the original crime. It is likely that

Long rediscovered his feelings for Severance at this point and began to follow him. Severance made a report to Ryan regarding these concerns. A report which was never followed up on. Please consult HOLMES to read the report following the briefing.'

Just like last night, Parkinson's hand was waving in the air.

'DC Parkinson?' Yorke said.

'I've read it, but there was no evidence to show that Long was actually pursuing Severance.'

'That is the case,' Yorke said, wanting to add: *but wouldn't it have been prudent for Simmonds to at least question Long?* However, he didn't add this, because the team were raw, and he didn't want to give Parkinson fuel to initiate a campaign of bitterness against him.

'Is it fair to blame Ryan for not acting on a gut-feeling?' Parkinson said.

'No one is blaming Ryan,' Topham said. 'Apart from Severance, that is.'

'Yes,' Yorke said, 'this seems to be the case. Severance was badly damaged by the subsequent run-in with Long. He was shot in the face and lost his tongue. So, it can be no coincidence that Ryan had his tongue cut out. We can only assume that Severance thinks that Ryan could have stopped it getting out of hand and so is partly responsible.'

'Why didn't Severance attack Ryan himself then?' Parkinson said.

'I'll get to that in a moment. As many of you are aware now, Ryan's killer, David Sturridge, also has a history that doesn't make for pleasant reading.'

Yorke went through the details of their investigation last night: the visit to the squat; the prostitution; and the brutal rape of Sturridge by Alex Drake. He also added that Alex was missing but did not elaborate on this for the time being.

'Last night, myself and DI Topham spoke to Sturridge. He communicates with cards because he has no tongue either.'

Until this point, many of the team had been unaware of this. A nervous chatter spread throughout the group.

'Did Severance cut his tongue out?' Willows asked.

'We don't know,' Yorke said. 'But he did offer some suggestions as to why this may all be happening. Sturridge has clearly emerged from an unhappy background which includes homelessness and male prostitution. In the interviews, he has referred to his loneliness and desire for vengeance.'

Yorke pointed at a picture on the whiteboard. 'Alex Drake, pimp, drug-dealer, and rapist of David Sturridge. He's also been missing for over a week. Sturridge has told us that he is dead.'

Another hand shot up. 'Did Sturridge kill Alex Drake?'

'He claims not. And he will not implicate Christian Severance. But I suspect Severance is the killer.'

Parkinson said, 'This isn't a Hitchcock movie! Seen *Strangers on a Train?* Two people swapping murders, so they don't get caught? Come on!'

Yorke took a sharp breath through his nose, and slowly exhaled through his mouth. *The man was dicing with disciplinary action. He was being antagonistic in situations which required teamwork.*

He filed the thought for post-investigation.

'Sturridge claimed to have *shared* his suffering with others, and *healed,*' Yorke said, recalling the details of the interview. 'There's something bigger at work here than just two people covering their tracks. Which, incidentally, they have not tried particularly hard to do. No, there's a much bigger picture here, especially when you consider the fact that the story to date, doesn't end there. Last night, Marcus Long was rushed to the hospital after biting his own tongue off.' There was more nervous chatter from his audience, but Yorke wasn't going to allow them breathing time. 'He received a letter from Christian Severance. The letter, now in our possession, will be discussed in more detail by DS Pettman, but it demanded that Long bite off his own tongue at eleven o'clock last night or his daughter would be murdered.'

Now, he allowed breathing time. Parkinson was mumbling something, but Yorke couldn't make out the words. Sheepishly, he kept looking up, which made Yorke wonder if he'd finally realised he was marking his own card for a disciplinary.

'I've read the letter,' Jake said, 'and again, it can be found on HOLMES. His letter is calm and thoughtful. There doesn't appear to be any bitterness or resentment. In the opening, he describes his understanding of Marcus Long's pain.' Jake looked down at his notes. 'I'm reading from the letter directly here: *I appreciate the love you felt for me. I was a young boy, and I know that plagued you with guilt. I know that your own domestic situation drove you to behave in unthinkable ways. I know all of this now. I know all of this because I have healed.*'

Yorke said, '*Healed*. It is the same expression that Sturridge used.'

'*I've accepted what I have become*,' Jake continued. '*Accepted and shared*. The letter continues like this for some time before he outlines his demands. Bite off your tongue or

Susie will have to die. He was also told to completely destroy the tongue so he couldn't have it reattached.'

'A demand he complied with when he flushed his tongue down the toilet,' Yorke said. 'He is recovering in hospital now and has been interviewed, briefly, by DS Pettman. I know I am pointing out the obvious here, but the priority of the case at this point is to recover Susie Long if he does not honour his end of the bargain to release her.'

'Not likely,' someone muttered.

'But our concerns stretch much further,' Yorke said. 'Who else does Severance have earmarked for revenge? He seems to have gone to a lot of trouble over Ryan and Long, so if anyone else is in his crosshairs, they could be living on borrowed time. This morning, while we were organising assignments, I prepared a list of those involved with Severance during those years of abuse, leading up to the attempted murder. If we can somehow anticipate where he may strike next, we could pre-empt more tragedy, find him, and recover Susie.'

He handed a wad of paper to Jake. 'Could you hand these out, please? These are the notes I made.'

CHRISTIAN SEVERANCE always stopped to look in the mirror when he was in the cellar. If ever there was a need for motivation, he could find it in his mangled reflection.

Behind him, Susie Long was kicking and shouting. 'LET ME OUT! PLEASE! I DON'T UNDERSTAND WHY YOU ARE DOING THIS!'

She was strong. He'd sprayed the gas into the opening on her plastic container minutes ago and the adrenaline was keeping her going. He wondered if she would need another dose of it? That would be remarkable.

He closed his eyes and stroked his face, imagining for a moment the fingers of one of his previous lovers caressing him. He longed for touch. The Conduit helped him find it in their meditations, but sometimes he wished the Conduit himself would just touch him.

The kicking and shouting stopped, and Severance opened his eyes.

He stepped over the rusted bikes and worked his way to the back of the cellar where the body was wrapped in plastic. He'd moved it out of Susie's line of sight to avoid her waking up and screaming in terror during the night.

After unwrapping the body, Severance slid it free from the plastic, leaving a trail of blood on the floor. He stared down at the victim he'd held captive in the house for over a week.

His trousers were around his ankles and his genitals were missing.

YORKE THOUGHT of Harry Butler and looked at his watch. The meeting was at 1:00 p.m. and it had only just turned 10:00 a.m. He figured he would be looking at his watch a lot today in the build up to that meeting. He'd tried already to call him six times, failing each time.

I've found him. Harry had hung that titbit out, initiated a frenzied state in Yorke, and then had switched his bloody phone off.

Well, Yorke thought, *if you want a face-to-face that bad, fine, but don't expect pleasantries.*

Everyone in the incident room looked up at Yorke eagerly, wanting him to continue the tale of Christian Severance and the events that had led up to his disappearance into silence.

He began with a potted history of his childhood. Nothing too significant there. Excellent academic record, close family relationships, everything going well until ... the grooming and the sexual abuse. The first person on Yorke's list of Severance's potential targets was Amanda Werrell, current principal of a secondary school near Old Sarum. She was the vice-principal during Severance's years in attendance and was investigated during the incident.

'There's a file, I want you all to look at after briefing,' Yorke said. 'Several members of staff reported that they'd approached Werrell with reports regarding inappropriate behaviour from Marcus Long. Not just towards Severance, but towards other teenage boys too. She was accused of not following up on these reports but was eventually cleared of any wrongdoing.'

'What kind of inappropriate behaviour?' An officer asked.

'Long periods of time talking alone with the children after school, lending them books and DVDs, connecting with them on social media. Stuff that could either be innocuous, or the backbone of grooming. The two members of staff were adamant that they'd made these reports to her. She was *adamant* that they hadn't. The trial didn't last long. Their words against hers.'

'Innocent or not,' Topham said, 'this could put her on Severance's radar.'

Yorke said, 'Which is why myself and DI Gardner will be going to speak to her first thing today. I've also assigned

DC Willows to speak to the two teachers who made the accusations against Werrell – neither are in the teaching profession anymore, but both are working in Salisbury.'

Willows nodded and made notes.

Yorke then talked them through the next stage of Severance's life. The investigation, the trial, the jail sentence of four years for Marcus Long.

After Long's imprisonment, Severance's life followed a productive path. He worked towards a PHD in researching snake anti-venom for third-world countries, funded by the Bill Gates' foundation.

'By all reports, he was an excellent public speaker who travelled all over the world to deliver hope. He drummed up significant funding, and at one point became the 'face' of research for these disadvantaged countries. All was going well until Marcus Long came back into his life.' Yorke paused for a mouthful of water. 'Things get hazy after the attack. Following Long's imprisonment, Severance moved off the map somewhat. He spent a long-time claiming disability, and a long time under the care of the NHS for psychological, as well as physical, damage. He was living with his mother – who has been spoken to at length during the Operation Autumn investigations, but there'll be no harm in paying her another visit. Then, about a year ago, he disappeared.'

'This disappearance provoked its own investigation. I have learned nothing significant from a brief look at this investigation; however, I have assigned this investigation to DC Johnson for thorough scrutiny.'

'I am also keen to pursue the Alex Drake angle too. Sturridge claimed that he is dead and has insinuated that it was Severance. If we can retrace Drake's final movements, then we could find ourselves in Severance's territory, so I believe that this angle is crucial. DI Topham will pursue this lead.'

Yorke took another mouthful of water. 'Once again, I ask you to revisit everything on HOLMES, and then check your assignments on the board at the front. I understand there is a lot going on right now, and I'm hoping that we can narrow down the field of investigation as the day wears on.'

AT THE FRONT DOOR, Susie looked up at her father's face. He swooped her up and pinned their faces together; she liked it when he did that, even when his stubble left an itchy rash.

While he continued to rub their cheeks together, he said, 'Susie, Susie, I love Susie,' over and over in that familiar sing-song voice she never tired of.

Eventually, she felt stifled, and tried to pull away, but couldn't. 'Daddy, you're squashing me!'

He pulled her tighter still and her whole little face seemed to fold into his cheek. She tried pleading again, but her voice was muffled. Her heart beat faster, and she opened her mouth to draw breath, but simply sucked in his skin.

She beat her tiny fists against his chest, and desperately tried to pull away, but his grip tightened further. Her father was suffocating her...

She opened her eyes, snapped her head back, banging it on the plastic behind her, and then drew breath. She threw an arm in the air, but it rebounded off the plastic back towards her. Awareness flooded in.

Trapped in a coffin.

Her eyes widened, her heart thrashed wildly, and she

flattened her body against the side of the container as hard as she could, willing it to crack, burst open and release her. She was no longer alone in here.

She'd had her mouth against the face of the man lying beside her. Breathing in his skin as if it were the skin of her father.

She felt sick rising in the back of her mouth, tasted it, and clutched both hands against her mouth for when it came out. But it never did.

The man's eyes were open, but the way they sunk into the blue face, and pointed slightly inward, confirmed the lack of life. His lips were also parted slightly, exposing front teeth; he'd either been sneering or grimacing in pain when death struck.

Her eyes rolled over his body and settled on his exposed groin which was a pulpy mess of congealed blood and torn flesh. Adrenaline came again, white-hot, but she didn't feel the need to vomit this time. She sucked in a breath, turned on to her back and with the balls of her fists pounded at the plastic roof again and again. Her heart thrashed so hard it hurt. But she didn't care. She was happy for it to explode in her chest rather than be trapped in here.

'LET ME THE FUCK OUT!'

She pounded and pounded.

'WHAT THE FUCK ARE YOU DOING TO ME?'

Christian Severance now loomed over the plastic coffin. She'd recognised him earlier when he pumped some sort of gas into the coffin and knocked her unconscious. She could never forget seeing his image in the newspapers over and over following her father's attempt to kill him. Except the papers had never revealed a picture of the destruction wrought on the boy's face. That special surprise had been saved for today – the day she realised that she would be the one being punished for her father's crimes.

'LET ME OUT YOU BASTARD!'

He lay a bloody knife on the coffin and a piece of paper with the following words:

Beside you sleeps the last person who tried to escape. Now lie still or join him in his eternal slumber. The choice is yours.

9

YORKE AND GARDNER were led through a large academy that resembled a prison; a huge open space with long staircases leading up to a succession of floors with classrooms pinned back against the sides like cells. Yorke imagined the children overhanging the balconies, dropping text books on fire, chanting and demanding a shorter school day in return for ending the riot. The reality was that the students were all contained within the classrooms studying silently, giving the expansive, modern structure a quiet, and therefore, eerie feel.

They passed some modern toilets; two facing rows of individual cubicles which led into an open-plan area with basins. 'At least there is nowhere to hide in this building,' Yorke said, recalling a time when he was pinned up against a cubicle door by three older lads, who threatened to extinguish their cigarettes on his forehead. 'Should cut down on the bullying.'

'Were you bullied?' Gardner said.

'Can't you tell?'

The receptionist stopped them outside the principal's office and knocked on the door. It opened immediately.

Amanda Werrell was a severe, looming woman with cropped grey hair. She wore bifocals and a cardigan – an odd choice considering the heatwave throttling England.

She offered her hand. Her handshake was firm. Yorke and Gardner introduced themselves. She didn't smile. Despite the solid exterior, Yorke immediately detected a fragility. His years in the force had made him wise to such pretences.

'Please sit,' she said, standing aside to let them pass. She closed her office door.

Yorke surveyed an immaculate desk headed with two framed photographs of a young man and woman in graduation gowns. She came around to the other side of the desk, and Yorke noticed a wedding ring. Another pretence. Yorke had done his research and knew she'd been divorced for three years now – he'd left soon after the children. She was a pillar of the community, so she was clearly just keeping up appearances.

She flattened her skirt and took a seat. Finally, she offered them a tilted smile. If Yorke hadn't realised that she was trying to feign a pleasant demeanour, he would have assumed she was sneering at them.

Yorke began with a pleasantry. 'I visited this school, several years ago, it's definitely moved forward.'

'Yes,' Werrell said. 'When we were converted into an academy, we were granted a new build. We were also sponsored by one of the private colleges in Hampshire.'

'All I can remember about my own school are the leaking roofs, boarded windows and frozen pipes, Mrs Werrell. I'm glad things have moved on. Thanks for seeing us.' Yorke pulled out a notepad and readied a pen. From the corner of his eye, he saw Gardner do the same. 'We wanted to ask you when you last saw or heard from Christian Severance.'

It was Yorke's turn for pretence. He had his pencil poised over the paper ready to write. He knew she'd be stunned by the question. He allowed it to play out for ten seconds.

'Sorry.' Yorke looked up. 'Would you like me to repeat the question?'

Amanda Werrell took a sharp intake of breath through her nose. 'Let me see ... over fifteen years ago, I think. If you need the exact date and time, I will have to consult SIMs, our database.'

'You can provide that later today, Mrs Werrell. What happened the last time you saw him?' Yorke looked back down at his pad.

'You know what happened, Detective, or you wouldn't be here!'

'Please answer the questions, Mrs Werrell,' Gardner said.

'Christian Severance disclosed his experiences with Marcus Long to the designated safeguarding lead. His parents came to pick him up. For obvious reasons, he never returned to this school.'

'Obvious reasons?' Gardner said.

'He accused Marcus Long of sexually abusing him, but why are you asking me questions to which you already know the answers?'

'It is quicker, Mrs Werrell, if we just ask the questions,' Yorke said. 'Did you believe the accusations?'

Werrell adjusted her glasses. 'He's been found guilty, so the answer is yes. I trust in our system.'

Yorke looked up at her. *People who trust in this system aren't usually so hostile,* he thought.

'How about before he was found guilty? Did you believe the accusations then?' Gardner said.

Werrell chewed her bottom lip for a moment before answering. 'It wasn't my position to judge him. It was simply my position to act on the accusations and safeguard the child.'

'That is the correct stance, no question, Mrs Werrell, but, could you tell me, deep down, whether you believed Marcus Long was capable of this?'

Again, she paused before answering. *Not impulsive, are you? You are a very measured person.*

'I never saw anything in his behaviour to suggest this was to be the case. But when the disclosure occurred, I behaved only in the young person's interests. Records will show that Marcus Long was immediately suspended.'

'Was your relationship with Marcus Long completely professional?' Yorke asked.

Werrell ripped her glasses off and started to clean them with her cardigan. 'What do you mean by that?'

'Did you have a relationship outside of work?' Gardner said.

'We were friends, yes. But I was also friends with his wife. Myself and my husband used to go out for meals with them.'

'And how long were you friends for?'

'Marcus started working here at roughly the same time I did – we were close, yes, I won't deny it, but as I've said, on countless occasions, I never suspected that anything was happening.'

'Were you approached by two members of staff regarding his unprofessional conduct?' Yorke said.

'You will know, Detective, I have denied this vehemently

since the accusations were made, *and* I was cleared of any wrongdoing.'

'Still,' Gardner said, 'I can understand one false allegation, but two. This strikes me as more unlikely.'

'The two male PE teachers in question, who I may add, are no longer in education, were unprofessional themselves. I had spoken to both, on countless occasions, about behaving in a more adult manner with children. Granted, these two newly qualified teachers were young themselves, but that does not justify flirtatious behaviour with Year 11 girls. I caught both men changing their shirts in front of the class after a PE session. I was pursuing them for their conduct, so they saw an opportunity to turn the tables. This was all recorded, Detective, following the hearing in which I was cleared of any wrongdoing. Feel free to take a look.'

'We have looked, Mrs Werrell,' Yorke said. 'And have you been in contact with Marcus Long since?'

She flinched. 'No, I have not.' She looked away. 'He let us all down.'

Yorke looked at Gardner, then back at Werrell. 'There have been some developments since then.'

Yorke had to be really careful how he explained recent events to Werrell. There were many details that the press wasn't privy to yet. He tried to explain the link between Simmonds and Christian Severance. She knew what had happened to Severance, including the details of his disfigurement, as this had made it into the press many years previous. Yorke stressed that he wanted her to be vigilant.

Werrell shrugged. 'But I'm innocent. Cleared of any wrongdoing. Surely he would know that?'

'Like I said, Mrs Werrell, this is all precautionary. I need you to be aware that this investigation is ongoing, and you may be considered, by Christian Severance, as part of the chain of events that led to the incident.'

She rubbed her forehead. 'Poor boy. He'd done so well for himself. His work for the Gates' foundation was inspirational. I really thought he'd put the bad times behind him.'

'We are going to station an officer outside the school, and outside your home until this is over,' Yorke said. 'As long as you are okay with that?'

'I really do not think there is any need, but yes, Detective, do what you must.'

───────

AFTER AMANDA WERRELL had closed the door behind the two officers, the tears came.

She approached the desk from which the detectives had grilled her and then warned her, put her hands flat on the surface, and used it for support as her body racked with sobs.

She pulled the wedding ring from her finger and threw it across the room. It disappeared behind a bookshelf loaded with science textbooks. How she missed those days of just teaching science! Why had she saddled herself with so much responsibility?

After slipping back into the chair on which the pompous officer had sat, she closed her eyes, and remembered a time when Marcus Long had clutched her hand tightly and said, 'I saw them together, around the back of the restaurant, all over each other. I'd suspected for a while – that's why I followed them outside when they went for a cig. They were so engrossed in each other, they didn't even see me standing there, watching them. It wasn't the first time either. They knew their way around each other. Bastards, the pair of them. Didn't you notice my shock when we were all sitting back around that table? Come here, lean on me, I've cried for days, don't feel embarrassed about crying now. It's your right. Well, I just came right out and asked her yesterday, couldn't stew on it any longer. They've been at it for six months! Six *fucking* months! Last time was last week when we were at parent's evening. Can you fucking believe it? While we were working to support our families! Selfish, selfish idiots.'

Werrell came out of the memory, lifted her glasses and brushed away tears.

Get control of yourself.

She closed her eyes and took some deep breaths.

She couldn't blame the police for reopening old wounds; they were trying to protect her. Not that she believed she was in any danger, Christian Severance would have no reason to come after her. She'd been cleared of any wrongdoing and no one knew that she'd lied - apart from Marcus Long.

She closed her eyes again and remembered a time when he'd stroked her back. She'd been sitting naked on the side of the bed with her head in her hands.

'Try not to feel guilty. We didn't start this. Yes, they've told us it's over, but does that excuse six months? Six months! Come on. We deserve this too. Some happiness. Besides, do we even know they've stopped? Are we tracking their every move? Their lunch breaks? I don't trust them. Come here, Amanda, lean back. Let's not forget. We didn't start this. I love you.'

The thing is, at that point, she'd loved him too.

Back in the present moment, she took another deep cleansing breath and wondered if she still did.

THEY KEPT their voices down as they followed a male receptionist through the building to the exit.

'Of course she's lying,' Yorke said. 'She's fragile, defensive, holding onto the remnants of a long-dead marriage. We may never know exactly what went on, but one thing is for sure, she tried to protect Long.'

'But the question is – does Christian Severance know?'

'I can't answer that for sure,' Yorke said, 'but let's assume he does. And if he does, this is a hot spot. Until the officer I requested arrives, Emma, can you stay in reception and keep an eye out? I'm not seriously expecting Christian Severance to just stroll in but let's not take any chances. And remember Severance could have enlisted others like Sturridge. Anything is possible.'

He looked at his watch. It was past twelve. He wanted to arrive at *The Wyndham Arms* before Harry, so he could make it *his* territory.

Just before they reached reception, Yorke put a hand on her shoulder. 'Emma, you'd tell me if you weren't alright, wouldn't you?'

Gardner flushed. 'Of course, why do you ask?'

'You seem quieter lately. You don't seem to be bollocking me as much as you usually do.'

'You've not been smoking, so there's been no need.'

Yorke smiled, thinking about his willpower failing last night in the garden. 'Still, you can always talk to me.'

Gardner smiled. 'I would Mike, but honestly, there's nothing to worry about.'

The door into the reception area opened before they reached it, and a strong smell of perfume mixed with tobacco smoke wafted over them. Walking out of reception, wearing a low-cut top and a pair of white leggings, was a woman in her late twenties. Her make-up was bold and Yorke could see it was a desperate attempt to cover up a bad case of acne. She wore oversized hoop-earrings and clutched a small pink handbag to her side. A visitors' lanyard bounced off her exposed midriff.

While marching behind her, a female receptionist said, 'This is Ms Lang, sir. Here for a meeting regarding her daughter.' She then rolled her eyes, suggesting that Ms Lang's child was troublesome.

In reception, Yorke explained that Gardner would be staying on duty until a plain clothes officer arrived to add extra security. The receptionists were inquisitive as to why this was the case, but Yorke brushed them off as politely as he could.

He turned to Gardner. 'I've got an appointment. I'll be off the grid for an hour. Then, we'll rendezvous back at the station for afternoon briefing unless anything else comes up. Do you have your tic-tac's?'

Gardner smiled and tapped her jacket pocket.

Yorke smiled back when he heard them rattle.

It was boiling hot in the plastic coffin, and judging by the stench, the body next to her was decomposing. Biology was one of her interests and strengths at college, and she knew how death worked. It was clear to her that the corpse was well into self-digestion. Enzymes were eating the cells of the organs from the inside out.

Susie gagged but, as she'd done on many occasions these last few hours, managed to hold back the vomit.

She'd taken off as much as she could to cope with the

extreme temperatures. Her bra and knickers were damp, and a sheen of sweat sparkled on her pale skin. However, she wasn't prepared to remove her underwear, and allow this man, Christian Severance, to see her naked. Next to her, the face of the dead man sparkled too, not because of sweat, but rather because of the small blisters rupturing all over his body.

His skin looked loose, hanging free, and she closed her eyes to stop herself staring at him. Another day, trapped in here with him, and he would start to bloat. Then the odour would really kick in and the insects would make an appearance.

She started to cry. *What could she do?* Severance had shown her the murder weapon. Silence was her only option. If the mutilated corpse beside her didn't show her that he meant business, nothing would.

She closed her eyes and remembered the day her father had emerged from jail. This time, the *first* time, he'd gone to jail, she'd forgiven him. *Why?* Because she adored him. Always had. She'd clutched him hard outside the jail walls. Begged him to be her father again. Accepted his countless apologies - that he'd loved the boy, but knew he'd done wrong.

'Do you still love him?' She'd asked.

'Of course not,' he'd lied.

She opened her eyes.

Why? Dad, why? Why couldn't I be enough? Why did you have to go back?

She thought of the bloody knife, the note pinned to the plastic coffin, and his disfigured face.

Why did you create this monster?

A sudden thought occurred to her.

She lifted her knees, so they were just beneath the lid, and shuffled partway down. When she was within reach, she manoeuvred her hand over the corpse's destroyed genitalia and clutched his jeans. She tugged them up his legs to the point she could investigate the pockets.

She pulled out a wallet first. A collection of credit cards and a couple of points cards for various supermarkets. All labelled with the name: *Alex Drake*. There were also a couple of VIP cards for various strip bars.

She continued to root through his pockets but could only find a collection of keys. When she brought them up to her face to examine them, adrenaline shot through her.

A red Swiss Army knife hung from the keyring.

THE YOUNG LADY doused in perfume seemed timid. She stood at Amanda Werrell's office door with her face lowered slightly, and although she smiled, there was a slight tremble in her lips.

'Come in, Ms Lang, I'm so glad you could make it today.' Werrell stepped to one side, allowing her visitor the space to enter the office. 'I know it isn't under the best circumstances, but I'm sure we can get to the bottom of what's bothering Alicia.'

Ms Lang entered the office, clutching her pink handbag tightly.

Werrell lifted her glasses and rubbed her eyes as she rounded to the other side of the desk, concerned that the mother of this child would see the evidence of her earlier tears. That would be unacceptable. Her position as head of this school was a strong one. She should appear unshakeable.

They both took their seats and then Werrell pointed at the phone on her desk. 'Would you like me to phone through for a coffee, or a cup of tea, perhaps?'

Ms Lang shook her head.

'Well,' Werrell said, 'let me know if you change your mind.'

She nodded.

Werrell opened up the folder. 'Over a fortnight ago, I suspended Alicia for two days for swearing at a senior member of staff. We spoke on the phone about it and you seemed to accept our decision?'

She nodded again.

'Well, things had been going smoothly. I received a couple of glowing reports from Maths and French. Unfortunately, this morning, it happened again. She swore at another member of the senior team.'

The mother didn't respond.

'Sorry, Ms Lang, did you just hear what I said? It happened again. Your daughter swore at Mrs Friars after being asked why she'd been sent out of her English classroom.'

Still, no response. The situation was beginning to feel rather peculiar to Werrell.

'She is in isolation, and I am going to issue another suspension. Can you please indicate your feelings over this matter?'

Ms Lang pointed at her mouth and slowly turned her head from side to side.

'Sorry, I don't understand...'

From Werrell's desk, Ms Lang picked up a pile of post-it notes and a pen. She started to write.

The phone on the desk began to ring. With her heart

thumping in her chest, Werrell picked it up and placed it to her ear. 'Yes?'

'Sorry, it's Clark, we just wanted to let you know we have Alicia in reception, when you've finished your meeting with Ms Lang—'

'Clark, what did Ms Lang say to you at reception?'

'Well, nothing, but I guess you'd know that by now, wouldn't you? Dentist has left her mouth a little worse for wear – she communicated with me using handwritten cards...'

Ms Lang handed a post-it note to Werrell.

The handwriting was messy but she was able to read it: *im not ms lang*

The phone slipped from Werrell's hand.

10

YORKE GAVE A salute, as he always did, to Dionysus, God of Wine, pictured above the door to *The Wyndham Arms*. To say that Dionysus looked like the fawn from *The Lion, the Witch and the Wardrobe* wouldn't be inaccurate. This pub housed the *Hopback* brewery, responsible for the finest tipple known to man – *Summer Lightning*.

To his disappointment, Yorke found Harry Butler, ridiculously early, in the front parlour. *So much for making this my territory*, he thought.

Harry was chewing his way through a pint. Yorke suspected it was *Crop Circle*, Harry's favourite. A clean flaxen-coloured beer brewed with flaked maize. Yorke chewed his lip. The smell of beer was strong in here. It was always a real test of his willpower.

'Sorry, Mike, should have made it a coffee shop. I just remembered that you would never drink on duty.'

'If you'd left your phone on, Harry, I might have been able to remind you of that.'

When Yorke sat opposite Harry, he was surprised to see how dramatically his hair had thinned. His face was also gaunt, and his eyes sunken.

'Before you ask ... *chemotherapy*,' Harry said.

'I'm sorry, Harry.'

'Don't be. Had a noticeably low count of something or other last check they did. It's going well enough.'

'Well enough for you to drink that?' Yorke pointed at his pint.

'It's always going well enough for that!' Harry smiled. 'There's a time when you would have agreed with me on that one.'

'That time was long ago.' Yorke looked at his watch. 'Can we make this quick?'

'Why? You came early – it's not even one o'clock yet.'

'I'm short on time. The fan is wallowing in a lot of shit right now.'

'Congratulations by the way.'

Yorke looked confused.

'The ring on your finger.'

'Thanks, Harry, but really, can we push this forward?' Despite his need, *his desperate need*, to be away from the man who had failed him, guilt prickled him, and not just because of the cancer. Harry had lost his wife in violent circumstances, and nobody was ever coming back from that experience. Not properly. 'Don't take it personally, Harry ... it's just time I don't have.'

'I get that,' Harry said. 'I remember it well. One of the hazards of the job ...' He took a mouthful of beer. 'I miss every one of those *fucking* hazards.'

'William Proud?' Yorke leaned forward. 'You drop that name on me ... you might as well drop a bomb on me.'

'Remember I told you a long, long time ago, Mike, that I'd put it right?'

'And I told you that I didn't want you to, *remember that*?'

Harry reached down beside him and lifted an A4 sized brown paper envelope. 'Then I guess you won't be interested in these then?'

Yorke reached out and Harry pulled them back. Yorke tried to keep his voice down. He failed. 'Not now, Harry. *Seriously*. Not right bloody now.'

'Michael, it's been a fair old time!'

It was Kenny, a seventy-plus local legend, who frequented most of the Salisbury public houses, *most days*, and was considered a good-luck charm by nearly all the landlords. If old Kenny stopped by for a pint, takings were sure to increase before the night was through.

Kenny swayed at the end of their table. The last dregs of beer were sloshing around in the bottom of his pint glass. *And fortunately*, thought Yorke, *not down the old man's cords as witnessed on previous occasions*.

'Has work been murder?' Kenny smiled. He wagged his finger. 'Get it, *murder*?'

'The old ones are the best, Kenny,' Yorke said.

'That's what everyone keeps saying about me.'

Yorke faked laughter. 'I've been busy. You? Kenny? How are you?'

Kenny took a step back, held his arms out and twirled. 'Well, I'm still fucking here, aren't I?'

Yorke smiled and looked over at the envelope in Harry's hands. Harry was staring right at Yorke rather than Kenny.

'And the secret of my success is ...' Kenny slurred with a thick Wiltshire accent. 'Go on, what do you reckon it is?'

Yorke said, 'Fuelled by the *Lightning?*'

'Nah ... well ... maybe that's part of it ... rather, it's the freedom I allow myself.' He stroked his forehead. 'In here. I don't carry anything that doesn't need to be carried. A friend of mine says I'm a *minimalist.*'

Yorke thought a *minimalist* was someone who kept his possessions to a minimum, but he chose not to challenge Kenny's train of thought.

'I learned a long time ago Michael that even the smallest thing.' He clicked his fingers. 'Can make you go *boom!* So free your mind. That's the secret. Always has been and always will be.' He smiled, opened his hand to bid farewell, and turned to leave.

The smallest things can make you go boom!

How true that sounded right now. *How long had he been carrying this? His dead sister? Could he have even saved her? Had he not tried so many times before she died?*

Free your mind.

He looked up at the door out of the *Wyndham Arms*, and considered standing up, and walking away.

Then, he looked back at Harry and said, 'Give me the sodding envelope.'

He tore open the envelope and emptied the photographs on the table.

Every photograph was of William Proud – his sister's killer.

'He's back,' Harry said, 'and I'm going to kill him for you.'

THE YOUNG WOMAN's lips twitched, and a tic flared up on the left side of her face. She clutched the handbag so tightly in her lap that her bony hands resembled the legs on a hunched tarantula.

'Let me help you,' Werrell said, showing her hand to the woman, before moving it slowly over the table. Just when it seemed that Werrell would succeed in running a reassuring palm down her arm, the woman thrust her chair back and bared her teeth.

Werrell pulled her hands back and held them in the air. 'I only want to help.'

The woman clicked open her handbag and reached inside. Werrell took a deep breath and stood. 'I think we should—'

The last word stuck in her throat when she saw the knife the woman was holding. Then, before she had decided how to react, the woman was on her feet. She cast the handbag aside, drew the knife above her shoulder, and lunged.

Werrell managed to sidestep, but the tip of the blade tore through her cardigan and into her shoulder. The knife didn't stick, and the woman floundered on the table. Werrell raised her eyes to the office door. She circled the desk and scrambled across the office. The wound in her shoulder was burning.

She practically tore the door off its hinges and threw herself out the room, spinning as she went, so she could grab the handle.

The woman was already on her feet, knife raised again, and charging.

Werrell slammed the door closed and listened to the knife thud into the wood. She looked down at the lock on the door and swore. The *fucking* key was on her desk.

Werrell gripped the handle in both hands as her assailant

tugged at the door. Despite appearing frail, the woman was anything but. The door came ajar. Werrell took a deep breath and wrenched back with all her might. The door closed. But the driven woman dragged it ajar again.

As they wrestled with it, the burning in Werrell's shoulder intensified, and she gasped when she glanced down to see the arm of her cardigan glistening with blood. The knife must have bitten deeper than she'd realised. She was bleeding freely.

Even though her hands were drenched in sweat, she maintained her grip, but she knew that once that blood reached her hands, it was game over. She'd slip free and her assailant would be on her.

'HELP! HELP!'

The door opened.

'FUCKING HELP ME!'

The door banged close.

Recent budget cuts had left her school short on staff and, as she glanced down the bare open corridor, she cursed the government.

Her best bet was the reception, to her right, and the police officer that those detectives had promised.

'AMANDA?'

She looked up. Pauline Thompson was leaning over the second-floor balcony, looking straight down at her.

'PAULINE, HELP ME. THERE'S A FUCKING MAD WOMAN WITH A KNIFE IN HERE!'

Several students came alongside Pauline, mirroring their teacher's same gormless expression.

'NOW!'

Pauline finally responded and bolted for the stairs. She could hear a build-up of nervous chatter. Children and

teachers were emerging from the classrooms above. She looked at the reception. The door was still closed.
'SOMEONE TELL RECEPTION!'

The office door opened further with each aggressive tug, and Werrell caught a glimpse of wide eyes and bared teeth.
'WHAT DO YOU WANT?'

She managed to close the door, but now her blood had found her palm. When the woman pulled again, the door handle skidded free.

The woman flew backwards. Werrell seized her moment. She turned and ran for the reception. Above, she could see Pauline had reached the first floor, and was just starting on the second flight of stairs.

'THE RECEPTION!' Werrell pointed forward as she sprinted. Behind Pauline, other members of staff followed, continually shouting back up to the balconies, instructing the children to keep their distance and remain where they were.

Despite the chaos, Werrell could hear the breathing of the woman behind her. *Shit.* She must have been close. She couldn't look. If she did, she'd lose ground and then she wouldn't just be hearing the bitch's breath, she'd been feeling it on the back of her neck. She gritted her teeth. Reception was only a hundred yards or so away.

And then the most wonderful thing happened. The reception door opened and the detective from earlier was standing there with wide eyes.

She was saved. *Fucking saved.* That vile woman was going to jail for stabbing her.

She glanced up. Children's faces, on both floors, were looking over.

Then she tripped.

YORKE KEPT his voice to a whisper. It was early and quiet in the pub, but there was still the barman to consider. This was one conversation that mustn't be overhead.

'Have you lost your mind, Harry? You just informed me of your intention to commit a crime.'

'Yes, on your behalf.'

Yorke struggled not to explode. 'What the *hell* are you talking about? On my behalf?'

Harry finished his pint in two gulps and threw his hands out over the photographs of William Proud, and dragged them back. 'You've lived without justice for too long, Mike, because of me. Let me get it for you.'

'How are you going to get justice from the inside of a prison cell, Harry?'

'I'll never see the inside of a prison cell, Mike, look at me!' He dragged his t-shirt down from the collar to reveal his chest. His ribcage was bursting through his sallow skin.

'The chemotherapy ... you said it was working!' Yorke said.

Harry released his t-shirt. 'Stopped it months ago. Too busy...' He grabbed a handful of photographs and shook them. 'Finding this fucker.'

Yorke massaged his temples. 'This is lunacy.'

'Yes,' Harry said, 'it is. But I'm dying, and before I die, I want to make it right.'

Yorke took a deep inhalation through his nose. 'All of this for *my* forgiveness?'

'I don't want your forgiveness. I wouldn't expect it. My actions have tortured you.'

'So it's just for you, then? A selfish man's last selfish act.'

'Is that really how you see it, Mike? Could it also be because this fucker doesn't deserve to draw breath? He's destroyed many lives, and it's time for it to stop.'

'You are not walking out of here to kill a man. Not with my knowledge and complicity. It does not matter who that man is ... I won't let it happen.'

'You will, Mike, you have no choice.'

'Listen to yourself! You have always had a tendency towards the ridiculous, but this is a whole new ball park. I'm going to arrest you...'

'And I'm telling you now that if you arrest me, you will never know William Proud's location. He's slippery, as well you know, and he currently resides under a different name. It has taken me years to find him. Do you really want him in the wind again? If you arrest me, Mike, I will not give you his address, I will die with it in custody.'

'That doesn't sound like atonement to me!'

'If you cannot grant a dying man's wish then you don't deserve it. It seems you are not the man I thought you were.'

'If you truly knew me, Harry, you would know where I draw the line. Accepting murder? I mean, why are you even telling me this if you've already made up your mind?'

'Because, tonight, both William Proud and I will disappear from your life forever and I wanted you to know that. I *never* want you to wonder again where the man who killed your sister, and the friend who betrayed you, are. You don't deserve to live in doubt. My last action is to give you closure.'

GARDNER TOOK in the scene quickly: many students looked down from the two balconies above; several members of staff were scurrying down both flights of stairs; Amanda Werrell was kneeling on the floor; and the young woman, who had walked nervously past her and Yorke a short while ago, was wielding a knife at shoulder height. 'STOP! POLICE!'

The young woman slammed the knife down into Werrell's face.

The nervous chatter from the students above turned to silence.

Gardner's eyes widened, she took a deep breath, adrenaline whipped through her body and she started to run.

The woman struggled, but managed, to free the knife from Werrell's face; it had entered her left cheek and burst out through the right.

'POLICE!'

The gap was closing, but the woman was unconcerned. She drew the knife back and plunged it into Werrell's face again and again.

'JESUS, STOP!' Gardner said.

Around her, silence turned to screams. The students above had started to move in droves. The staff on the stairs were running back up the stairs to try and calm them. One teacher had reached the bottom of the stairs. She was sprinting over to Gardner.

Gardner was close enough to hear the woman's ragged breathing as she drove the blade in and out of the kneeling principal's face. She threw an arm out to grab the woman's wrist.

And missed.

The woman swivelled, their eyes met, and then the knife came again.

'*Shit!*' Gardner felt the burn in the palm of her left hand.

Her eyes flew to the damage. The blade had gone right through her hand. 'What the—'

The bitch drew the blade out. Gardner screamed in pain and clutched her mangled hand.

The woman pounced, the knife raised again, but Gardner was quick, and she turned around her assailant, clutched the wrist of her free hand, and pulled her arm behind her in a solid arc.

Gardner gritted her teeth through the agony of making this manoeuvre, but all she could see was her child Annabelle, motherless and sad, and she wasn't about to let that happen.

The woman was still waving the knife in front of her, frenzied and uncaring. Several metres away, the teacher, who had not fled back up the stairs with the other members of staff, stood, uncertain of her next move.

'Back away,' Gardner told her. 'You don't want to get too close.'

The woman refused to submit. She tugged and raged in Gardner's grip.

Gardner felt something on her leg and glanced down.

Werrell had looped her arms around Gardner's leg. The principal was trembling in a pool of her own blood. Her face was a red mask. The dark lines, and folds of skin demonstrated how extensively she'd been cut. 'Help me.' Her whole face seemed to open as she spoke. 'Help me.'

Gardner tried to shake her leg free. '*Let go!*'

Werrell's grip tightened. 'Help me.'

'I am doing, *let go!*'

Gardner saw white, felt hot pain, and heard her nose splinter. The woman had seized on the moment of distraction, thrown her head backwards, and broken Gardner's nose.

And now the bitch was free again.

Instinctively, Gardner's hands flew to her nose. She took a quick step back, and readied herself for the woman again, but things moved quickly in the dizzy haze. The woman turned, the knife flashed, and Gardner felt extreme pressure on her chest. She looked up to see the teacher who she'd told to stand back, holding her mouth in shock. Then, she looked down at the blade buried in her chest.

Refusing to accept that she was beaten, especially with this dangerous creature on the loose, Gardner used the last of her strength to punch the woman as hard as she could in the face. The woman flew backwards, relinquishing her grip on the knife, which still protruded from Gardner's chest, and fell into the arms of the teacher. The teacher wasted no time in getting the exhausted woman into a headlock, dragging her to the ground, and climbing onto her back to pin her still.

In the haze, Gardner watched other people run in the fray to assist. Then, she started to cough up blood.

YORKE WAS NO LONGER WHISPERING and was pointing at Harry's face, who sat barely a metre away. 'If you had an ounce of integrity left in you, *an ounce*, then you would give me the address of that murderer right now.'

'And then what would you do, Mike?'

'What the bloody hell do you think I would do? My duty.'

'Arrest him? You'll have to prove who he is first. He's changed his identity.'

'Then we'll prove it.'

'And in the meantime, he catches wind and runs? No, my way is cleaner.'

'My way is the *right* way.'

'It might be, Mike, but I'm not giving you the choice.'

'I don't believe you, not for a second. If I take you in, you'll give me the address rather than let him get away. I know you ... you forget that.'

'Look at me.' Harry opened his arms to present himself. 'I'm not the man you knew. Can you really take that gamble?'

Yorke's phone rang. He saw that it was Topham.

He pointed at Harry again and said, 'Don't move or I'll put an APW out on you.'

Yorke went outside to answer the call, and what he heard over that phoneline was pestilence. A pestilence that burned deep into his soul. A pestilence that Yorke knew, as he steadied his trembling body against a wall, would scar him forever. No amount of time, healing, or even memory loss, would ever numb this moment. It would be with him for the rest of his days.

After the call ended, he charged back into *The Wyndham Arms*.

He towered over Harry, wiping tears from his eyes.

'What's wrong?' Harry said, starting to rise.

'Stay in your seat,' Yorke said.

Harry obeyed.

'Just make me one promise. Just one. You owe me that much.'

'Of course,' Harry said.

Yorke took a deep breath; it was all he could do to stop himself from crumbling.

'Do not do anything until you speak to me again.'

'When will that be?'

'Later today.'

'Okay, you have my word.'

Yorke wiped more tears away. 'And leave your *sodding* phone on.'

With that, he turned and exited the pub to seek out the pestilence.

11

SUSIE LONG LEANED, sweaty and half-naked, over a mutilated and decomposing corpse, working the corkscrew on the Swiss Army Knife into the lock on her plastic coffin. She was inches away from the dead man's blistering face. Every breath she took, rebounded back, carrying a sweet, yet foul smell, which made her gag, but she ceaselessly worked the Swiss Army Knife into the lock, because she wanted, with all her heart, to live.

And she had only two choices.

Get free and survive or stay here and die.

SEVERANCE ALWAYS FOUND the movement into hypnosis gentle because the Conduit used *soft* words and *serene* visualisations. However, the end destination was always turbulent.

In fairness, it was difficult for the Conduit to manipulate the visualisations because Severance could no longer speak, and writing in this meditative state was tedious, and often ineffective. So, the Conduit made do with his detailed notes and Severance's physical responses to guide him.

'Is she still not listening to you?' The Conduit said.

Severance shook his head.

'Christian, tell her everything again, *all of it*, from start to finish. Even if she continues to stare at you with that disinterested expression, *tell her.*'

Severance leaned forward in his chair and told his vice-principal, Mrs Werrell, again. Her gaze remained watery; in fact, her expression didn't even change when he referred to that first moment Marcus made him feel special – made him realise that he wasn't a *nobody* anymore. That his interests in sixties music was a real passion to have; that a fascination with Charles Dickens and reading wasn't an anomaly; and that a dislike of football wasn't a reason for concern.

To Severance, it felt good to be able to speak again, even if the response was anything but pleasing.

Severance looked up at Mrs Werrell with eyes full of tears – *tears she could clearly fucking see, heartless bitch –* and said, 'And then he made me do these things, which I knew, were wrong, but...'

At this point, her eyes would move away from him. *Was she embarrassed by what she'd heard?*

'Have you told her about the moment he said he loved you?' The Conduit said from outside the visualisation.

Severance told her and she flinched.

'He said it more than once,' he said.

'*Nonsense!*' Mrs Werrell said. '*Nonsense, nonsense, nonsense!*'

The conduit spoke in Severance's visualisation again. 'And after she tells you it is *nonsense*, I want you to fight against your natural instinct to cry, to clam up, to say nothing else and walk away, *broken*. This time needs to be different.'

Severance nodded.

In the visualisation, Severance leaned forward, pointing. '*It is not nonsense!* And you listen to me, you old witch. You have a duty of care to me. You told me that whatever I disclose to you here, *now*, had to be reported. That is what I've done, so you will report it!'

'I will do nothing of the sort,' Werrell said. 'Mr Long is a decent man. An honourable man. I've heard about your recent outbursts towards him—'

'Because he's a liar!'

'No, it is because you cannot control your behaviour, and someone has called you out on this. And this is how you respond? With slanderous comments?'

'I'll take it to someone else.'

'You do that – if anyone wants to report this vile poison, let it be on their heads!'

'I'll report you for ignoring—'

'Your word against mine. Did you really think this was a place to air your grievances? To pollute the air with your poison?'

'Now, calm.' The Conduit spoke into the dream again. 'Draw back. *Freeze*. You have altered the outcome of the meeting. You did not internalise the frustration, and the pain, over Werrell's betrayal – you've *accepted* her betrayal for what it was – her own failing. And by voicing that, you have *shared* your frustrations.'

Severance nodded.

'But I understand,' the Conduit said, 'that this isn't enough. It can never be enough to mitigate the pain she has brought you, so I want you to *displace*.'

So, Severance placed Werrell on her knees and made her scream. Her face was chopped up and she mumbled incomprehensibly because her tongue had been destroyed by the blade.

'This is more than a visualisation, Christian. This is a reality. Chloe has succeeded. It has been reported on the news. So, you can come back now, feeling even more whole, feeling healed, because you have succeeded in releasing your affliction, and pain. You have *shared* and *displaced.*'

The Conduit drew him back gently with more serene visualisations and soft words. And when Severance emerged, he kept his eyes closed, and drew in long, deep breaths through his nose, revelling in the pleasure and paradise this relief brought.

Only minutes later, while bathing in a warm contentment, his phone rang. He opened his eyes and looked at the Conduit, an older man, who was large and strong. The Conduit played with his long white moustache and then nodded. Severance took the call.

And after the call, Severance closed his eyes again, and sighed, because that feeling of euphoria returned. Ten times stronger than before.

The person on that call had been his contact in prison. It was confirmed. Marcus Long had severed, *and disposed of,* his own tongue.

He sat upright in his chair. Susie Long didn't need to be a burden any more.

'I have to go now,' the Conduit said. 'I can't be late. Keeping up appearances, and all that.'

Severance's saviour rose, loomed over him for a moment, placed a hand on his shoulder and then headed for the front door.

After the Conduit had closed the door behind him, Severance rose to his feet.

It was time to rid himself of the burden.

THE BUILDING ahead wasn't a monstrosity, but it still felt overwhelming. He steadied himself against a bollard and closed his eyes. He tried to gather his thoughts and end the sudden instability. It was no use. The last twenty minutes were a blur. He could barely remember driving here, and he had no idea where he'd left his car.

Time and time again his attention returned to the moment when Topham delivered the news, or at least *attempted* to. '*Someone came ... Werrell ... stabbed ... but, sir, Emma ... God, sir, Emma too ...*'

Focus, Yorke thought. *Right now, focus, like everything depends on it ... because it does. Everything and everyone is depending on you. So bloody well*

'*Focus,*' he said out loud.

A young lady, pushing a patient in a wheelchair, paused in her journey to ask him if he was okay.

'Yes.' Although he was anything but, and would certainly not appear so, hunched over and hyperventilating. 'It's just hot, I'll be fine when I get in.'

'Well, let me help—'

'No, no, ma'am, thank you all the same.' Yorke straightened himself up. 'It's not me that needs the help, other people do. And you are busy. Thank you for your kindness, but I'm ready to go in now.'

When he arrived inside the hospital reception, Jake intercepted him. Yorke took him tightly by the upper arm and his friend gripped him by shoulder. Yorke took a deep breath and squeezed his eyes shut. 'Emma?'

'She's still fighting. In surgery.'

Yorke exhaled but didn't dare to feel any relief yet.

When he opened his eyes, he saw that Jake's face was puffy and red. He envied him this ability to expel the raging turmoil inside.

'The knife punctured a lung, but they got to her in time.'

'Are the doctors confident, Jake?'

'I haven't spoken to them personally. Barry is here, but I would give him a few more minutes before asking him.'

Yorke rubbed his forehead. *Shit. Poor man.* 'And Anabelle? Please don't tell me that Anabelle is here...'

'No, Mike. She's at pre-school.'

'Good. Okay.' Yorke rubbed his forehead again. 'You have the assailant in custody. Werrell is also in surgery?'

'Yes, and she'll survive. Her injuries are life-changing ... but she will survive.'

'What else do I need to know?'

'Well, there is something—'

'DCI Yorke?' It was a familiar voice. A voice that could in equal parts both soothe and intimidate. And could both crush and rebuild you. Superintendent Joan Madden.

'Ma'am.' Yorke turned.

Joan was a tall woman, strong and agile, testament to a life of extreme exercise. She wore a tailored suit, and her hair was pulled tightly back, and sharpened into a hard knot.

'How are you feeling, Michael?' Madden said.

'Okay,' Yorke lied.

'Compromised?'

'I'm not sure I understand, Ma'am.'

'Take a walk with me, Michael. DS Pettman, will you please excuse us?'

'Of course,' Jake said.

Outside, in the hospital garden, the skyline shimmered. Madden peeled off her suit top. She had a short-sleeved shirt on underneath, and she exposed lean, sinewy arms. They sat on a bench. Yorke tried desperately to control his breathing. Hearing that Gardner was alive had calmed him somewhat, but his body was still drowning in adrenaline, and he could feel his innards twisting and turning. He needed to prove to Madden that he was not *compromised*. If he didn't, finding Christian Severance, and ending this would fall at someone else's feet.

'Michael,' Madden said, 'did you meet with Harry Butler earlier today?'

The whole world tilted. Yorke looked down. He closed his eyes – *how did she know?*

'Michael?'

He opened his mouth to speak, perfectly prepared to tell her he had seen Harry, as she obviously knew, but he couldn't speak, he was simply too disorientated by the line of questioning.

'I think the world of you Michael, so I'll ask you again—'

'Yes, I did.' He felt relief at finally letting the words out.

'Why?'

And now what? Have Harry arrested? Call him out on his threat to die with the truth of William Proud's location?

He answered as honestly as he could without taking that risk. 'The usual, ma'am. To apologise and to tell me he doesn't have long left – he's dying of cancer.'

'Anything else?'

How much did they know? Had the conversation been

overheard? Had Harry been wearing a wire? Was Yorke being stitched up? And why would anyone want to do that to him?

His mind could wade through this tarry stew of questions all day, but he had to call it. He took a gamble. 'Not really.'

'Anything about William Proud?'

She knew the subject of Harry and Yorke's conversation then – *what the hell was going on here?*

'Yes, of course, as always. He promised to find Proud before ... before he dies. I brushed it off – this is all usual from Harry.'

'How would you feel if I told you that we think Harry may actually have found Proud?'

Yorke rubbed sweat from his forehead. 'Surprised? Harry's at death's door.'

'Listen carefully, Michael, to what I am about to tell you. And think very wisely about your next move. Harry has been calling in old favours from some of our colleagues. We've had to suspend two officers over the last couple of days.'

'Who?'

'Not relevant to you just now, Michael, but we do believe that Harry has been able to locate William Proud.'

She allowed him time to respond. He had to be very careful here. If Yorke admitted that Harry had confessed his intention to commit murder, his neck would be on the line. But, in a way, he liked what he was hearing. If Harry had used information from these officers to locate Proud, they could repeat the process. Harry no longer had ownership of the truth. The location of Proud would not die with him. 'So, do *we* have Proud's location?'

'The two officers in question have not been very forth-coming with this leaked information since we suspended them. They want to use it as an olive branch to save their jobs.'

'And are you going to offer it?'

'Of course not! They're finished, but we are working them now, so it won't be long. They might avoid some jail time.'

'So, can you pull in Harry?'

'On what grounds? Has he suggested to you that he is about to act on this information in some way?'

'I told you everything. The meeting was brief. I received a phone call from DI Topham very shortly into our meeting. The details of the events at the academy.'

'Yes. A disaster, and the other reason we need to talk.'

'You think I'm compromised over the attempt on Emma's life?'

'It will be a miracle if it remains as an *attempt*. I've just spoken to the doctor.'

Yorke flinched.

'So, yes, I think you're compromised. It is no secret you are close friends. It is no secret that you're the godfather of her daughter.'

'You're right...'

'But it's no secret that you're the best we've got.'

'Thanks ma'am. Not sure I agree, but thanks anyway.'

'You can beat yourself up over this all you want but remember we all make mistakes. Admittedly, because of you, I'm facing the biggest shit storm of my career. Potentially, I have two dead officers in two days, *yet* we were actually at the scene of the crime following good work by yourself in identifying potential targets. But that doesn't get away from the fact that this actually happened on our watch. Martin

Price and his press buddies will be baying like a pack of wolves.'

'I can do—'

'Don't even suggest it, Michael. Look at the *fucking* state of you. Compromised. That's what you are. You've got Harry fucking Butler snapping at your heels, a best friend lying in ICU, and an open murder investigation that just became very fucking personal. How many times did I just use that profanity, Michael?'

'Three times.'

'How many times have you heard me use that profanity before?'

'Never.'

'So, do you appreciate the severity of the situation?'

'You know I do.'

'Here is the *fourth* time I use it for good measure. Get in there, say goodbye to your friend, just in case, round up your team and close this *fucking* case down.'

'I will.'

As SOON AS Severance stepped into the cellar, he knew something was wrong.

He looked around and saw the usual: the mould eating the walls; the rust chewing on the bikes; the flies bashing against the bulb; and the blood trail from the castrated man.

His eyes widened when he saw pieces from the broken locks beside the coffin. He ran over to confirm that she was gone.

She had to still be in the cellar because the door at the top of the stairs had been locked.

His eyes flew around. Boxes were piled up everywhere. Some old chairs were stacked in one corner. In another corner were two seven-foot-high shelves.

The shelves.

It would be the most obvious place to hide.

He surveyed the bike, and other pieces of scrap beside the plastic coffin, and lowered himself down to secure a large spanner. He did this quietly, although he knew that she would be aware of his presence – his entrance had been rather dramatic – and he also knew that she would have had the sense enough to arm herself.

With his right hand, he readied the spanner. With the left, he drove the sweat back off his forehead into his hair, and then put this other hand on the spanner too. Holding it head-height, he quietly approached the shelves.

His heart beat quicker than usual, but not fast. He felt in control. As he did most of the time these days. The Conduit had seen to that. He stood at the edge of the first shelf. She'd been wetting herself for days and the smell of urine was intense here. He curled his top lip up.

He would turn in and swing. Bash her head again and again until the stink of her piss was drowned out by the scent of blood and grey matter. He thought of Marcus Long's reaction when he heard the news. Then his heart *really* did start to beat fast...

He swooped in between the two shelves and brought the spanner down onto emptiness. Confused, he looked at the floor, saw her clothes in a pile.

There was a flash and the whole world seemed to burn. He collapsed to his knees. Another flash, and his face was in the pile of sodden clothes. He rolled onto his back. Above him, the world swirled, but he could see Susie holding what looked like a wrench.

Everything disappeared.

'I'M SORRY,' Yorke said, embracing Barry in the waiting room.

Barry's eyes were bloodshot, and his body shook. It took him a while to get any words out. 'It's not your fault.'

But it is, Yorke thought, *it really is.*

'I know you can't see her, not yet, but when she's out of surgery and I'm in there, do you want to say anything? I know how much she thinks of you. She might not be awake, but she may be able to hear.'

Yorke forced back his own tears. This wasn't his *time* to cry. It wasn't his right to steal that moment. He put a hand on Barry's arm. 'You tell her I'll be in as soon as they let me.'

'I will.'

And tell her, thought Yorke, *I'll never touch another ciggie again if she recovers. I absolutely bloody guarantee it.*

'She's the best police officer I've ever worked with,' Yorke said. 'You can tell her that if you want. But she already knows.'

'Yes, she's told me you say it often.'

Yorke smiled. 'It's true.' He forced the tears back again.

The surgeon came over, peeling off his mask.

'Mr Gardner?'

'Yes.'

'It went well. Better than I hoped.'

'Is she going to be okay?'

'It's too early to say. If you come and sit over here, we can talk it through.'

Barry looked at Yorke, who nodded back at him. He reached out one more time to clutch his arm. Then, Barry and the surgeon wandered over to the couch.

Yorke turned to the exit because, in the words of Super Joan Madden, he had to *close this fucking case down.*

———

SUSIE LOOKED DOWN at the bastard lying in his blood. She didn't think he was dead, but she wasn't about to bash his skull in to make sure. That was something she didn't have in her. Not really. Yes, she'd screamed at many movie heroines to finish off the bad guy, but now she was in that position for real, she knew that such behaviour would only come back to mentally haunt her. She wasn't about to hand Christian Severance victory in ruining her life. Hopeful that she'd be miles from him before he woke, she turned and ran.

Half-way up the cellar stairs, she realised that she was only in her bra and knickers. Was this a positive? If she reached her destination outside of this house, being practically naked would bring her more attention from neighbours. Then she really would be free.

As she turned at the top of the stairs into a narrow hallway, she tried to listen out for the sounds of Severance giving chase. *Was he coming after her? Charging up those stairs?* Blood rushed in her ears.

The hallway was lit. It led directly to a front door. Her pathway to freedom was a thing of beauty. She ran alongside the staircase and bumped into a cabinet. A vase toppled to the ground, but it didn't smash on the carpet.

Now, she was at front door and, it seemed as if the gods were smiling down on her, because it was unlocked.

Bursting from the dungeon in which she'd spent those days in terror, incarcerated within a plastic coffin, she felt like whooping in delight.

She was actually free. *Fucking free!*

It was a bright day and she was half-blinded, but she didn't care. The street, ripe with large, modern detached houses, basked in sunshine. Freshly mowed green lawns and colourful flowers. The world had never looked so delightful. She almost cried in happiness when she saw a man in his car mounted on the pavement.

She charged across the lawn. He had started his car, and was indicating to move out, but there was no other traffic, so he would be gone in seconds.

'HELP! HELP!'

He turned to look at her. She must have been a sight! A young lady in her underwear, streaked with dirt and sweat. Her hair drab and limp. She waved as she neared.

The man stepped out of the car. 'Are you okay?'

He was a muscular, older man with a friendly face.

'*Help me.*' Tears streamed down her face.

'Of course, come here, my dear. Sit in this car and tell me what's happening.'

'*Get me away from here.*'

'Of course, get in.'

They both climbed into the car. 'Please,' she said, wiping tears from her eyes. 'Please just drive.'

He looked at her, smiled and then started to play with the ends of his white moustache.

12

BACK AT WILTSHIRE headquarters, in his office, Yorke watched the CCTV footage from the academy with Topham. He shook his head throughout the entire recording and flinched when Gardner was stabbed. Afterwards, he trembled. He worked his way through a large glass of water before voicing a response. 'She walked right past us ... right past us.'

'But how could you have known?' Topham clutched his shoulder.

'I was telling Emma she needed to double check everyone that checked-in at reception, and then, at that point this woman passes, and we didn't speak to her? Do you not see the problem with that?' Yorke put his head in his hands.

'Look at her! There's nothing in her appearance to suggest that she was on her way to ... you know ... do what she did!'

Yorke pulled his head from his hands and glared at Topham. 'Since when did we judge on appearances?'

'You know what I mean.'

Yorke sighed. Nothing Topham said would lift his guilt. The fact of the matter was that Yorke had been in too much of a bloody rush to get to that meeting with Harry, and now Gardner was fighting for her life.

'Listen, *Mike*, it was your *hunch* that put us there in the first place! Give yourself some credit. At least Werrell was warned. It could have ended a lot worse if she'd been caught completely unaware.'

'Her face was cut to ribbons!'

'Yes, *but she's alive.*'

'Give myself some credit? Mark, do you hear yourself? Emma wouldn't have been there *if* I hadn't told her to stay there.' He paused to rise to his feet. 'Now, go out there, Mark, and find out if this woman is ready to be interviewed. Get a stack of cards for her to scribble on. I'll just wait for final confirmation that she is who she says she is.'

The woman in custody had already identified herself as Chloe Ward. She'd also shown her driver's licence to back this up.

Topham left and closed the door. Despair was coming, but Yorke managed to close his blinds just in time. With the tears streaming down his face, he paced the room like a caged animal, images from that moment when Chloe Ward walked past them burned in his mind.

The strong smell of perfume mixed with tobacco smoke. The bold make-up. The small pink handbag. The knife inside?

He thrust out his hand, scattering folders and the papers all over his office. He grabbed a coffee cup and hurled it against the wall. He sat down on his hands. He was making too much noise. People would now be staring at his office.

He released one of his hands and rubbed tears away.

He'd been a fool. And if Gardner died, he'd never be able to forgive himself.

Yorke received confirmation that the woman in custody was Chloe Ward and gathered some background on her. She was a twenty-nine-year old who had been through the ringer. Adoption, taken into care, foster families – she'd had the full English of support from Social Services. Recent years had seen her mixed up with drugs which would eventually see her linked to Sturridge and the squats in Tidworth.

She'd had a string of lousy boyfriends. Records showed that she'd pressed charges against one of them for beating her before eventually dropping them.

Six months ago she'd dropped off the radar. Her benefits had been frozen and her disappearance had been reported. A brief investigation had ensued, but she'd not been found.

And now here she was, in custody, minus her tongue, with the blood of a respected principal and a decorated police officer on her hands. Figuratively, of course. Once, samples, fibres and other traces had been taken, she'd been cleaned up.

Yorke and Topham observed Chloe on a monitor, waiting in the interview room. They'd dressed her in blue overalls and a guard watched over her. She looked rather nonchalant. At least she wasn't grinning inanely like Sturridge had been.

Where have you been for six months? Yorke thought.

Dots needed to be joined, and he was certain that Christian Severance would be one of those dots.

When Yorke and Topham sat opposite her, it was as if they didn't exist. They'd supplied her with a pencil so she could write her responses to their questions on the cards, but instead she just sat there and drew. Intently.

Yorke managed three unanswered questions before he slammed his fist down on the table. Not hard enough to concern Topham, and the guard towering above the young lady, but hard enough to draw Chloe's attention from the drawing.

Only when she slid the picture over did Yorke realise that she hadn't really been distracted by his fist. She'd simply finished her sketch.

Yorke's eyes widened. Beside him, Topham murmured, '*Jesus.*'

It was an impressive sketch of Gardner's face. As impressive as any forensic artist Yorke had ever come across. She'd captured her face, eyes and hair perfectly.

What was even more impressive was that Chloe had only clamped eyes on Gardner for a brief moment, and not just any old moment, but a moment filled with chaos and blood.

Yorke was too stunned to speak, so Topham took the reins. This was unfortunate because his question was wholly inappropriate. 'Are you taking the piss?'

She looked confused for a moment. She then glanced down at the blank piece of card, paused, and wrote again.

sorrie

Her writing, unlike her drawing, was atrocious. Topham read it out for the recording.

'The woman you stabbed,' Yorke said, 'is the mother of a young girl.'

She wrote again. Her spelling was poor. *im reallie sorrie I came for the other one that was a mistayk*

'Why did you come for Amanda Werrell?' Yorke said.

Chloe looked at Yorke, swung her eyes to Topham, and then committed herself to another sketch.

'Do you know Christian Severance?' Yorke said.

She nodded but continued to sketch.

'How about David Sturridge?'

Again, she nodded.

'Chloe, do you understand the severity of the situation you are in?'

Chloe didn't respond this time. She just continued to draw. Yorke and Topham exchanged glances and then allowed her a couple of minutes to finish her sketch in the hope that it might offer some kind of enlightenment.

Eventually, Chloe pushed over a pencil drawing of a little girl, no more than five, sitting by a lake. Again, it was an extremely impressive image.

Yorke looked up at her. She had tears in her eyes. She wrote the following onto a piece of card: *plise give this to her tel her im sorrie she shouldnt be hert*

Topham read it out for the camera.

'Chloe, we do not know if she will survive.' Yorke forced back his tears, desperate to keep this whole sorry situation professional.

She wiped tears away with her sleeve. She then paused to scratch her stomach. Yorke noticed this. He remembered Sturridge scratching his forearm. *An infestation of bedbugs at the squat perhaps?* More evidence that she'd been there for the last six months after she'd dropped off the Social Services radar. He'd already emailed DC Jeff Powers an image of Chloe to see if he'd seen her in the squats during his time there. Yorke's phone, lodged in his jacket pocket, was yet to vibrate with a response.

'Why did you just draw a picture of a little girl, Chloe?' Yorke said.

She slid over another card: *thats how i immajin she would look now*

'Who?'

my dorter

'Your daughter?'

Chloe nodded.

'Where is your daughter now, Chloe?'

ded

'We have no record of you having a daughter,' Yorke said.

Chloe wrote another card, slid it over and then pointed at her stomach.

ded in side here

Over the next ten minutes, Chloe revealed the circumstances surrounding her miscarriage. An abusive ex-boyfriend had pushed her down a flight of wooden stairs, killing her seven-month unborn daughter in the womb, and leaving Chloe haemorrhaging to death on the bottom step. She'd been saved in hospital, but the cost had been great; she would never again be able to conceive.

Yorke glanced down at the sketch of the young child again. *That's how I imagine she would look now.* Chloe Ward was another broken person like Sturridge. Was she another person recruited by Christian Severance?

The interview continued at a very slow pace. She struggled with her writing and was clearly sounding out the words in her head as she committed them to paper.

But she was more forthcoming than Sturridge had been, and what she lacked in intelligence, she seemed to make up in emotion and kindness. The longer the interview wound on, the more Yorke struggled to believe that this was the woman in the CCTV footage that had mutilated Werrell's face and stabbed Gardner in the chest.

She made it clear that it was Severance who had initiated the incident at the school today. She referred to him as her *brother* over and over.

The complete details of how he went about this were sketchy, because Chloe herself didn't fully understand them, but it went something like this: Christian Severance had coerced someone within the school, using threats against family members, to access and report on the online diary of Amanda Werrell. When the parental meeting with Debbie Lang, parent of troubled student Alicia Lang, had been scheduled, Severance had sent Chloe in instead. Debbie Lang had spent the day at home, drugged up on heroin, administered to her by a man called the Conduit.

'Who is the Conduit?' Yorke said.

the man who heeled us

'Sorry? Healed you?'

She wrote four cards and handed them to Yorke. Yorke read each card in the order she'd written them:

heeling

exseptanse

shairing

displasmernt

Topham reeled backed in his chair. He was as white as a sheet. 'That's not possible.'

Yorke turned to him. 'Sorry, Detective Inspector, I didn't quite—'

'I said, that's not possible.' He glared at Chloe. 'HASD? Are you referring to HASD?'

She nodded.

Topham turned to look at Yorke. He'd started to tremble

slightly. '*Healing from Acceptance, Sharing and Displacement.*'

Yorke's eyes widened.

'I think we need to take this conversation outside, sir.'

Yorke terminated the interview.

'HASD IS a ground-breaking new cognitive-behavioural treatment for PTSD,' Topham said. 'It's in its infancy but is yielding excellent results.'

'Sorry, Mark,' Yorke said, pacing around his office. 'But how do you know about this?'

Topham took a mouthful from a glass of water. He was still pale and trembled slightly. 'Neil.'

Yorke nodded. He knew Topham's partner Dr Neil Solomon reasonably well. He had been at his wedding the previous day. 'Go on.'

'While HASD has been gathering pace, they've been recruiting more practitioners to really put the techniques on the map. Neil is well respected within his field for his work on CBT as a treatment for PTSD, so he met the pioneer of HASD, Martin Adams, and was invited onto the team.'

'I see. Okay. So, how does the treatment work exactly?'

'From what I understand of it, the person *heals* from a process of *accepting* the trauma, *sharing* the knowledge of the painful experience with others, and finally, by *displacing* the pain onto those willing to accept – namely, the psychiatrist.'

'Does it involve drugs?' Yorke said.

'I'm not sure.'

'So, *if* Chloe Ward has been treated with HASD – how would that have worked exactly?'

'I think you are asking the wrong person here. I can only give you my version based on several long evenings listening to Neil drone on. To begin with the patient revisits the trauma – in Chloe's case, I guess, the assault and the miscarriage. In Sturridge's case, it would have been the rape. The patient is guided into *accepting* the trauma as part of their life, rather than as a vicious external force. New thoughts are introduced to replace the traumatic ones, so they view this event as nothing more than part of their being – not something that defines them. Obviously, the event will continue to be some kind of battery of anxiety, so the next stage is to *share* with others – to explore and describe the anxiety and event in as much detail as possible so others can *feel* and *empathise* with the trauma. This process of *sharing* is done as part of a group. The final stage, *displacement*, is conducted in a controlled environment with the therapist. The patient can visualise and push the pain and experiences onto others. It allows them to be free of their own personal trauma for a short period of time and observe others experiencing it rather than themselves. It has two functions: it makes them feel less isolated and alone in their experience, and it allows them to see, that they are still the same person without the trauma. They can continue to be who they always were and who they really want to be.'

Yorke stared at him with wide eyes.

'Are you okay, sir?'

'Yes. Just stunned you know so much, and how articulate you are on the subject.'

'Thanks – I did some psychology modules at university. Is Neil in any danger?'

Yorke continued to pace. 'I don't know, but if you ask him to come to the station now to help us unravel this whole thing then he won't be. Can you make the call while I go back into see Chloe?'

'Of course.'

'Insist though, Mark. We need someone in the know here. I have called an emergency briefing to begin straight after I finish with Chloe and I want a professional that can go through everything you just told me. Also, get some officers to Debbie Lang's house to see if she is alright after being drugged up to the eyeballs by this wacko called the Conduit.'

'BUT WE NEED YOUR HELP,' Topham said down the phone to Neil.

'I get that, but I'm sitting in front of my first patient in two minutes, and you want me to walk away, without any clue as to why?'

'Well, it's about HASD.'

'Who is talking to you about HASD anyway? It's not even really out there yet.'

'A suspect. But that's as much as I can tell you. Look, Neil, this is big. Very big. It's connected to everything that has happened recently – everything you've read about in the papers. I cannot stress enough how important it is that you come.'

'It's just over a minute until I'm in a room with my first patient, and you want me to jeopardise everything I've worked towards. *Everything I've ever wanted.*'

There was silence on the phone line. Topham did not know how to respond to that.

'Less than a minute, Mark.'

Topham broke. 'How long will the session last?'

'One hour.'

'And then you'll come.'

'In a heartbeat.'

Topham sighed. 'Okay. I love you so much.'

'I hope you love me as much as I love you.'

DR LOUIS MAYERS WAS LATE.

That was fine by Neil because it gave him another couple of minutes to read over his file for the umpteenth time.

Mayers had been a successful psychiatrist for thirty years and, like Neil himself, had followed a clinical path which involved CBT therapy. Mayer's speciality had been insomnia, and he had a range of published works on the subject. He'd spoken all over the world and was renowned right up in the upper echelons of psychiatry.

Life had been good to Mayers, and Mayers had been good for life in general, until one fateful day five years previous.

Two of Mayers' long-term insomniacs, both high-flying bankers, addicted to cocaine, had entered a state of psychosis due to prolonged sleep deprivation. Both patients knew each other well. In fact, one of the patients had recommended Mayers to the other. In this state of psychosis, these patients found common ground. They believed that it was actually Mayers and his practice that was preventing them from sleeping. They believed themselves the victims of a conspiracy; a corrupt scientist's experiment on the effects of sleep deprivation.

Being wealthy, and connected, made acquiring guns much easier.

Three other patients, two receptionists, and Mayers himself were gunned down that fateful day. Only the doctor survived. The two bankers then turned the guns on themselves.

After suffering a nervous breakdown and leaving his family, Mayers embarked on his own personal journey into CBT to counter his PTSD. Over this time, he attempted suicide three times. Two years ago, he became one of Martin Adam's first patients in HASD. He was now one of Adam's closest friends and helped wherever possible in the development of this treatment.

Neil wasn't stupid. He knew this was a training run. Mayers was so far into his HASD treatment that Neil would be unlikely to help *or* fuck this up. He was certain that Mayers would have been briefed by Adams on how to respond, and how to help Neil in his professional development during this session.

It was a session based entirely around *acceptance* and involved *accepting* the trauma as part of your life rather than as an external force.

Neil had intensely researched Mayer's traumatic experience all morning. He knew the ins and outs of every moment of Mayer's horrendous experience that day; right up until that bullet shattered his ribs and grazed his heart.

His survival had been a miracle but, two days after he'd woken up, he'd told the doctors that it was a miracle he hadn't wanted.

There was a knock at his door. 'Come in,' Neil said, rising to his feet.

The door opened.

'Dr Mayers,' Neil said. 'Very pleased to meet you.' He held out his hand.

'Likewise, Dr Solomon.' Mayers came across the room to shake his hand.

He was a big man and his handshake was firm.

Neil was nervous but was immediately relaxed by Mayer's wide smile. He exposed coffee-stained teeth framed by a thick, white moustache that curled right out to the corners of his cheeks.

13

O N THE WAY back to Chloe Ward, Yorke took a
phone call from DC Jeff Powers from Vice.

'Yep. Chloe Ward was at the squat. I recognised her
instantly from the image. I've also just stopped in to speak to
Sylvia to confirm it and get a timeline together. Chloe started
staying, and working there, six months ago. She disappeared
from the squat two months ago. Sylvia describes her as a
fragile young woman, who avoided the plague of drugs
sweeping the squats, who did 'service' a few clients. Her
heart clearly wasn't in it, and she refused to turn tricks most
of the time.'

'Someone is recruiting from those squats. Someone
called the Conduit.'

'Just a minute, sir, let me get a pen. The Conduit? What
kind of name is that?'

'You tell me? Can you support me with this investigation? Take a couple of your officers down and interview
everybody who works there. I could use my people, but I

suspect you would appreciate using officers more sensitive to the needs of these particular interviewees.'

'Yes ... of course. What approach are we taking?'

He explained, in detail, his understanding of the situation so far. Chloe's personal trauma, the fact that she'd been treated with HASD by the Conduit, and a potted version of what HASD was.

'So, this man has treated Chloe and David for trauma and the result is that they go out and mutilate other people?'

'That's the gist of it.'

'Doesn't sound like the most effective treatment, does it?'

'I don't think it's going to get a glowing recommendation from the World Health Organisation at this rate *unless...*'

'Unless what, sir?'

'Unless, he's doing something different. Altering the treatment, perhaps? But first, we need to identify him. Take a picture of Christian Severance with you – I think he is the third man that has been recruited by the Conduit. And take a picture of Martin Adams too. He is the founder of HASD. And please call me as and when you learn anything.'

'Of course.'

Yorke paused at the door of the interview room. He undid two buttons at the top of his damp shirt. His phone buzzed in his pocket, and he looked to see who was calling. It was Patricia. She would know about Gardner now and would be going out of her mind worrying about him. He owed her a quick phone call. He made a mental note to do it as soon as he'd finished with Chloe.

When he sat down, opposite Chloe again, he realised that she was just like a child. Not just because of her youthful appearance, but rather the faraway look in her eyes and her innocent, uncluttered expression.

How could she be responsible for those atrocities? Really? How?

'What are you drawing now, Chloe?'

She slid over a picture. Again, the likeness was remarkable.

'Christian Severance?'

She nodded.

'You are a talented artist, Chloe. Did anyone ever tell you that?'

She shook her head.

'Did this man, Christian Severance, make you cut out your tongue?'

She shook her head again.

'Did the Conduit?'

She wrote on a piece of card: *nobodie it was my choyce*

He read her response out for the recording.

'Will you explain to me how it was your choice?'

Chloe nodded and began to write.

Chloe's disclosure was long and arduous. The air con in the room was still on the blink. Yorke and the guard sweated profusely. But no one sweated like Chloe, who wrote long passages in response to Yorke's probing questions. She clearly struggled to convey herself in words. Her brow creased, and she repeatedly chewed her bottom lip. Sweat ran down the side of her face and darkened the collar of her blue overalls.

Chloe had met Severance and Sturridge at the squat in Wiltshire. Although she didn't write this, Yorke surmised that they had all been drawn to this 'option' due to catastrophic experiences in their younger years. Severance had been abused before becoming a successful scientist, helping millions of people suffering from snakebites in third-world countries. All of which was brought to a crashing halt by Marcus Long and his undying obsession with him. There was Sturridge, who had been rejected by those who should have loved him and made homeless. Then there was Chloe, child-like and low on intelligence, abused by the people she'd loved, beaten into infertility.

All of them drawn together at Alex Drake's squat.

They all rejected the scourge of drugs but were made to sell their bodies for their accommodation. It was not surprising that they had found solace in each other.

And then came the Conduit.

we dont know his name he never told us his nayme
he never wanted sex he just wanted to tallk
then he wanted to hellp
we went to him for hellp

The Conduit had visited the squat time and time again, but not for sex. *Had he been looking for damaged individuals?* A destination such as this was likely to yield results in that regard. He probably met many – but then settled on these three. Severance, Sturridge and Chloe. Three extremely damaged individuals he could treat.

And make better?

Could self-mutilation, and committing heinous crimes be considered better?

'How did he treat you Chloe?'

Chloe tried her best to explain the ins-and-outs of her treatment, but she found it difficult for many reasons. She had to write it all down, and not only did she struggle with spelling, but she struggled with vocabulary too. She also explained that her memory was very hazy.

he mayde me eet and drink things

Yorke had read a few books on self-hypnosis following the murder of his sister to try and improve his state of mind.

He remembered reading that drugs like LSD and alcohol would significantly increase your susceptibility to hypnosis. He remembered thinking that this was a good thing at the time because he was drinking a hell of a lot.

'What *can* you remember?'

Chloe remembered that there had been a lot of sessions. To begin with, he'd conducted the sessions in her room at night while he was paying for her services. She claimed that many of these sessions revolved around reliving her most traumatic experience – the miscarriage – repeatedly until it was *accepted* as part of her life, not something external and influential, just a memory to own and reflect on in much the same way as you reflect on the first time you try ice-cream. She explained how the experiences were painful but made her feel better. A lot less ashamed and more at ease.

i fellt normal

Severance had been the first to go. Chloe explained how he'd just upped and left one day and, it was only later, when she'd left too, that she'd realised where he'd gone. One-by-one, the Conduit had taken them to his house. He'd arranged to meet them at the carpark at Tidworth skate-park after dark. She'd journeyed to his home in the boot of his car – so she would not be able to identify the location of his house.

'How about when you left his home this morning to go to the academy? Do you remember the journey then?'

She didn't because the Conduit had taken similar precautions then too.

She then described her experience at the Conduit's house, what she could remember of it. For months, she had been treated by the Conduit up to five times a day. She'd been subjected to a range of medicines and visualisations.

She wrote: *i was hole again*

But at what cost? Yorke thought.

They'd *shared* their afflictions. At first, this had been done in a group discussion. Severance, Chloe and Sturridge had sat together with the Conduit as he'd unified them in the pain. They would have been able, as Topham described it earlier, to *feel,* and *empathise* with one another's trauma.

True healing came, Chloe reported, when the Conduit made us physically *share* our afflictions.

Yorke took a deep breath and sat upright in the chair. Most of the day, he'd been fighting back a need to burst into tears; right now, he was fighting back a need to retch.

To share Severance's trauma, the Conduit had removed Chloe and Sturridge's tongues. But it hadn't stopped there and, as Chloe continued to disclose, Yorke brought a closed fist to his mouth. To share Chloe's trauma, the Conduit had sterilised Sturridge and Severance. Chloe wasn't aware how he'd done this, but Yorke assumed he'd given them both vasectomies. Finally, in order to share Sturridge's experiences, the Conduit had raped both Chloe and Severance. Chloe claimed that the Conduit had taken no pleasure from any of these actions.

but it workd we fellt that we really understood eetch other

Then, Chloe took him through the third stage of the treatment – *displacement* – and everything fell into place.

It was deep into Dr Louis Mayer's session of *acceptance* that Dr Neil Solomon realised there was a problem.

Despite being treated with HASD for nearly two years, it was clear that Mayers hadn't really *accepted* anything.

Could this be the true reason that Dr Martin Adams had

given Mayers to Neil as his first patient? Not as a test, but rather as an example of the more resistant patient, the one that was more difficult to crack? Maybe Adams believed that he could be the final piece of the jigsaw? The person who could take this treatment to the finishing line?

Or maybe, thought Neil, this was just wishful thinking?

Again, and again, under hypnosis, Mayers relived the moment that he'd been dragged from his office by his hair and thrown to the floor in the blood and brain matter of his colleagues and patients. He'd cowered under a table, but the gunmen hadn't taken long to find him.

The gunmen. *His* patients.

And that was Mayer's problem right there, Neil realised. He was completely focused on the fact that they had been his patients, and that he *should* have treated them and prevented this. The dead bodies which had been littered around him were a knock-on effect of his *failure*.

After he'd woken up in hospital, Mayers had told the doctors, 'They are all dead and, unjustly, I am alive.'

Even now, with Neil, after reliving the moment he'd been shot in the chest, and had woken up in hospital with a damaged, but still functioning, heart, he repeated the same thing, 'They are all dead and, unjustly, I am alive.'

So, Neil tried for almost an hour to try and alter thoughts, which surely, Adams and others had tried to alter for years now.

He tried: 'These men were that high on cocaine – there was no stopping them.'

And: 'You cannot be expected to halt such ruthless behaviour on only one hour of therapy a week!'

Also: 'You tried to help them remove the stressors from

their lives – if they chose not to follow advice, how much responsibility should you really take?'

None of these reasons were helping Mayers reach *acceptance* in this session. So, if he couldn't accept these specific alternative thoughts, Neil would have to try for the more philosophical. He told him that this event was part of him now, like countless other events.

'It is important to be *defined* by everything,' Neil said. 'Not just this one moment.'

And as Neil did this, he noticed something that filled him with great concern. Mayers kept rubbing at the wrists that he'd sliced opened on three occasions since the traumatic experience.

'They are all dead and, unjustly, I am alive.' Mayers said, and then opened his eyes. He had broken from hypnosis. 'I'm sorry, my mind is being rather stubborn today. It has a tendency to do that. Especially when it is so very hot.'

'You should let me bring you out of hypnosis properly, Doctor Mayers—'

'And risk you running into your next session?' Mayers nodded at the clock on the wall. He was still rubbing his wrists.

'I don't have another session.'

'Well, I do have somewhere to be, I'm afraid. Don't worry, Dr Solomon, I'm a seasoned hand at this myself. Going in and out of hypnosis is like turning the television on and off. Do not take my stubborn mind personally.'

'Dr Mayers, you repeated the statement: *they are dead and unjustly, I am alive*, several times. It suggests that you still believe your life is unjust. That leaves me ... concerned.'

'Well, don't be. I've said this statement, under suggestion, thousands of times. I've challenged it repeatedly. You have unearthed nothing new here today.'

'But you have made three attempts on your life to date, and now you've made this suggestion today. I'm worried that you may be a danger to yourself.'

'*Poppycock!*' Mayers stood up. 'I like you, Dr Solomon. My first impression of you is sound. And I am close friends with Dr Adams, as well you know. He allowed you to treat me first for obvious reasons. We want you to experience stubborn resistance. A resistance that cannot be broken down, or even chipped at, in a first session. If you wish to report that I am a danger to myself, be my guest, but if you want to present yourself as a laughing stock in front of Martin on your first day, don't say I didn't warn you. Now, young man, shake my hand, and let me make my dinner appointment.'

YORKE SENT a text message to Patricia claiming that he was holding it together despite the morning's shocking events. He really should have phoned her, but he was running a briefing in a matter of minutes, and he didn't want to risk tears by having a heart-to-heart with his wife.

As always, Yorke was first in there. He paced the front of the incident room as the officers filed in. Many looked tired, and emotional, having put in a long shift already. HOLMES was teeming with new information. He'd already been briefed on some of the more salient facts over the last thirty minutes since concluding Chloe's interview.

Debbie Lang, the parent impersonated by Chloe, had been discovered drugged up. She'd regained enough composure to explain that the empty needle lying beside her was not hers, and she had a vague memory of opening the door to an elderly man with a kindly demeanour. She'd also noted his unusually long white moustache. This man, who Yorke suspected was the Conduit, had claimed to be from Social Services, there to follow up on a concern reported by the academy. At first, Lang had been taken aback, but then he'd offered her a calming word. He'd told her that it was just a chat, that he was on her side, and nothing serious would come of all this. His ID had been very realistic. She couldn't remember taking note of his name. In fact, she remembered very little of the next few minutes. She'd been forced to the ground and stuck with this needle. SOCOs were currently crawling over the scene for fibres and trace evidence. The usual door-to-door was in session. CCTV cameras in the local area were being scrutinised for comings and goings.

Interviewing officers at the school had already identified the leak as single mother Julia Hayder. She was PA to the headteacher and had crumbled immediately, admitting her actions before the questioning had even really started. Her ordeal had begun when a picture of her thirteen-year old boy was pushed into her letterbox late on a Sunday evening. The picture had an email address and a message scrawled on the back. The instructions had been clear: every appointment Amanda Werrell had scheduled in for the forthcoming week were to be emailed the following morning. The sender had kept the threat traditional: *do as you are told or I will take your son from you. Let the police know and I will take your son from you.* She'd even received a reply to her email the next day. *If any appointment changes, and you fail to email, I will take your son from you.* Analysts were currently trying to track the email reply to a location.

Use of manpower in Wiltshire was at an all-time high. A

dead police officer, another in intensive care, a mutilated headteacher, and a missing college girl certainly warranted it.

Yorke paced back-and-forth at the board, examining the pictures from both Operation Autumn, and Operation Coldtown, which had blended themselves together into one noxious concoction. Then, he used blue-tac and added a photo of Chloe. He had another piece of A4 paper in his hand, folded. He started to unfold it, weighing up whether to pin it up on the board too. He decided against it and held it against his side.

Eventually, the officers were assembled, Dawson from HOLMES and his female counterpart had their laptops humming and ready to roll.

He noticed the smell of summer was strong in here. A floral smell had drifted in from the outside and mingled with the pungent body odour of the large crowd. Sitting right in the middle of the crowd with his arms crossed, looking squat and smug, was Parkinson.

Yorke felt his irritation surge. If the oppositional cretin started to pass comments, like he'd done in the previous two briefings, Yorke wasn't sure he'd be able to hold it together.

He nodded over at Jake, who was running his hand back-and-forth over his crewcut, clearly not used to it. Topham stood alongside him at the front, staring at Yorke, shaking his head, indicating that Neil was still not here yet. Yorke looked to his other side where he would have asked Gardner to stand. He grimaced.

He began by dimming the lights, switching on the projector and showing them all the school CCTV footage of the violent assault on both Werrell and Gardner. No one spoke. Very few officers *seemed* to breathe. Everything was deathly still. Yorke felt tears prick his eyes. He decided he was past caring how he appeared. At least if it was noticed he'd be considered human. *Was crying really such a weakness?*

Silence continued for seconds after Yorke stopped the footage. He was allowing them time to digest it, to press on them the importance of, in the words of Madden, closing this *fucking* case down.

Seconds felt like minutes. Some officers stared down at the table.

'We're dropping like flies,' Parkinson said.

Yorke drew a sharp breath in through his nose. It was clearly audible. Most officers kept their eyes down. Some made notes. Some glanced at their watches.

Parkinson, with his arms still crossed, stared right at Yorke.

Topham stepped alongside Yorke and replied to Parkinson, 'And your point, DC Parkinson?'

Parkinson shrugged. Yorke looked at Topham with gratitude because his own response to that comment would probably have caused problems. He diverted the sudden irritation, and rise of adrenaline, into bringing the incident room alive. This was the beating heart of the investigation and, now more than ever before, this heart needed to beat.

Yorke bounced around the wall, drawing the threads of the case together. He provided the background on the recruitment of Chloe, Sturridge and Severance by a man called the Conduit. He explained that many of the events disclosed by Chloe in the interview room had been corroborated by Sylvia and several other witnesses from the squat. Many of these witnesses recalled the Conduit. Many of them had experienced time alone with him after he paid for their services. He never had sex with any of them. He just asked them about their past. When he returned, he usually asked for someone different.

'They obviously weren't damaged enough for him,' Yorke said. 'So, he kept on returning until he found the three he wanted.'

'At this point I am going to hand you over to DI Topham to explain HASD to you. I'd suggest taking notes. There is a lot to get your head around here.'

Topham talked them through the practise of HASD in a similar fashion to how he'd done with Yorke earlier in the office. At the same time, Yorke wrote the list on the board in permanent marker, capitalising the initial letter of each word to spell out the acronym.

Healing.

Acceptance.

Sharing.

Displacement.

Willows asked a question. 'So, would it not be reasonable to assume that this Martin Adams, founder of HASD, is the Conduit?'

Yorke said, 'It's a very good question, Detective Willows. We will come back to that in a moment.'

He circled the word *Acceptance*. 'Let's consider this phase one of the process. I've no idea if they actually refer to it in this manner, but until we have our expert in,' he paused to glance at Topham, who gave him a shrug, 'we will consider this phase one. I think he managed, phase one, *acceptance*, in a straight-forward manner at the squat. He returned again and again for sessions with them, while their pimp, Alex Drake, just assumed they were having sexual relations. Not that Alex would have cared either way as the Conduit was still paying for their time. So, at the squats, using visualisation, hypnosis and CBT techniques, he helped them to come to terms with their past traumas. Consequently, they started to trust him, so he could convince them to come away with him. To his house.'

Yorke explained how the Conduit kept this part of the journey secret by taking them in the boot of his car.

He then circled the word *sharing*. 'This is where things get creepier. Phase 2. Now, I want you to consider what DI Topham has just told you about *sharing*. It sounds very traditional – yes? People *sharing* past traumas in groups, using each other for support, sympathy and empathy. After intensively interviewing Chloe, and I emphasise *intensely*, we have discovered that she is rather childlike in her understanding of the world. Her ability to communicate, as you can imagine, is limited. But her confession indicates that Phase 2 is where the Conduit started to adapt the normal approach to HASD.'

He paused for a sip of water and a deep breath.

He pointed at all three pictures. 'They all *shared* their afflictions. *Literally.* Not just through visualisations, but physically, too.'

There was a moment of nervous chatter. Yorke let it pass, and then elaborated. 'Christian Severance's trauma was the loss of his tongue. Chloe and Sturridge have shared this. Chloe's was the loss of fertility. Again, this is shared by Severance, and Sturridge - I'm guessing through vasectomies. Finally, Sturridge was raped,' he paused, every eye in the room was on him, 'and so Severance and Chloe were both raped by the Conduit.'

'Sick,' said Willows.

'So,' Yorke said, 'we can surmise that the Conduit is adapting Adam's HASD technique outside of a scientific setting. Which brings us to Phase 3.' He circled *displacement*.

He held a hand up and gestured at the board, and all the victims displayed on it.

'This is the *displacement*. Gone is the controlled environment in which the psychiatrist uses visualisations to actually displace their pain onto others to offer temporary relief. Those visualisations just became very real.'

'So,' he said, pointing at the photographs of Simmonds, Long, and then Werrell, 'we know why their tongues were removed.'

'To offer relief to Christian Severance?' Jake said.

'Yes. And we can assume Alex, the pimp who raped Sturridge, has also experienced this *displacement*. In what form that is, we can only hypothesise, but we have been informed by Sturridge that he is dead. Chloe, when I questioned her, wasn't aware of the specifics of his fate.'

'And Chloe's aggressor? The one who caused the miscarriage?'

'Checked already,' Yorke said. 'Fate beat them to it. He was involved in a fatal road collision five months ago.'

'Lucky for him,' Parkinson said. 'He probably avoided a grislier death.'

'And in all of this,' Yorke continued, 'Susie Long is still missing.'

Topham said, 'And now it really doesn't look good.'

'No,' Yorke said. 'If we assume Severance knows that his play to get Long to remove his tongue was successful, he would have no further need for her.'

'He could release her?' Willows said.

Everyone stared at her. No one graced her with a response.

An officer called Prior said, 'But sir, why would all these individuals go to so much trouble to heal themselves in such a barbaric, complex fashion only to spend the rest of their lives in jail?'

'It's a good question,' Yorke said, 'and one that I can't get out of my own head. They gave themselves up too easily. Why? Chloe and Sturridge both remained at the crime scenes. I agree, it makes little sense.'

'Maybe they think that true healing cannot be achieved?' Jake said. 'Maybe they are just giving up?'

'They could believe,' Topham said, 'in their own twisted way that if the process works, that they are the *evidence* that it works. Maybe the Conduit is revelling in the success of his adapted HASD programme and wants to show that it is successful?'

'I think this is the more likely explanation,' Yorke said. 'We must assume he is a doctor. Research is everything, and then the evidence is his bread and butter. Also, let us not forget that Severance is still out there, which means that he is not finished yet.'

'What if there are more recruits?' said an officer from near the back.

'The interviews at the squats, which are still ongoing, suggest otherwise. These are the three recruits. Unless he has recruited *elsewhere,* but we have no evidence of that yet.'

He paused for another mouthful of water. He noticed Parkinson whispering something in a colleague's ear, and smirking to himself. *Enough is enough*, Yorke thought. *I'm addressing him after this briefing.* Yorke realised he was clenching a fist. Embarrassed, in case anyone noticed, he thrust it into his pocket.

'Assignments are organised, but I can tell you what the

priority is right now.' He held up the A4 piece of paper. 'Chloe is quite the artist. This is the Conduit.'

On the paper was a large burly man, leaning forward over a desk, smiling. Jake looked closely. 'No one will miss that moustache.'

Yorke said, 'I will put this on the board after it has been copied, familiarise yourself with the image. Earlier DC Willows asked me if we should be interviewing Martin Adams. And yes, we will be. But after seeing an image of Adams earlier, I do not believe he is the Conduit. He has no likeness to the man in this image. However, we need to see Adams immediately because the Conduit may be connected to the HASD team in some way.'

It was at that point that Yorke noticed that Parkinson had his mobile phone out. Yorke's surge of irritation could be contained no longer. '*Detective Parkinson. Get to your feet now!*'

The room fell silent. Parkinson looked up. Yorke started to move towards him. '*I SAID NOW!*'

Parkinson stood. He expressed confusion with a creased brow, but his flushed cheeks showed he was embarrassed.

Yorke stood a metre in front of him, towering over the smaller man. He widened his eyes, lowered his voice to a hiss. '*Give me your phone.*'

'No, I will not...'

'Are you disobeying a direct order?'

'No, but it is an inappropriate—'

'*Now.*'

Parkinson handed it over with a trembling hand.

Yorke marched over to the window, opened it, and glanced down to check that there was no one two floors below. Then, he dropped the phone out of the window, and watched it smash on the concrete below.

He closed the window, turned to the crowd and pointed at Parkinson. 'If you ever contaminate my incident room again, I will end your career.'

He left the silent room.

14

O N HIS WAY to see Dr Martin Adams at Southampton University, Yorke took the scenic route, so he could pull over in a quiet country lane. He reached under a seat and pulled out a disposable phone. Over ten minutes ago, he'd texted Harry the following message: *phone this number from a payphone at least fifteen minutes from your house.*

He quickly phoned Jake on his main phone to tell him that he was running a little late in meeting him at the university to see Adams. He lied, saying he'd had to stop and queue for fuel. He'd no need to contact Topham, because he'd left him back at the station to wait for Neil's arrival and coordinate the rest of the team in their assignments.

After five minutes, Yorke's frustration grew. *Where are you, Harry?*

He didn't want to have to phone Jake to apologise again.

Finally, the disposable phone started to ring.

'Yes, Mike?'

'They know all about it,' Yorke said.

'What?'

'Your plan. Joan Madden confronted me. You're being watched. The information you pried out of two of our officers has been compromised, and they've been suspended.'

'What? Bradley? Suspended?'

Bradley. An older officer, close to retirement; he'd be taking it early now. Yorke was well aware of Bradley and his old school methods.

'Yes. Precisely, Harry. Your efforts continue to ruin lives. And the irony is, we now have the information to act on it *ourselves*, so I'm telling you to stand down, before you cause any more problems.'

'I can't do that, Mike.'

'What the hell are you talking about, Harry? It's done. Finished. Madden and company are watching you.'

'Well, thanks for the heads-up. I'll make sure I give them the slip later.'

'But they know! They'll probably get to Proud before you.'

'But do they know? Really, Mike? Have they worked it out yet?'

'Of course.'

'So, tell me Mike, where is Proud?'

Yorke pounded the steering wheel with his fist. 'I don't know *but* I'm sure they do.'

'Well, I'll take my chances.'

'I could just go to Bradley myself, right now, and get the location.'

'You could, and you may even get there before me, but then what? You'll have to admit you are working with me.'

'Still, I'll take my chances. No one will believe it. And I'll do anything to stop you committing murder.'

'I'm dying anyway.'

'That's not the point.'

'Yes, it is. You were there. I held my dead wife in my arms. She was riddled with buckshot. Do you not remember?'

'Of course, I remember.'

'Now, I have the chance to put *something* right for once. To even the scales.'

'It won't bring her back and it won't earn my forgiveness.'

'Maybe not, but I'll try. Goodbye, Mike.'

'Wait, Harry...'

But the phone was dead. Yorke punched the wheel again. He bit his bottom lip to hold in his anger. He didn't want to be heard. He exited the car and worked his way through some bushes, picking up scratches on his hands. Eventually, he made it to a narrow stream.

Checking there was no one about, he smashed the phone to pieces on a rock, and scattered the debris into the stream.

Susie Long's world pulsed like the heart of a demented creature.

She was aware that she was in a living room, because out of the swelling, bloated chaos around her, she identified a television and some sofas.

The large man with the moustache came through the soup and knelt before her. He dabbed at her face with a handkerchief. It took her a while to remember him from the car earlier.

'There, there, Susie. The medicine can make you dribble

to begin with, but it'll pass, as will the wooziness. Then we can begin.'

'What are you doing?' she said.

'I cannot understand a word you are saying, Susie, just try and relax for a moment.'

'LET ME FUCKING GO!'

'Please calm down. Half of your mouth is not currently moving, you may feel like you are speaking right now, but I can assure you that you're not.'

She started to cry, but just like the speaking, she wasn't sure if it was actually happening. She'd never felt so *disassociated*.

'Please nod if you can understand what I am saying to you, Susie?'

She assumed that she'd managed to nod because he continued to talk.

'My name is the Conduit. I am a channel. I become the piece that is missing from inside people, and I allow the thoughts, feelings and behaviours to move fluidly through me and within them. Nod if you understand.'

She nodded again.

He tilted her head so she could see Severance sitting on the sofa. He had one leg thrown over the other, and he stroked his chin as he observed. He presented himself almost professionally, like a doctor, rather than a vicious killer who had castrated that man in the plastic coffin.

'You have, of course, met Dr Severance already. He was a successful doctor, you know. He achieved so much in his short career.'

Severance turned away.

'And he would have gone on to achieve so much more if your father hadn't destroyed his face. But you know all of this already, don't you? If it wasn't for me, Susie, you'd be dead already. Did you know that?'

At such a comment, she expected her heart to beat wildly. The fact that it continued to drum slowly in her chest made her feel even more unstable. Everything was at odds with itself.

'I'll repeat the question - did you know that?'

Susie shook her head.

'So, I saved you, and you owe me. I hope that with some time together, with some more of my medication, you could help me further my research? Would that be okay?'

'No ... I want to go home.'

The Conduit shook his head and tutted. 'I understood your refusal, but not what you said after that.' He held up a syringe. 'Would it be necessary to administer more of this medicine? I was hoping that it would be unnecessary.' He held her arm and pointed her wrist upwards and towards him.

She tried to pull it away, but it didn't move. Whether it was the tightness of his grip, or her lack of motor control, she wasn't sure.

She shook her head. 'No more.'

'Good,' the Conduit said, releasing her arm.

She flinched, or at least thought she flinched, when she noticed that Severance was now standing behind the Conduit. He was stroking the tangle of welts and scars that twisted around his mouth like spindly animal claws.

'There is darkness in all of our lives, Susie. *So much darkness.* No one is exempt. That is what I have learned over the years, through my own experiences, and the count-less experiences of others. Rather than always trying to smother the darkness, push it away, contain it – sometimes we need to embrace it. The sense of freedom that comes from that is indescribable. Just ask Dr Severance behind me.'

She glanced up and he was nodding.

'So, I'm going to help you find that darkness inside yourself.'

He pulled a small contraption from his pocket and switched it on. It produced a slow flashing light. 'To do that, I must hypnotise you. The drugs in your system will help with this. If you consent, the impact will be more powerful. Let me be your conduit, Susie, let me find the darkness inside you, and let me help you embrace it. Do you consent, Susie?'

She couldn't pinpoint the exact reason she nodded. It may have been the Conduit's voice, which was soothing and protective like her father's had been so many years ago. It could have been the scarred man intimidating her. Possibly, it was the drug tangling her system in knots.

Having consented, the Conduit held the flashing light in front of her eyes.

WEARING SUNGLASSES, Christian Severance left the Conduit to his work. His time, like Chloe's and Sturridge's, was drawing to an end. He glanced at his watch, noting the hour. His final plan had already been initiated, the flies were being drawn in, and he needed to ensure that he, the spider, was there, within plenty of time, to spring the trap.

As he descended the path, he enjoyed the sunshine. The Conduit had been referring, at length, to the darkness in their lives only moments ago. And he was right, Severance had experienced more than his fair share. The light, the burning brightness, was something to savour in these final hours.

He scratched his thigh. There was an itch there that was really starting to bother him.

When he got into his car at the end of the driveway, he pulled his wallet out of his inside pocket and looked down at a picture.

Whenever he was under any doubt as to whether he was doing the right thing, he looked at this picture.

He started the car. It was time to finish what he'd started.

FOR SUCH A SUCCESSFUL MAN, breaking new ground in the world of psychiatry, Yorke was surprised by how poky Dr Martin Adams' office was. Littering the desk were a couple of half-drunk cups of tea; piles of lecture notes and essays; and an old desktop computer which hummed louder than the fan in the corner of the room. Yes, he still lectured, but surely, his fame, published works, and treatment of many would have earned him a reasonable amount of money? Maybe this was all a University offered to a mini-celebrity?

Yorke was still shaken up by his phone call to Harry which had ended abruptly and without resolution. He knew his only course of action was to locate the suspended officer, Bradley, and acquire the information that had led Harry to Proud. However, he couldn't do it right now. Interviewing Adams was the number one priority. Not addressing this first would seem all too obvious to Madden and his other colleagues. Yorke felt like he was running out of time in both situations. He felt suffocated.

Not only were the surroundings a surprise, but so too was

the man himself. He was a jittery fellow, who shuffled papers and teacups around to clear space, muttering, 'Sorry for the mess, Detectives.'

Eventually, he took a seat opposite them. He pulled off his glasses and chewed on the arm as he listened to the reason Yorke and Jake were here. Yorke congratulated him on his success with HASD and queried him as to why he wasn't achieving more recognition and reward.

'It always takes a while for people to realise the impact of newer techniques. HASD has been a long and arduous process.' He smiled. 'But one I've relished. I've never been a person to rush into success, Detective Yorke. It will come in its own time.'

You might realise that it is not coming any time soon when I explain why I'm here, Yorke thought. 'Have you heard of a man called Christian Severance?'

'I'm afraid not.'

'Chloe Ward or David Sturridge?'

'No, and no again, Detective.'

'I have only just been introduced to the basic principles behind HASD today, Dr Adams, and as you will soon be aware my knowledge is just that ... basic. Could you tell me how many patients have been treated by HASD?'

'Why hundreds of course!'

'So,' Jake said, 'is it possible that Chloe Ward and David Sturridge were treated by HASD?'

'I suppose. I could double check, but I suspect that the answer will still be the same. My memory is exceptional. I have studied my case studies to within an inch of their lives.'

'How many people are there on your team?' Yorke said.

'Eight in total.'

'We will need to speak to all of them. Today, if possible.'

'Of course, I will give you their names. Five are on campus. Three are off-campus today. I also have one new starter today...'

'Dr Neil Solomon?' Yorke said.

'Yes ... that's right. You've done your research.'

'Yes.'

'So, are you going to tell me *why* the sudden interest in HASD?'

Yorke and Jake looked at each other. This was always the most difficult bit. Revealing the important information, but not all of it. Control filters needed to stay in place. When people approached them with information, they had to be sure that the information was fresh and not contaminated by knowledge which had been strategically held back.

'We have reason to believe that a series of crimes has been committed using the HASD treatment.'

Adams raised an eyebrow and shook his head. 'I don't understand. That sounds ... ridiculous.'

'Do you know someone called the Conduit?'

'The what? The Conduit? No, of course not.'

Yorke talked through the way HASD could have been adapted in a similar fashion to how it had been explained back in the incident room at HQ. He left out names and specific crimes. Adams turned pale, and started to tremble.

'So, this is connected to what happened to that police officer, DC Ryan Simmonds, and that school principal, Amanda Werrell?'

Yorke looked at Jake and then back at Adams. 'You do have a good memory for names.'

Adams nodded. He took his glasses off, stood up and sighed. Then he started to pace around behind his desk, stopping occasionally to stare out of his small, dirty window.

'The adaption of medical practice is nothing new. But I have never heard of anything so ... barbaric. You'd have to go back to the Victorian ages to find such despicable actions.'

'So you have no idea who could be responsible for this?'

'No, but I hope you find them and stop them soon, because it sounds like the last three years of my work is about to go up in flames.'

Yorke looked at Jake and then pulled out Chloe's picture of the Conduit.

'Do you recognise this man?

Adams turned to one side, clutched his mouth for a moment and gagged violently; then, he vomited on the floor.

Susie Long could feel the Conduit in her head. Not just his voice, which seemed to sporadically vary between the hypnotic and the soothing, but rather *him* – his whole being.

As a result of this, he was able to drag her back to her darkest memory.

Susie remembered being only eight in this memory, but she was yet to make an appearance. He'd brought them into this room earlier than she'd originally been there. She looked at the Conduit, who stood alongside her in the visualisation. He reminded her of a spirit in A *Christmas Carol,* showing Scrooge the way to enlightenment.

The room was well lit. The windows were open, allowing in the fresh air. The curtains flapped gently.

Because they had arrived early, her beloved grandmother was still alive. Her breathing was shallow, and she was slipping in and out of consciousness frequently, but the woman who'd been such a huge part of Susie's life until this point was still present.

Susie approached. She could feel the Conduit beside her, but he stopped at the foot of the bed, while she came around the side to look down on her grandmother's face. She was asleep, dreaming away her final moments. Susie looked back at the Conduit. He offered her a sympathetic expression.

Then, she looked over the bed at her uncle Roland. He was readying a syringe.

She told him to stop, but it was of no use, because she wasn't physically there yet. Her real self would, just about now, be leaving her grandmother's living room where other members of family waited for their turn to spend some final minutes with her. Everybody expected her to die tonight; nobody, except her uncle, expected it to end this very moment.

He was doing it *for* her, she realised, to alleviate her great suffering.

But, still, despite her great pain, it felt wrong. Not only was her uncle playing God, but he was taking on a burden that he shouldn't have.

So, she tried again, to tell him to stop, but he didn't hear her, *couldn't* hear her, and he pushed the needle into her arm. At that point, eight-year-old Susie came into the room. She watched her smaller self look up at her uncle in surprise. 'What are you doing, Uncle Roland? What are you putting in Granny's arm?'

Her uncle withdrew the needle and placed it in his inside jacket pocket. He beckoned the younger Susie over and put an arm around her. Clutching her grandmother's hand together, they watched her take her final breaths, and disappear.

The older Susie spoke to the Conduit in the visualisation. 'I didn't fully understand what I had witnessed then. Not until years later did I realise. But I accepted it. I loved her, and it was mercy. He did it because he loved her and her pain was destroying him.'

MAYERS LOOKED DOWN at his dribbling patient. He'd understood most of what she'd just said. His cocktail, which included a higher dose of lysergic acid diethylamide than he normally used, had almost reduced her to an incomprehensible wreck, but now, she was becoming more coherent.

This, of course, excited him. She was poised delicately between clarity and disarray, making her incredibly malleable. She had let him into the site of her trauma, and under normal circumstances, they would now work on *acceptance*. But this had never been about normal circumstances; and, besides, she'd *accepted* the trauma already.

So, he would have to work on undoing that *acceptance*.

What could he term this technique? Rejection?

He would work on making her *reject* her trauma, and then when she was at her lowest point, he could *alter* her behaviour.

He ran his fingers over his moustache. *It could take a long time.*

He looked at his watch. Severance would be back early evening.

Which meant he did have a couple of hours to kill.

Dr Neil Solomon sat alone in his car and watched the house he had followed Mayers to, feeling more and more unprofessional with every passing second.

He was parked several houses back, on the opposite side of the road, buffeting himself with the aircon. If he didn't, he'd be asleep by now. The outside temperature gauge on his car read thirty-five degrees.

He couldn't believe this was happening, but this man, Mayers, had him spooked. Three past suicide attempts coupled with a disastrous therapy session could not be ignored.

Was this a test by Adams? Was he supposed to flag up Mayers to Adams as a suicide risk to prove that he knew what he was doing?

Or, had Mayers been accurate in his warning that Adams would view it as ridiculous and condemn him to paper-pushing in a back room until his contract expired?

Whichever way you viewed it, he was certain of one thing: following him to his house to check on him was unprofessional and dangerous.

However, two things had kept him glued to the spot. Firstly, Mayers had drawn the lounge curtains when he'd arrived home. Why? It was a hot, sunny day. Of course, there could be a thousand and one reasons – the light was shining on his television screen, perhaps? But still, it had been enough to send a further bolt of adrenaline through him and keep him rooted here for longer.

Then, there was the man who left. Who was he? Mayers' file painted him as some sort of recluse with very little in the way of family. He had no sons, and his wife had left him a long time ago. Was this a new partner? Was Mayers gay? Again, there could be a thousand and one reasons, but his curiosity was piqued further.

But he had to call it sooner or later - leave or commit himself to the ridiculous task of knocking on Mayers' door. He ran through the scenario. He would have to admit that he'd followed him, then he would have to claim that it was out of the goodness of his heart, and finally, he would have to pray Mayers didn't report him.

Bloody hell! Is this where paranoia got you?

His phone rang. *Mark Topham* flashed up.

'Shit.'

He hadn't completely forgotten that he was due at the station. How could he? That in itself had been a curious request, and under normal circumstances, he'd have bolted there. But these weren't normal circumstances.

Yet, seeing his partner's number now, just sent a bullet of guilt though him, to add to the already mounting catalogue of neuroses.

'Fuck it,' he said.

He got out of his car, locked it with the remote over his shoulder, and headed to Mayer's front door.

15

AFTER DR ADAMS had stopped vomiting, he became tearful and identified the man depicted by Chloe's talented hand as Dr Louis Mayers.

'But ... there must be some mistake.' He dabbed vomit from the corners of his mouth with a handkerchief. 'He's been with us since the beginning. He was the first patient.' He moved the handkerchief to the tears. 'And ... he's my friend. Who drew that?'

'A victim of the Conduit. I believe this depiction to be accurate.' Yorke turned to Jake. 'DS Pettman, you know what to do. Let me finish up here. You join the team, but collect as much information on this man as you can, on route.'

'Yes, sir.' Jake would request Armed Response to Mayers' house. There were now clear grounds to believe that Susie was there, and her life was in jeopardy. Jake left the room without further comment; he had to return to Salisbury at pace.

Yorke said, 'Tell us as much as you can, Dr Adams, we

have a situation here, based around your project, and it has spiralled out of control.'

Yorke took notes as Adams told him everything he knew. Dr Mayers was the first person he'd treated three years ago. His experience had been particularly harrowing – a shooting in his office that had resulted in the deaths of patients and office workers. They'd made ground-breaking progress. It was his treatment that had made Adams believe anything was possible. 'If it wasn't for him, we wouldn't have gotten this far.'

'If it wasn't for him,' Yorke said, 'I wouldn't be sitting here.'

He described their relationship in-depth. 'He is brilliant you know. The best psychiatrist I have ever worked with. His wisdom, enthusiasm and, most importantly, his *creativity* are second-to-none.'

Adams was avoiding eye-contact. He was distraught; social norms had flown out of the window.

'Look at me, Dr Adams, and listen carefully to the next question.'

Adams complied.

'Do you think that he was creative enough to modify, adapt and, potentially, develop his own treatment from yours?'

Adams sighed. 'Isn't that the sign of any good doctor?'

IT WASN'T how Susie remembered it. The windows were closed. The curtains didn't flap gently under a welcome breeze. Instead, there was the cloying smell of death.

Because they had arrived early to the event, her beloved

grandmother was still alive. Her breathing was shallow, and she was slipping in and out of consciousness frequently, but the woman who'd been such a huge part of Susie's life until this point was still present.

Susie approached. She could feel the Conduit beside her, but he stopped at the foot of the bed, while she came around the side to look down on her grandmother's face. She was thin, and she was yellowing. Susie looked back at the Conduit. He offered her a sympathetic expression.

Then, she looked over the bed at her uncle Roland. He was readying a knife.

She told him to stop, but it was of no use, because she wasn't physically there yet. Her real self would, just about now, be leaving her grandmother's living room where other members of family waited for their turn to spend some final minutes with her. Everybody expected her to die tonight; nobody, except her uncle, expected it to end this very moment.

Her grandmother opened her eyes and looked at her son. Within seconds, her cheeks were wet with tears. Susie's uncle looked down on his mother with malice.

So she tried again to tell him to stop, but he didn't hear her, *couldn't* hear her, and he bared his teeth.

'You bitch,' he said. 'You always made me feel so worthless.'

He put the blade to her throat. She widened her eyes, and looked up at her son. 'I loved you,' she murmured.

At that point, eight-year-old Susie came into the room. She watched her smaller self look up at her uncle in surprise. 'What are you doing, Uncle Roland? What do you have against Granny's neck?'

He dragged the weapon over the loose folds of skin, and there was a tearing sound.

There were tiny spurts of blood from the weak flickers of a fading heart, and the red blossomed on her white sheets.

Her uncle pulled the weapon away and examined its bloody blade while his mother gurgled her final breaths beside him. When she finally stilled, he turned to the younger Susie and beckoned her over.

She turned and ran.

Mayers noticed that Susie Long was sweating. It was an extremely hot day, but still, the excessive perspiration surely came from her visceral experience, and the adrenaline bubbling within her.

After he finished talking her through the visualisation, he sensed success. Already she spoke of the event as if it was a fully realised occurrence, rather than a work of fiction.

Excited, he left her in her drug-induced state of hypnosis, and prepared to start the visualisation again. How many times he would have to do this to achieve full *rejection* of the actual events, he had no idea, but he didn't mind. It was enjoyable and this was what he did best.

He began the visualisation only to be interrupted by a knock at the door.

Severance was out of breath, but he was content. It was done and it had been successful.

As he looked into the small unit at his handiwork, he

reached down and scratched his thigh. He winced. It was now starting to burn.

He paused at the door to his storage unit, and instinctively reached out for the light switch, checking himself just in time.

No. Light was needed. He turned one last time and looked on the final strands of his web.

Two voices collided in his memory.

Anthony Morris and Andrew Salton.

Severance smiled. Here was the final stage of his *displacement.*

He sneered at the prone figures, looked down at the blood on his shirt and left the unit.

JAKE MADE it back in time to watch the BMW X5s pile in. Armed Response. They only usually came when there was a report of firearms, but Jake hadn't found it difficult to get Superintendent Joan Madden to authorise it in this instance. A seventeen-year-old girl's life was in the balance. There wouldn't be a fight to deliver the press release if she didn't survive and they hadn't thrown the kitchen sink at it.

As Jake sat on the bonnet of his car, he noticed the light dimming, so he glanced up at the rounded and bumpy cumulus clouds. A thunderstorm wasn't long off. Not a bad thing. The humidity was unbearable, and it needed to rain, but he didn't want to get caught in a downfall. *Let's get this done quickly.*

Armed Response assembled outside Dr Louis Mayer's bungalow. It wasn't the best-looking bungalow, Jake considered. The concrete was crumbling, and the red-tiled roof was patchy and in need of work. It stood out on a street of well-kept properties.

A small man appeared at the fence that ran the perimeter of the garden beside Jake. He was wearing shorts and a T-shirt and held a grease-stained spatula in one hand. Jake noticed the barbecue smoking away in the man's garden.

'What's happening?' he said. 'There's a lot of you here.'

'Please ensure you take cover, sir. I'd like you to move back into your house.'

'Why are the police armed?'

'Please, sir … if you could just go inside.'

Shit. Jake noticed other residents were emerging into their front gardens to take a look. Not that you could blame them. This was not an everyday occurrence on Elm Grove Road.

He hoped there wasn't a show. This needed to go smoothly. The phones were already starting to emerge. He grimaced when he thought how hungry the press would be for that footage.

He moved down the street, instructing the phone-wielding residents to move indoors. Some went back into their houses, some gave the appearance that they were complying, and then lingered.

Behind him, he could hear the armed officers knocking on Mayers' bungalow and demanding entrance. They weren't getting it.

Jake flinched when the officers crashed through Mayers' front door.

Several residents ran into their houses.

That did the trick.

He wiped sweat from his brow and turned around, noticing that one female resident was still standing in her garden. As he crossed over the road, he held the palm of his hand in the air, beckoning her to leave her vantage point and head inside.

He paused when he reached the other side of the pavement. *He recognised her.* He felt a swelling in his stomach that threatened to explode. He clutched hold of a lamp post to steady himself and took a deep breath.

It was his sociopathic ex-girlfriend, Lacey Ray.

'Dr Neil Solomon,' Mayers said, looking at the dishevelled psychiatrist in his doorway. 'I would say I was surprised to see you, but I'm not really.'

'Yes, sorry, Dr Mayers—'

Mayers shushed him with a finger to his mouth. 'Don't be, Doctor, I know why you are here. When has caring about your patients ever been a crime?'

'Yes, forgive me. It's hot. *Relentlessly* hot. And it's my first day ... and I just felt that our session went badly. And I was worried.'

'About me?' Mayers held out his arms. 'As you can see, I'm just fine. Don't be so hard on yourself. In fact, while you are here, Doctor, you can help me with something.'

'Of course, anything.'

Mayers stepped to one side and let Neil into the house. He closed the door behind both of them. 'This way please, the first door on your left. The lounge.'

Neil walked ahead of Mayers. 'What do you need my help with?'

'Fixing something.'

'Okay...' Neil looked back and smiled. 'I warn you my DIY skills are not the best!'

'No, you misunderstand, I need help fixing a patient.'

Neil paused before reaching the door, and turned. 'You have a patient in there?'

'Yes,' Mayers said. 'A young lady. Her name is Susie. And she's troubled, and needs fixing.'

'But, you are not practising anymore?'

Mayers shrugged. 'What can you do? Once a doctor, always a doctor.'

Neil grew pale. 'Still. This doesn't feel right...'

Mayers shushed him again. Gently. 'Just hear me out. This girl has suffered immensely. Do you know what she witnessed, Doctor? Murder of the most heinous design. Her own grandmother, whom she adored, having her throat cut by her uncle, whom she also adored.'

'Jesus.'

'Yes, and she was eight.'

Neil sighed. 'What a thing to see.'

'I know,' Mayers said, nodding, 'so, here I am, treating her with HASD. I know, inappropriate. And, by all means, when you leave this house, report me. I am tired. So, so tired. But first, you must let me finish what I've started. And you can help me with that, Doctor, you really can. She's *accepted* and *shared* her experience. Help me finish this now. Help me with her *displacement*.'

'But my training with *displacement* is limited, Doctor. My guidance from Dr Adams is clear. I am to perfect my approach to *acceptance* before practising *sharing*. I mean, what process are you following for *displacement*?'

'You know *Route 4*, don't you?'

'Of course. To visualise the experience happening to

another person, to truly *share* the experience, and to completely free yourself from that crushing sense of isolation. It's the pinnacle of the treatment. But it really is the most extreme treatment, and is only done with months of preparation, and several practitioners.'

'That's why I've asked you for help.'

'But we are not even in a clinical setting, Doctor! I really must insist, the treatment is in its infancy.'

'Just take a look at her first, Doctor, that's all I ask. See, and then decide.'

'I have decided already.' He sighed, turned and opened the door. 'But I will look—'

Mayers watched, and smiled, as Neil ran to Susie Long, who was slumped back on the sofa, drooling. She was murmuring to herself, and her eyelids fluttered. Neil fell to his knees and clutched her hands.

'My God, Doctor! She's sweating and trembling. You need to call an ambulance. What's happened? *What have you done?*'

Mayers approached Neil from behind and bent at the knees so he was low enough to loop his left arm around his neck. Then, with his right wrist, he applied as much pressure to the back of Neil's head as was necessary to cut off his blood supply.

'I broke her.'

Neil tried to fight, and writhed in the headlock for a few moments, but Mayers was strong, and it wasn't long before he was unconscious.

'And now I'm going to fix her.'

'Are you okay?'

Jake looked down at the manicured hand on his arm, and then up at the attractive face of the woman he'd mistaken, thank Christ, for Lacey Ray.

'Yes.' Jake relinquished the lamppost, and stood up straight, adjusting his suit. 'It's too hot for a suit. Took a dizzy spell.'

The woman had bobbed blonde hair with a razor-sharp fringe, and shapely eyebrows. She wore a summery, flowery dress and expensive Louis Vuitton sandals. It had been an easy mistake to make at a distance; she did look like Lacey Ray.

'You with them?' She nodded over at Armed Response.

'Yes.'

'Are you in charge?' A ghost of a smile floated across her face, and again he thought of Lacey Ray, who was always the master of the flirtatious comment.

'Partly,' he said.

'Thought so, the suit gave it away.'

Jake realised that she still had her hand on his arm. He also saw that she didn't have a wedding ring on, and then admonished himself deep inside for checking.

Go easy on yourself, he thought, *you've just had one hell of a scare.*

She withdrew her hand and then quickly thrust it back out for a handshake 'I'm Caroline.'

'Jake.' He shook her hand.

'Detective?'

'Yes,' he said, deciding to leave off the Sergeant, for fear that he might end up admonishing himself again for trying to impress her.

'Do you need to come in for a glass of water? You still look rather pale.'

'No, I've got to get back on duty, really. But, ma'am, could I ask you to go indoors for the moment, at least until response have stood down?'

'Caroline, please.' She smiled. 'And yes, of course. If you take my card.'

She handed him a card. She was a beauty therapist.

'Thanks.' He felt the word scratching at the sides of his throat as it exited.

She smiled. 'Tell your wife about my micro-blading service – I'm running a discount at the moment for new customers.'

'Yes.'

She smiled. 'And whenever you need a glass of water – you know where I am.'

'Yes ... thank you ... Caroline.'

Jake's mind whirred as he headed back towards Armed Response.

Why Lacey Ray?

He'd pushed that woman so far to the back of his mind these last months that she'd been struggling to find any air time whatsoever. But, here she was, sneaky as ever, emerging from his sub-conscious, re-announcing herself, clawing at his sanity.

But it was hot. Operation Autumn and Operation Cold-town had taken their toll on his sleeping. No good detective slept when the investigation peaked, and the adrenaline flowed. He shouldn't read too much into it.

So, as he approached Mayer's house, he tried to focus his thoughts.

And that's when his mind drifted back to the beautiful

woman he'd just met.

Caroline.

Yorke was driving away from the University of Southampton when he received the call from Jake telling him that Dr Louis Mayer's house was empty. A build-up of post at the front door and the rotting kitchen bins indicated that it had probably been standing empty for weeks.

According to Dr Adams, Dr Louis Mayer's had attended an earlier appointment with Dr Neil Solomon. If this was confirmed, then at least they would know that Mayers was still in Wiltshire, and not halfway to Australia.

At the end of the call, Jake said, 'Are you alright, Mike?'

'Mike instead of Sir, eh? Guess you are worried! Why do you ask?'

'Well, it's just...'

'Go on! Spit it out!'

'Well, chucking Parkinson's phone out the window. Wow. I've never seen you react like that before.'

'It's nice to be less predictable.'

Jake laughed. 'But really, sir, with what happened to Emma today, nobody would expect you to keep pushing yourself like this.'

'It's nothing to do with Emma, Jake. It was to do with Parkinson. You know what he's like.'

'Yeah, I agree that he's a colossal bell end, but it's just not your usual style.'

'And what's my usual style?'

'I don't know. Quieter, more formal, I guess.'

'Silent assassin?'

'Hmmm. Something like that, although you're not really sly.'

'I'm fine Jake. Thanks for asking. I saw red. There were a million and one better ways to react. Lesson learned. It won't happen again.'

'I'll see you back at the station.'

After Jake had hung up, Yorke acknowledged to himself that his over-the-top reaction to Parkinson was inevitable. One of his most loyal colleagues, and friends, lay critically ill in hospital. Couple that with the fact that there was an imminent threat to Proud's life. A threat he was doing nothing about.

And why was that? Why was he doing nothing?

Is it because he secretly wanted it to happen?

He shook his head. *Ridiculous. Get a grip! You're finding issue where there isn't one to find!*

I mean, how could he do anything right now? He'd not had a second to breathe, and getting DC Bradley's contact details, and finding Proud before Harry required a second's breath.

It took him over an hour to reach HQ in Wiltshire. Along the way he noticed the clouds swelling and darkening; the sky looked fit to burst. While he was parking outside the long red-bricked headquarters, he answered another phone call from Topham.

'I'm outside now,' Yorke said. 'You were the first person I was coming to see.'

'Neil is *still* not here, and he hasn't been in touch.'

Yorke stepped out of his car. He felt his heart flutter. 'Okay, keep trying his mobile.'

'I've phoned him again and again. This is unlike him, sir, he said he'd be here.'

The flutter in Yorke's chest was becoming faster now. 'What time did you last speak to him, Mark?'

'He was just about to meet a patient. Just before one o'clock I think.'

Keeping the phone pinned to his ear by his shoulder, Yorke took his notebook from his pocket and flicked back through his notes.

Neil's appointment with Dr Louis Mayers had been at 1 p.m.

And now Neil was missing.

Shit.

'Okay, Mark, sit tight, I'll be up with you in five.'

Yorke put his hands on the roof of the car. *Think ... think.*

What would the Conduit want with Neil? Would he really have taken him from the session? To what end? There had been no connection between them until today...

Had there?

His mind was on overdrive. He could really do with a calming word from Gardner right now. She always knew exactly what to say to bring back focus.

It took him three minutes to formulate a plan.

He assigned two officers to head back to the university, and the offices in which Dr Louis Mayers would have received treatment from Neil today, to form an immediate picture of what happened after that session. Car park CCTV footage would show Mayers and Neil leaving, separately or together, and then cameras could be used to track the vehicles to their destination, if they didn't drift into zones that had no monitoring. He also made a phone call to have Neil's mobile phone tracked. Triangulation could be used, but that would require Neil making or receiving calls to hit towers. According to Topham, he wasn't making or receiving calls right now, so it was a long shot.

All of this would take a considerable amount of time. Time they probably didn't have. But at least the ball was rolling.

Following the phone calls, he approached HQ. The many windows stared at him from the long building front. It would be so easy to consider every room in this place a separate entity, but they weren't. Every room was a part of a whole. On so many times in its history, it had worked so smoothly as one.

But not today. This whole sorry investigation was a mess of parts, not working smoothly. Each piece of this bloody puzzle circled each other, with teeth bared, unwilling to share, unwilling to unify.

Susie Long, Louis Mayers, Neil Solomon, David Sturridge, Chloe Ward.

To unify all of this – he knew he would have to go back to the source of it all.

Christian Severance.

And the secrets of his past.

16

MAYERS DID NOT have to worry about Neil waking. He'd mixed water with an anaesthetic and then, using an oral syringe pressed against the interior of his cheek, he'd squirted it slowly in. Neil's reflexes had taken over and he'd swallowed.

Meanwhile, the concentration of the chemicals in Susie's bloodstream had subsided slightly. Her eyes were now fully open, and she was observing her surroundings. He dragged an arm chair around to face her and propped Neil up in it.

Susie stared at Neil's unconscious face.

'This is Uncle Roland,' Mayers said.

She creased her face in confusion.

'Who is this, Susie?' he asked.

She tried to shake her head from side-to-side to indicate that she didn't know, but it simply flopped against one shoulder and then the other.

'This is Uncle Roland,' he said.

Again, she showed her uncertainty.

So, he repeated the statement and the question again and

again, noticing, each time, her expression becoming less and less confused.

After pressuring her for a considerable length of time, he made one last attempt. 'Who is this, Susie?'

This time she murmured something. It was incomprehensible, but it was enough to give Mayers cause for celebration. He smiled. *Progress.*

So, he pressed on. He went through this process countless times for the best part of an hour, until he was able to ask, 'Who is this Susie?'

And she was able to reply, 'Uncle Roland.'

Then, he gave her more of his cocktail, readying her for the final visualisation.

THE FIRST THING that Yorke did in his office was something that would surely come back to burn him. *Severely.* He looked up DC Wayne Bradley's details, knowing, as he scribbled it down on a post-it note, that this search would be flagged up if Madden and company decided to trawl through his account at a later date.

But, for now, he shrugged it off. The way it was going, he was unlikely to have any time later to pursue Harry before the vigilante mission was done and dusted anyway. And, if by some miracle, he did have time, *and* he prevented Proud's murder, would these not be mitigating circumstances?

Would they not be *turn-a-blind-eye* circumstances?

Somehow with by-the-book Madden involved, he doubted it.

Then, with the matter of Bradley's location ticked off his

list, he went to the incident room where Topham was staring at a board swollen with information.

Yorke stood back for a moment, watching Topham working from picture to picture, scribbling notes onto a pad. His colleague was so lost in thought that when Yorke came up beside him, he flinched.

Yorke knew that this was the moment he should tell his friend about Neil's appointment with Louis Mayers AKA the Conduit, but doing so, would fling him all the way from useful to God-knows-what, and the only way to put this *whole fucking thing to bed*, to coin a phrase from Madden that plagued his every thought, was to have someone as useful as Topham beside him.

'The chain belongs to Severance,' Yorke said. 'Always has done. From the word *go.*'

Topham nodded.

'The answer is there,' Yorke said, pointing at the soup of information dripping down the board. 'It always has been. In Severance's chain.'

'So, what do we do now then?'

Yorke went back to the beginning and put a finger on a photo of Christian Severance as a schoolboy. 'We start at the beginning of the chain, and we *go* again.'

MAYERS HAD ALWAYS BEEN FASCINATED by how much of the real world you could alter within a visualisation. Tweaks with the lighting; manipulation of the temperature; adjustments of sound... To a certain extent, the world could be your playground. However, to *alter* the narrative of the real event was a whole different ballgame. Not only was that unethical, but it was also futile.

The patient's mind would always fight back.

But things felt different this time. The combination of both his cocktail, and the adapted process of HASD, had led him down a promising avenue.

He still began with the basics. *The tweaks*. The room in which Susie witnessed her grandmother's final moments was darker now; a slight parting in the curtains allowed a slither of moonlight for some visibility, but that was all. The window was closed, and the room was stifling hot. Finally, he crowned it with a stench; not just of sweat, but of excrement, and the foulness you'd associate with only the most death-ridden of locations – abattoirs, and places of genocide.

Mayers allowed some of the original narrative to play out: the grandmother's shallow breathing, her fight between consciousness and unconsciousness, and the despairing uncle leaning over her. The main difference this time was that the older Susie was no longer a passive observer. She *was* the eight-year-old forced to endure her uncle's actions. Mayers was overjoyed when Susie, from within this visualisation, questioned the appearance of Uncle Roland. 'He seems different somehow. Looks different. But I know it's him. I know it's that ... that ... murderer.'

Mayers played with one end of his white moustache, holding back whoops of delight.

She saw him. She saw Neil Solomon in place of her original uncle! It was working.

He took her through the part of the adapted narrative in which Roland readied the knife.

'Watch him,' Mayers said. '*Watch* Uncle Roland look down on your grandmother with hate.'

'She's crying,' Susie said.

'Yes! And what's he saying now?

'He's saying: *you bitch! You always made me feel so worthless.*'

Mayers rose to his feet. *To think,* he thought, *I could alter a real narrative to this extent – Adams you would stand in wonder!*

'God!' Susie cried. 'He's got a knife to her throat.'

'And where are you, Susie?'

'I'm at the door. I was told not to come. I said I was going to the toilet. I lied.'

Mayers moved into the next part of the altered narrative. 'But you sensed something was wrong, didn't you?'

'Yes, somehow I knew that he was going to hurt her.'

'Look down at your hand, Susie, do you see the knife there? The knife that you collected from the kitchen on the way here?'

'No ... I'm confused ... the knife is in *his* hand.'

Damn, he thought. *Trying to run before I can walk!*

He needed to teach her to collect the knife from the kitchen.

'A big knife,' he would tell her, again and again. 'A bigger knife than him.'

Then, after that part of the narrative was ironed out, he taught her what to do with that knife. He told her again and again to 'save her grandmother.' He explained to her, in detail, how she could do this.

And she followed his instructions with more enthusiasm than he'd anticipated!

Mayers realised he was on the cusp of something very special. *What better displacement is there? To totally eradicate the experience – as if it never happened!*

He sighed when he realised, with great sadness, that the only people he would ever share this experience with were Christian Severance, Susie Long and, of course, Neil Solomon.

ANTHONY MORRIS' mouth felt like it was full of sandpaper. Awareness came in little sparks, and it took a while before consciousness finally blazed. He had no idea how long he'd been out; it could have been weeks for all he knew. As he emerged from the swirl, his eyes homed in on a solitary strip light, which appeared to tremble. As comprehension of his predicament grew, he realised that it wasn't trembling, it was simply swarming with flies and midges.

He sat upright against the concrete wall of what must have been a three-hundred square-foot storage unit. To his left was a steel roll-up door. Ahead of him was nothing. To the right of him was a man chained to a metal chair with his head slumped forward.

Memory came at him like a bulldozer; a disfigured man spraying him in the face with something. He gulped air and his hand flew to his mouth.

It took him a minute or two to regain composure and to acknowledge that he, unlike the other man, was not chained up.

He looked at the steel roll-up door. Even if it was locked tight, he could bang on it and scream merry hell.

'Don't worry, I'll get us out of here,' he said to the unconscious man.

When he started to stand, which was difficult as he felt weak and woozy, he noticed there was a mobile phone pinned down under his thigh. He picked it up and pressed the button. The phone was unlocked, and the image used as its wallpaper made him gasp out loud.

It was his ten-year old daughter, playing outside in their front garden, smiling at whoever had stopped to take this photo.

TOGETHER, Topham and Yorke worked methodically through Severance's chain again. Pausing only for Topham to try Neil again, and for Yorke to get an update on Gardner.

She wasn't out of the woods yet. Yorke looked up at the heavens – he wasn't a religious man, but knew a quick, silent nod to the legend, be He real or otherwise, wouldn't do any harm.

And when Yorke lowered his head back down from the prayer, his eyes settled on a newspaper clipping of Severance collecting an award for a remarkable discovery. He'd read it before, but he read it again, to confirm his sudden realisation.

Severance thanked his mentor, a man called Robert Webster, a total of three times during that acceptance speech.

Yorke acknowledged the sudden rush of blood. Robert Webster was the key to unlocking this whole sorry chain.

He picked up the phone and made the necessary calls.

THE CONDUIT OPENED the front door for him.

Severance noticed the pride on his doctor's face, and raised his eyebrows.

'Yes, I do look rather happy, don't I?'

Severance nodded.

'Made a remarkable breakthrough. You could fill books with the progress I have made today. *What I have shown*. It's actually quite sad that I have to go away for a while.'

The Conduit looked over Severance's shoulder at the old Fiesta he'd driven up in; he had a hungry look in his eyes. 'Where's the girl? In the boot?'

Severance shook his head, and thought, *enough is enough. You've had your fill, Doctor. No more.*

The Conduit closed the door behind Severance. 'I don't understand, Christian, where is Anthony Morris' daughter?'

Severance led the way to the lounge. He found some notepaper and wrote the Conduit a message: *It is in hand. We don't need her here with you.*

'I disagree. It would have been safer if you'd brought her here.'

I went to Robert's grave first. I made my decision there. We are finished now, Doctor.

'You'll be finished when I tell you we've finished.' The Conduit's face flushed.

Severance maintained eye-contact with the Conduit. He'd never challenged him on this level before. It was essential that he showed no weakness.

Severance waited until the red faded from the Conduit's face and then wrote him another message: *Finished. And now I'm going. As was planned.*

The Conduit sighed.

Severance noticed a phone on the sofa he didn't recognise. He wandered over to pick it up.

The wallpaper image was of two middle-aged men he didn't know. They had their cheeks pressed together. One was holding the camera at arm's length to take the selfie. He noticed that there were twelve missed calls on this phone. All calls were from a *Mark Topham*.

Severance raised his eyebrows to express curiosity.

'Yes, my breakthrough! You really must come and see.'

Severance nodded and slipped the phone into his trouser pocket.

Severance followed the Conduit down the steps to the cellar where he'd been knocked unconscious by Susie many hours earlier. He could hear movement coming from within.

The Conduit turned back to look at him. 'Don't worry, Christian. It is perfectly safe. I have her on a loop. Frozen in a moment. It will not stop until the drugs wear off, or she passes out from exhaustion.'

He nodded and opened the cellar door.

Christian Severance had seen and experienced many horrifying things in his time.

But never anything like this.

———

INFORMATION ON ROBERT WEBSTER came in quickly.

Like Severance, Webster had been a remarkable scientist; and, according to this newspaper article, a phenomenal mentor.

When Severance had received the award reported on in this article, Webster had been three years from retirement. He'd been around the scientific block more than a few times.

Quick Google searches unlocked more evidence that Severance and Webster had been close. Webster had referred to him, in one interview in the *New Scientist*, as one of the 'most remarkable young scientists he'd ever met.' Another more informal interview had seen Webster referring to Severance as 'the son he'd never had.'

Yorke wouldn't have been doing his job properly had he not considered all explanations for this close relationship, including a sexual one; however, he considered it more likely that Severance had simply found a man he could idolise, rather than a man who just wanted to exploit him. A man like Marcus Long.

After the attempt on Severance's life, two years prior to his planned retirement, Webster had suffered a stroke.

'Was this stroke brought on by the fact that his protégé had just had his life destroyed?' Topham said.

'Well, it wouldn't have helped,' Yorke said. 'I guess it comes down to Severance's interpretation of events, so I suspect it would have something to do with it.'

Further phone calls indicated that Webster had left all of his possessions to his brother, Frederick Webster, who currently resided in Australia.

Yorke managed to contact Frederick. After apologising, and providing some context behind his phone call, he asked him why he'd left his brother's house sitting empty for so long.

Frederick had emigrated at an early age, so his Australian accent was strong. 'Well, it isn't sitting empty.'

Yorke rose to his feet with his heart beating wildly.

'Robert asked me, less than a year before he died, to allow a good friend of his to live there for free should he ever fall on hard times.'

Yorke stared at Topham with wide eyes.

'I told him to change his Will, obviously, and leave this lad the flaming house. He said he would, eventually, but he was always so busy. He said he'd get to it in retirement. He didn't have to worry. I'm not short of a few dollars. He could trust me.'

'What's the name of the boy, Mr Webster?'

'Christian Severance.'

WHEN ANTHONY MORRIS heard someone walking past the storage unit, he felt frustration like he'd never felt before. It would only take a simple rattle of the steel fold-up door or a sharp cry for assistance and he'd be tasting freedom. He looked down at the photograph of his ten-year daughter again. It implied she was in danger. Running for freedom now came with a risk. A risk he had no desire to take.

The phone had no reception on it. Not that it mattered. Calling the emergency services would have been too risky. He turned the phone over and noticed a small white label stuck to the back. Written on it in red biro were the words: *check the notepad.*

He turned the phone back over and went into the notepad app. There was only one file and it was called: *For Anthony.*

He opened it.

Anthony, please do not be alarmed. I would like you to enjoy these last few peaceful moments before you are required to act.

My name is Christian Severance. I expect you have paused at this point to try and recall who I am? Well, if you are struggling, I have a remarkable memory, so let me give you a clue. Do you remember these words?

"I ask the Right Honourable Salton to consider Christian Severance's role in all of this. I understand the controversial

nature of our counter-argument but consider the evidence we have shown you. The testimony from Logan Burns, his classmate, regarding Christian's sexual advances, and Logan's need to threaten police action to end the pursuit. Also, the diary entries that were entered into evidence which showed Christian's obsessive tendencies towards males he found attractive. None of these are excuses for Marcus Long's guilt, but we ask you to take into account these mitigating circumstances when passing sentence."

My memory is excellent but forgive me if I got a few of the words wrong. I'm sure you remember me now.

Today, I would like to ask you this: if your own daughter, a minor, that pretty young lady I currently sit with, experienced what I experienced, would you consider all of the above circumstances mitigating? Yes, I was a young man, struggling to understand my sexuality, but isn't it a step too far to consider my attractions to these individuals obsessive? I was fourteen years old! You are a lawyer, Anthony, not a doctor. At what point did you feel qualified to make this diagnosis of obsession? Maybe you never even believed it yourself. After all, you are skilled at creating narratives to suit your own ends. And you were convincing, I will give you that. Convincing enough for Judge Andrew Salton, who now sits beside you.

Anthony paused to look up at the elderly man with a shock of white hair. He was chained to a metal chair. Was it really Judge Andrew Salton? Anthony had come before him on many occasions in his career. It was difficult to tell right now because his head was slumped forward. Anthony's eyes fell back to the notepad on the phone.

Do you remember Judge Andrew Salton's words before he passed sentence? I do. Maybe when all of this is over, you could look them up? Refresh your memory. There is no need for me to do that. These words haunt me. Daily.

You succeeded with your mitigation, Anthony, didn't you? Two years and he was out. Two years for what he did.

'Yes,' Anthony said out-loud, 'but what happened to you, would have happened anyway. It was many, many years later. So, this does not make me responsible!'

Anthony felt tears in his eyes. This was one case he was not going to be able to present to a judge and jury.

What I am going to ask you to do now will be quick. Can you see the camera in the corner of your room?

A small, black dome CCTV camera was attached to the ceiling.

I am watching your every move.

At this moment, I am running a hand through your daughter's fine blonde hair. Don't worry, this is nothing sinister, I am not that way inclined. I have simply been combing the knots from her hair.

Who knows? If my life hadn't have ended up this way – I could be experiencing this with a child of my own.

She is asleep in my arms, Anthony. At peace. I am happy to keep it this way. It is your decision if it stays this way.

'FUCK YOU! I lost my wife last year, and now you come along, and threaten to take the only thing I have left in my life. FUCK YOU!' He pointed at the camera as he shouted.

After brushing away his tears, he continued to read. *Over in that chair sits the man who reduced Marcus Long's sentence. I imagine he still sleeps. He is far older than you are and I gave him a heavier dose. What I am going to ask you to do now will confuse you, but that is irrelevant. What is relevant is that you do everything I ask. Look at the camera again. Imagine it is my eye. You do everything I ask, then you will see your daughter again. You will be different, changed like me, but you will see her again. If you don't, I will break her neck. I will not do it while she is awake because I see the innocence in her. An innocence that we all had once upon a time. An innocence none of us deserve to have snatched away. So, I will do it while she sleeps.*

He drew away from the message, unable to read on. His heart was banging too hard.

'You hurt her, and I will kill you.' Anthony jabbed his finger at the camera again. '*I will fucking kill you.*'

He looked between the chained man and the fold-up steel door. He imagined his daughter in the disfigured man's lap. He heard the *snap* in his mind.

He could not live without his baby. That he knew. He read on, knowing that he would do whatever he was asked to do.

DESK SERGEANT LIVINGSTONE wiped the mayonnaise from the corner of his mouth when the police station door opened, and he quickly stuffed the chicken sandwich beneath the counter.

It was hot in Bourne Hill station, and the fan was several metres away from him, pointing directly at his head, so he quickly averted the fan's trajectory to stop the few remaining strands of his hair simulating a Mexican Wave.

A tall, thin man approached, wearing a freshly pressed white shirt, and black trousers. Livingstone averted his gaze, realising that he was staring at the scars and welts that twisted around the man's lower face, and said, 'Good afternoon. How can I help you?'

The disfigured man placed a piece of paper down on the table. The handwriting was neat and cursive.

I am Christian Severance and I believe you are looking for me.

YORKE CAME off the phone after directing Armed Response to Webster's house on the Salisbury Plains. He'd expressed caution. 'If Susie Long is still alive, I believe she is in there.'

He'd also stepped out of the room so that Topham wouldn't hear him mentioning the possibility of Dr Neil Solomon being there.

As he stepped back into the incident room, he received another phone call. His eyes widened as he listened to what the officer on the other side of the line had to say.

When he hung up, he was speechless.

'*What?*' Topham said.

'Well, I can assure you of one thing – Christian Severance will not be at Webster's house.'

'Why?'

'Because he just turned himself in at Salisbury station.'

Topham's eyes widened too.

17

AFTER THEY CONFISCATED his belongings and strip searched him, Severance was handcuffed and locked in the back of a police van. They didn't tell him where he was going, but they didn't need to. It was obvious. They'd be taking him to the HQ in Devizes to let the high and mighty detectives take a run at him.

They'd be desperate to know where Susie Long was.

Let them distract themselves with the inconsequential, he thought, *and allow time for the Anthony and Andrew situation to play out.*

Severance wondered if Anthony was staring at that dome camera right now, imagining that it was his eye. *Big Brother?* Not really. The camera wasn't even connected to anything!

One thing he'd learnt from this whole process was how easy it was to play on people's desperation and paranoia. Making them believe the unthinkable was enough to bend will. The Conduit had certainly taught him well.

Now, as this whole affair was coming to an end, he wondered if he had any regrets.

What he'd seen the Conduit achieve earlier had disgusted an older part of himself. The newer part of himself was, of course, desensitised and numb, so he'd just shrugged it off, but still ... *was this really a road he could have carried on travelling?*

No, he was done, burned out. But he had no regrets.

How could he have regrets when he thought of Robert Webster?

His best friend.

Yes, the Conduit had supported him. And there were moments when his family, in his younger years, had shown him love and kindness. But no one could come close to Robert.

He wished now he could look at his mentor's photograph, but he couldn't, because the police had taken it from him. So, he closed his eyes and imagined him instead. A wiry man, with wrinkles that stood out on his face like lines on a roadmap. The wisest man he'd ever met. This man had offered Severance an olive branch. He'd been spinning around in an empty world. An abused, suicidal young man searching for meaning, or death, depending on which came first. Robert had found him, nurtured the great intellect in him, without the sexual motivation of the likes of Marcus Long, or the self-serving interests of people like Amanda Werrell, and made him as complete as anyone could be after what had happened.

They had travelled around the world together, *discovered* things together, and *learned* from each other. Severance had offered so much, had helped so many people with his discoveries over the years, and Robert had helped him to understand that.

He remembered the day he'd found out that his mentor

had died. Severance had been lying in a hospital bed, under-going months of surgery to reconstruct his mangled face, and someone had come to tell him about Robert's fatal stroke.

Had he been killed by the shock of what had happened to his protégé?

Undoubtably.

No, there were no regrets from Severance.

Just relief, really, in the fact that soon he could rest.

YORKE WAS INFORMED by Jake that Armed Response was now at Webster's house taking, he was assured, a cautious approach because Susie, and maybe even Neil, could be inside. Then, he joined Topham in the interview room with the broken air-conditioning unit. They could have opted for the other room, where the air-conditioner had been fixed an hour ago, but as Topham had so eloquently put, 'Let the bastard sweat, it's the least he deserves.'

Severance was led in. As he took his seat opposite them, he gestured down at his handcuffs.

Yorke shook his head. *They were staying on.* Severance shrugged.

One of the two officers that had brought him in left; while the other, a rotund fresh-faced officer, hung back.

'My name is Detective Chief Inspector Michael Yorke, and this is Detective Inspector Mark Topham.'

Severance leaned back in his chair. He could have been smirking, but Yorke wasn't sure if it was the damage to his face that was giving this impression.

'You have refused a solicitor,' Yorke said. 'In much the same way as your predecessors, Chloe Ward and David Sturridge. I have no qualms about sharing their names with you now, Christian, we have already connected you all. We already know, beyond all doubt, that they acted on your behalf.'

Severance wrote on a card in front of him and slid it over the table.

Yorke looked up at the camera. 'Christian Severance has written: *that is correct.*'

'Let's cut to the chase. It is over, Christian. You have made the right decision in turning yourself in. This, and the other information that you give us now, could help you moving forward. The judge can take all of these factors into account when passing sentence.'

Severance wrote a response. *Yes, judges are very good at taking things into account when passing sentences.*

Topham said, 'What do you mean?'

Exactly what I just wrote.

Yorke jumped back in. 'Let's not get distracted from the situation at hand, Christian. Where is Susie Long? And where is the Conduit?'

He didn't look surprised by the mention of the Conduit. He had probably predicted that Chloe would share her knowledge of him with the police.

This is where I choose to exercise my right to remain silent.

Severance gestured at his mouth with his hand, and rolled his eyes. He also seemed to smirk again.

'We know about Robert Webster,' Yorke said.

Severance flinched.

Yorke took advantage. 'Surprised? Yes ... we know all about your friend and mentor.'

So? It changes nothing. He is dead.

'And we know about his house. I have a team there now, waiting to go inside.'

Severance took a hissing intake of breath.

It doesn't matter. It is too late to stop it. It is almost finished.

Yorke glanced at Topham. He was worried about asking the next question. Worried that the answer would reveal the whereabouts of Neil and expose Yorke's secrecy.

'Is Susie Long in that house?'

She is.

'Is she alive?'

Yes.

Yorke felt relief wash over him. 'Is the Conduit there?'

No, he left when I left. He has chosen a different path to me. He will not be coming.

'So is it safe to send my team in? She is in no immediate danger?'

She is not. You have my word.

Yorke leaned over to Topham and whispered in his ear. 'Pause the interview, please, and stay here, with the guard. I'll alert the team that it may be safe to enter. Then, I'll be straight back in.'

Outside, Yorke made the phone call to Jake before being grabbed by Tyler. He looked as white as a sheet.

'What's wrong Sean?'

'You have to see this, sir. I can't quite believe it...'

'*What Sean?* Spit it out, I'm in the middle of an interview—'

Tyler had already turned and was heading down the corridor. 'This way.'

They stopped outside of conference room 7. Inside, exhibits officer, Andrew Waites, was beavering away, grumbling as usual while he looked through evidence, ensuring it was appropriately logged and tagged.

Without communicating, he thrust a small plastic evidence bag in Yorke's direction. Yorke took the bag; inside, a phone screen flicked on under the heat of his touch. Topham and Neil, cheek-to-cheek, stared up at him from a selfie.

Waites spoke for the first time. 'It was in Christian Severance's pocket.'

Yorke's blood ran cold as his phone started to ring again. It was Jake. He answered.

'We've gone in, sir ... Jesus Christ, Mike ... I can hardly breathe!'

'Jake, for God's sake, talk! What have you found?'

TOPHAM WANTED to carry on interviewing the bastard. He wanted to ask him why he'd orchestrated all of this horror and destruction.

Yes, he already kind of knew why, and he also knew the answer he'd probably get, but it felt too unsatisfactory. *HASD? Healing, Acceptance, Sharing and Displacement? Was that really the answer? Come on!*

Topham had been one of the first people in the church that day. One of the first to feel the tingle of evil in that infected air. The first, other than Sturridge, to hold Simmond's severed tongue.

He drummed his fingers on the table. He glanced up at the sweating officer. He looked as if he was about to fall asleep on his feet.

'This isn't just about HASD is it?' Topham said.

Severance looked at him.

'I mean, who heals from murder and violence? I've never heard so much *bullshit* in my entire life.'

Severance started to nod, demonstrating that he was listening to Topham's train of thought no matter how provocative.

'We've come across people like you before, Severance. People wired all wrong. You've done all of this because you enjoyed it.'

Again, a ghost of a smile seemed to appear on Severance's face, but it was so hard to tell, his flesh was so badly damaged.

'Remember what Martin Luther King said? Hate begets hate; violence begets violence. There is nothing about *sharing* and *displacement* in that sorry tale. You are a fucking fake. You've enjoyed your revenge. You've enjoyed destroying lives around you. And now you will spend the rest of your life in jail.'

Severance reached down to scratch his thigh. He tilted his head to one side and stared at Topham again. Then, he started to write. He slid the card over to Topham.

I recognised your face when I came in, and then your name too. Do you want to ask me why?

Topham narrowed his eyes. 'What the fuck are you talking about?'

Severance continued to write. Topham looked up at the guard, who did seem to be taking a mild interest now.

It took Severance a while this time. Eventually, he pushed over a card. *The world is a place of coincidence, Mark Topham. Or so some would have you believe. These days, I see logic and sense in everything that happens. I learned about pain, and suffering, from an early age, and it has taken a lot of time to find relief. You talk to me as if I've enjoyed this journey. I've enjoyed the outcome, not so much the journey. I think Mark, it is time for you to go on a similar journey.*

Topham stood up. It felt as if all the blood was draining from his body. He pointed down. 'How do you know who I am?'

I've met Neil.

Topham started to sway on his feet. The walls suddenly seemed to be pulsing. 'You are talking nonsense.'

Severance wrote: *Or at least I've met what's left of him.*

Topham put a hand on the table to steady himself. *'You're lying.'*

Severance slid the next card over. Topham was struggling to read now, but he managed. God, how he wished he hadn't. *There were bits of him everywhere, Mark. He'd been stabbed thousands of times.*

'Shut the fuck up! Shut up now!' Topham felt ready to vomit. 'I will fucking kill you.'

And she was still doing it when I left. Stabbing him. Again and again.

Topham swooped the pencil from Severance's hand, gripped the killer by his throat and dragged him away from the table. He pinned him up against the wall, and placed the nib of his pencil against his eyeball.

As Yorke sprinted back down the corridor towards the interview room, he felt the contents of his stomach rising. Around him, the air seemed to press in on him. The evil invading their lives was now as palpable as the heat grilling the world around them.

He heard commotion from the interview room acknowledging, immediately, that his worst fears were realised.

Topham knew.

Yorke burst through the interview door.

Topham wasn't a large man, but he was bigger than Severance and he was pumped full of adrenaline. He'd lifted Severance partially off the floor by his neck. The prisoner's face glowed which was a good sign because it meant he was still in the earlier stage of strangulation, and saveable. The pencil to his eye was not such a good sign.

'You're a *fucking* liar,' Topham said.

Behind Topham, the officer was trying to pacify him. A pathetic sight. 'Sir ... please, sir.'

'Mark,' Yorke said, 'it's Mike.'

Topham glanced back at Yorke. 'Mike, you're not going to believe the bullshit pouring out of this vile fucker.'

Severance's mouth was open, and the remaining nub of flesh which had once been a tongue wiggled around in the air.

'Mark, you need to let go of him.'

'I should push this pencil into his eye, Mike, and I shouldn't stop until it is buried in the wall behind him. The monster has just told me that Neil is dead. That he's been stabbed to death. Can you believe it?' He looked back at Yorke again. There were tears running down his face.

'I don't know why he's said those things,' Yorke lied. 'But this isn't the right way to solve it. We both know that.'

'Just tell me it's not true. Tell me he's lying.'

The words stuck in his throat; lying to his friend was eating him up inside.

A bluish tinge was beginning to creep into Severance's face. The window of opportunity to save him was shrinking.

'Please?' Topham said.

'Mark, you are confused, and I completely understand. So listen to me, and focus on my words as much as you can. You need to let go of him, and then we will find out what has happened.'

'What did they find in the house?'

'I don't know.'

'*What did Jake find in the house?*'

'I haven't spoken to him, Mark.'

'You went to call him.'

'To tell him about Susie being there, alone. I've not heard back.'

'Then phone him back *now*. I need to know that this is bullshit.'

'By the time I've made that call, Severance will be dead,' Yorke said. 'You need to let go of him. If he loses his life now, there will be nothing I can do to stop you losing yours too.'

Topham didn't reply. Yorke prayed he'd gotten through to him. 'He isn't worth your life, Mark. *Not at all.*'

Topham threw Severance to one side as if he weighed nothing.

He looked at Yorke. 'You get me the truth.' Rubbing tears from his face, he marched out of the room.

For the first time since the incident began, the officer ceased his pathetic flapping, and dived to Severance's assistance. Yorke said, 'Officer, get this monster to his feet, out of this room and to the other side of the bloody building.'

Yorke chased Topham down the corridor. He was sloping side-to-side, like a drunkard. When Yorke had caught up with him, he steered him into an empty office.

Topham turned to look at Yorke. There were more tears running down his face, but it wasn't red. It was ashen.

Yorke put a hand on Topham's shoulder. 'Sit down, Mark.'

Topham pulled away and turned his back. 'Don't you dare, Mike. Don't you *fucking* dare!'

'Mark, I *need* you to sit down.'

Topham reached down and brushed everything off the desk: a telephone, a heap of files and some framed pictures. Everything came crashing down. 'You don't get to do this, Mike. You don't get to fucking lie to me, and then bring me in here to tell me something different.'

He paced through the mess he'd pushed over onto the floor, back and forth for a minute, before turning and pointing. His finger was inches from Yorke's face. 'YOU DON'T GET TO FUCKING DO THAT.'

Yorke brushed his hand away and put his own hands on both of Topham's shoulders. Firmly this time. He didn't struggle.

'I did speak to Jake, Mark. I'm sorry for lying to you.'

'No ... no ... no ...' Topham turned his head from side-to-side. The tears were coming more freely now.

'Susie Long was alive, but there were bodies there. Two. I suspect one of them is Alex Drake...'

'Please, Mike, just stop, I beg you.' Topham looked down at the floor.

'Look at me, Mark. Please, look at me.'

Topham looked up.

'We recovered a wallet from the other body in the room. I'm so, so sorry, Mark. I really am. We suspect that the other body belongs to Neil.'

Yorke was sure he saw something happen in Topham's eyes at that very moment. It wasn't as obvious as a light dimming or something dying in there. It was something so subtle that it would only be noticeable to a person incredibly close to Mark Topham. A person like Michael Yorke.

Yorke couldn't quite put his finger on it, but knew that this moment, this subtle movement in the character of Mark Topham, would haunt him for the rest of his days.

Topham slumped to his knees and Yorke clutched his friend's head to his stomach.

And the sound of Topham's despair tore Yorke's world apart.

18

I T IS ALMOST *finished.*

Yorke stood alone in the conference room looking at the savage collage on the whiteboard, contemplating Severance's words.

He'd left something in play. *What?*

He chewed the end of a pencil as he thought hard.

More of Severance's words resonated: *yes, judges are very good at taking things into account when passing sentences.*

He went through to his office, and logged on. He identified the judges from the two trials of Marcus Long. He contacted The National Archives and requested, immediately, the two transcripts of these trials. They acted quickly. His email pinged.

The email was encrypted; GDPR had tightened laws beyond belief. Once he was in, he looked at the closing speeches from both judges. It was Judge Andrew Salton who caught his eye.

'*I believe that Christian Severance pursued Marcus Long with great intent. In no way does this excuse his behaviour, but I have taken this into account when determining the length of his sentence.'*

Bingo. Andrew Salton was on Severance's chain.

Yorke rang through to Judge Andrew Salton. His wife told him that he'd not arrived home. Yorke started to sweat. He contacted the Salisbury Law Courts and asked them to check when Salton left for the day and requested access to the CCTV footage of him leaving in the car.

While he waited, Wendy dropped him in a strong cup of coffee. 'Is DI Topham alright? I can't believe it.'

'Thank you for your concern, Wendy, but can we talk later?'

She nodded. His phone rang. Wendy left the room. Something had happened in Salton's car. The law courts sent the CCTV footage over.

Yorke rolled up his sleeves as he watched the footage; he could feel the sweat running down his back now. He drank the entire cup of coffee in two mouthfuls.

The footage was clearer than he expected. It used to be so grainy. Modern day clarity on a small camera was staggering. When Salton climbed into his car, Severance darted out from behind another car and jumped into the passenger side. He was holding a spray can. There was some commotion in the car, which was difficult to see because of the tinted windows. Eventually, Severance stepped back out, dragging and manoeuvring Salton over to the passenger side. The judge had obviously been rendered unconscious by whatever had been sprayed on him. Severance then closed the door, ran around to the driver's side and climbed in. He started the car and drove off.

Now where?

Wiltshire Council had invested almost £450,000 in new

state-of-the-art CCTV for Salisbury City Centre. Recently the ownership of it, and responsibility for running it, had been transferred to Salisbury Council. He contacted the council control room and made his request clear. He gave the vehicle make, registration and a request to track its journey.

They contacted him back and told him that this vehicle had been driven into Salisbury Solutions Storage Unit on Churchfields Industrial Estate. He instructed them to keep the recordings as evidence to prevent them being erased in 31 days.

He took a deep breath and contacted the reception of Salisbury Solutions Storage Unit.

He gave his credentials and then said, 'Does Christian Severance rent a unit here?'

Yorke heard the receptionist tapping away. 'No.'

Yorke paused to think; a sudden rush of caffeine through his system aided this. 'How about Robert Webster?'

More tapping. 'Yes.'

'Has he been today?'

Another pause. Yorke was on his feet now. Wendy's rocket-fuel bubbled inside him.

'*Twice.*'

'*Twice?*'

'Yes.'

She gave the times. Over an hour apart. 'Can you watch the CCTV footage of his actions please?'

'We cannot see inside the unit if the door is closed.'

'That's okay. Just tell me what you can see.'

And she did.

Severance drove Salton into the unit and folded the steel door down behind him. When he emerged, CCTV footage showed Salton in the shadows at the back of the unit, propped up in a chair. Severance drove away. When Severance returned over an hour later, he was in a different car. There was someone else unconscious in the chair beside him. Again, he drove in, and when he left, the second man was sitting against the wall at the side.

Yorke had no idea who the second man was, and he knew he didn't really have the time to figure it out.

Salton and this other man were in danger.

He contacted Jake. 'I need you at Unit 42 Salisbury Solutions Storage Facility now. As fast as you can.'

'Why?'

Yorke gave him a brief summary of the information.

After he hung up, he put an alert out on the two vehicles. They had Severance already, but there may have been a possibility of Mayers using one of these vehicles. Automatic Number Plate Recognition might strike gold.

Then, he headed back down to speak to Severance again.

He had a different officer behind him this time. Yorke had insisted the other one was changed for someone more competent.

He stared at Severance long and hard, and didn't speak for a while.

Severance stared back.

'Unit 42 Salisbury Solutions Storage Facility,' Yorke said.

The colour drained from Severance's face.

'What can you tell me about it?'

Severance's lips twitched.

'What will we find there?'

Severance opened his mouth to speak, clearly forgetting, in this moment of surprise, that he no longer possessed this ability.

He reached down for a card and scribbled his answer. *You will be too late.*

Yorke put his phone on the table. 'I wouldn't be so sure.' He folded his arms and sat back in his chair, continuing to stare at Severance.

Yorke may have looked confident, but he felt anything but.

STILL LOCATED at Mayer's house, Jake asked several officers from Armed Response to follow him to the storage facility. He informed them that they were more than likely recovering victims, and that there shouldn't be any threat on site, but it was better to be safe than sorry, or even dead.

He asked Willows to accompany him and explained why. She was pale following the discovery of Neil's decimated body and Susie, drenched in his blood. She'd been rocking back-and-forth in the corner of the cellar, clutching a knife to her chest.

'I can't come to terms with it, sir.'

'Neither can I, and I'm sure Mark won't be able to either, but we need to finish this.'

These words pre-empted a twenty-minute journey of stunned silence in which they contemplated the sudden, unimaginable and violent loss of a loved one.

It was late, and the sky was dark and swollen. The storm was close, but until it came, the high temperature would persist. Jake increased the aircon.

As they turned into Churchfields Industrial Estate, Jake said, 'I know it might seem ridiculous to warn you of this, after what we have just seen, but prepare yourself Collette.

Severance put two people in here remember. Yes, they were still alive when he left them, but I don't buy into the possibility that they'll be fine. He's turned himself in, hasn't he? Salton and this other man are not just sitting in there having a quiet cup of tea.'

A woman stood by an arm barrier in a hi-vis jacket. Jake stopped the car, opened the window and she approached. He showed his badge. 'Detective Sergeant Pettman, ma'am.'

'Sandra North.' She looked and sounded shaken up. She must have been the receptionist who'd viewed the CCTV footage for Yorke. 'As requested, everyone has been exited and no one has been admitted. The facility is empty.'

But it isn't really, is it? Jake thought.

He saw a BMW X5 in his rear mirror. 'Ms North, we have armed officers with us. Please point us in the direction of Unit 42, and then please go and wait inside the office.'

She described the route to him and then headed back inside her office. Moments later, the barrier raised, and Jake gave a thumbs-up to the officers behind him. They started to move into the facility.

'THERE's one thing I still don't quite get,' Yorke said, rotating the mobile phone on the table in front of him. 'Why did you go to all this trouble to heal, and let's be honest, *you've gone to quite some trouble*, only to spend the rest of your life in jail?'

Severance considered for a moment and then wrote a response.

Someone once told me that time was the greatest healer.

But I was never that interested. What is the point of all that time, all that pain, on a promise that one day it will be okay?

'That doesn't really answer my question.'

Severance tried again. He slid his response over.

My time with the Conduit brought relief, escapism, togetherness, growth – all the things, Detective, that you take for granted in your life. Every single minute of my time in the Conduit's care, every single second, I felt healed. The time I have had was worth it.

Yorke smirked. 'You could have summed all that up by saying that you're a rather impatient bastard seeking instant gratification.'

JAKE DIDN'T WANT to delay. Armed Response did. An officer called Friars, who was of a higher rank than Jake, posed an interesting question at the roll-up shutter. 'What if there is a bomb in there?'

'There was nothing on the CCTV footage to suggest that was a possibility, sir.'

'There're ways.' Friars chewed gum. 'Suicide vests?'

Jake looked at him. 'Let me take the chance. Take your officers a suitable distance back, and Willows, too.'

'Sir, I'll stay with you,' Willows said.

He looked apologetically at her. 'That's an order, Collette.'

Friars looked uncertain.

Jake said, 'There are lives in danger, sir ... you saw what was back at the house.'

'That's what I'm worried about.' He nodded and threw

his chewing gum to one side. At that point, there was a low rumble of thunder. They all looked up at the black sky.

'It's going to be one hell of a storm, we could do with getting this wrapped up,' Friars said, looking at Jake. 'Okay, fine, I'll escort your officer back.'

Jake watched Friars escort Willows to the BMW. She climbed in, but Friars didn't. Instead, he got something out of the van. He came running back over with a semi-automatic carbine.

Frustrated, Jake said, 'Christian Severance is in custody. I don't think we're dealing with criminals. Please keep it pointing down, sir.'

'I will, until it needs pointing up, officer.'

They waited until the BMW had reversed to a suitable distance and then Jake rolled up the steel door.

THEY WERE NOW in the interview room with the working aircon, so Yorke used the remote to hike it up. No, he didn't want to make Christian Severance comfortable, but neither did he want to sit in a puddle of his own sweat.

Yorke turned the phone over and looked at the screen as if that would somehow encourage it to ring, while Severance scratched his thigh and sat with a nonchalant expression.

Yorke had never seen a prisoner looking so content. He knew that as time ticked on, he was closer to winning whatever twisted game he was playing.

'Help yourself, Christian. Tell me what is happening inside that storage unit?'

Severance shook his head from side to side.

'Louis Mayers. Where has he gone?'

No response.

Yorke still sweated despite the air conditioning. 'How could you stand by and let him harm innocent people. Neil? Susie? They tell me she's barely coherent. What did he do to her?'

Severance wrote: *abominable things*.

'Precisely. You can sit there and justify Werrell, Simmonds, Long and Salton all you want. In your own twisted way, you can share among them the responsibility for the tragedy of your life, Christian. But what did Susie and Neil ever do to you?'

Nothing. But this was not of my choosing. This was the Conduit's choice. The Conduit's research.

'And now what? Has he done with you?'

Yes, he has learned all he can from me. Now, he must learn from others. We have helped each other. It was symbiotic.

'Learned what? If this adapted version of HASD takes off won't we all be hiding behind locked doors?'

The Conduit never wanted it to become a method of healing. He just wanted to prove its success. He has taken Adam's research to a new level. Now it is up to someone else to find a way to bring it back, effectively, to a clinical setting.

'Christian, I appreciate the trauma that you must have endured, but really? Mayer's work is going with him to a jail cell for the rest of his life. For the rest of all your lives. A good person, one of the very best people, is lying critically ill in hospital. Another good person is broken, potentially beyond repair, because of your research. *Research?* You and Mayers are no different from that doctor in the Auschwitz concentration camp who performed abhorrent human experiments.'

Severance narrowed his eyes.

'They called him the Angel of Death. What do you think they will call Mayers? What do you think they will call you, Christian? You brought silence to all your victims. The Angel of Silence? No, I don't think so. I don't think they'll bother with a name. Hopefully, they will dehumanise you, like you've dehumanised all those people. Maybe you'll be a chapter in a book we can all look back on. Sneer at. A quiet, irrelevant chapter because no one wants to read it, or fathom what you or that other monster were trying to do. You never had anything to say, Christian, not really, not since you lost your tongue, and then your humanity. You'll be lost in silence. Yes ... that's a good name for the chapter.' Yorke nodded. 'The Silence of Severance.'

ANTHONY MORRIS COULD HEAR movement outside. Someone was about to come into the unit. It was no good. He was yet to fulfil the bastard's demands.

Judge Andrew Salton continued to sleep. When he finally woke, when awareness came, Anthony needed to act. He squeezed his eyes closed and snippets of Severance's demands struck him like bullets.

... garden shears ...

... super lightweight, easy to manoeuvre ...

... he must be awake, he must sense everything, like I did ...

... then, do it to yourself ...

... she sleeps while I stroke her hair ...

... you may even hear the snap of her neck, because I'm nearer than you think ...

The shears clung to a huge portion of Salton's tongue. Severance had been right in his claim that they were super lightweight and easy to manoeuvre, but he hadn't factored in Anthony's shaking hands. Blood dripped from Salton's tongue.

The steel door rolled up. Anthony glanced over his shoulder as a large man wearing a suit, flanked by a smaller wiry man pointing a firearm at him. They approached.

JAKE HAD NOT EXPECTED them to be *alive* in here. And, for that, he was thankful. He couldn't be too thankful about other aspects of this situation though. Most notably, trigger-happy Friars lining up a shot on the man holding the garden shears.

'POLICE! PUT THAT DOWN! NOW!' Friars shouted.

Deciding that there was little point discussing the situation with the highly-trained walking weapon beside him, Jake took a step forward. '*DS Pettman, step back, that is an order!*'

Jake held up a hand to Friars, requesting a moment's grace, knowing that this decision, disobeying an order, was probably going to cost him.

The man's sweat-covered face glistened and trembled. Jake could see the tears in his eyes.

'*DS Pettman, I will ask you one last time. FALL BACK.*'

Jake turned his head. 'Can you not see he is acting against his will, sir?'

Friars' nostrils flared. He paused to consider it. 'His hands so much as twitch, I take the shot, understand?'

Jake nodded and turned back.

There must have been some humanity in Friars, Jake

reasoned, because the man's hands were already twitching. It was fortunate Judge Salton slept on, because his tongue was fully extended, and the grip of the shears looked tight. If he was awake, the panic might send him reeling backwards, and that would make a mess.

Jake addressed the man holding the shears. 'We know who the sleeping man in the chair is, but please tell me who you are.'

'I have no choice,' the man said.

'Your name, sir?'

'*He has my daughter.*'

'*Name?*'

'Anthony ... Anthony Morris.'

'Who has your daughter?'

'Christian Severance.'

'No, he doesn't. He is in custody.'

Anthony's eyes widened; then, his face started to soften. Jake felt a sudden rush of optimism. He offered a nod and a smile. Anthony opened his mouth to reply, but then the chair-bound Andrew Salton started to groan.

Anthony looked down at his victim stirring in the chair and readied the sheers. '*No!* You're lying. He left me a message and he's watching. When he wakes, I must do this, and not a moment before.'

Jake took another step forward.

'DS PETTMAN!' Friars shouted.

Jake flinched. 'Listen to me, Anthony, he came into the station a couple of hours ago, after he left you and Judge Salton here. How do you think we know you are here? He confessed.'

Salton moaned again.

Anthony shook his head. 'She's all I have, *everything*. He

257

left me a photo on that phone over there. *He's got her,* and he's watching. That camera in the corner.'

Jake glanced back at the camera. 'Let me see if it is connected.'

'NO! He sees you messing with it, he'll break her neck. He said he would.'

Jake realised that he couldn't guarantee that she wasn't in danger. Mayers could have her for all he knew, but he needed to continue this pretence, or it was going to end badly. 'I guarantee you that he is in custody. Now, *please,* Anthony, you have to trust me, and you have to put that weapon down.'

Anthony looked at the shears in his hands. 'This is the only guarantee I have.'

'Anthony, you must listen. There is an armed officer behind me, not prepared to wait. If Salton wakes up, he will shoot you, and then you will never see your daughter again.'

'At least, she will live.'

'She will live, Anthony, *because* he doesn't have her.'

Then an idea flashed through Jake's mind, but he was low on time. Salton continued to groan. 'Where is your daughter now? We can phone her.'

'Her grandparents. They take care of her, since Maggie, my wife, passed away.'

'*Number?*'

Jake pulled out his phone. He had no reception, but he banged in the number as Anthony said it and then sprinted outside.

'Please, sir,' Jake said, on the way past, 'we can do this properly.'

'Make the call,' Friars said, keeping the gun trained on Anthony, 'that man will be conscious in minutes.'

SEVERANCE WROTE on a card and slid it over to Yorke.

I need the toilet.

'That's fine,' Yorke said, 'but after you leave this room, you are heading back to a cell. We're finished. Next time I see you, you will be in court.'

I understand.

Yorke gestured down at the phone. 'So, you're not interested in the outcome?'

I told you already. It is finished. You cannot stop it.

Yorke stood up and pointed at Severance. 'Don't you be so sure! We've stopped men before you. Men with intentions as cruel and vile as yours.'

I take all the responsibility for stopping myself now, Detective. It is over, and you can rest. Finality fast approaches.

Yorke looked up at the guard. 'I've changed my mind. Take him to the toilet and then bring him straight back afterwards. I want him here when this phone call comes in. I need him to experience failure.'

DROPLETS OF RAIN pounded Jake's face, but that was the least of his problems. He'd been sent through to voicemail twice now. Not wanting to share his anger with the occupants of the unit, he moved away from the roll-up shutters to kick the wall between units.

Then he tried twice more. *Please ... please ... for the love of God.*

No answer.

Okay, one last time, Jake thought, *or we really are fucked...*

Someone answered. 'Hello?'

'Robson Morris?' Jake said, his heart pounding.

'Yes?'

'My name is DS Jake Pettman. There is *no* time. Please answer me this question: *is your granddaughter safe?*'

'Err ... yes ... of course.'

'Thank God, thank God.' Jake started to move back towards the open unit.

'Why? *What is going on?*'

'It'll be fine. I just need to tell your son, Anthony, that you have her and she is safe.'

'*Have her?* Well, I don't actually have her. She's at a friend's at the moment, but she is quite safe, I can assure you.'

Jake's blood froze.

He heard Friar's shout. 'If he opens his eyes again, I will have to shoot. Please put the weapon down!'

We're fucked, Jake thought.

DAVID STURRIDGE YANKED down his trousers and sat on the toilet. Outside his cubicle, he could hear the guard pacing back and forth. Quickly, he rolled back the sleeve on his prison overalls to expose the plaster on his forearm. He brushed his fingers over the wound, feeling the small lump beneath his skin. Then, he peeled back the plaster, and dropped it between his legs into the toilet bowl.

He looked at the five stitches that held his skin closed, drew a deep breath through his nose, and started to unpick.

Once the blood started to flow out of the re-opened wound, and the pain became excruciating, he breathed out. He so desperately wanted to take rapid breaths as the hyperventilation would help with the pain, but the guard would be through the unlocked cubicle door in a second.

The blood was working his way down his arm, over his hands, and dripping onto the floor. He didn't have much time. If the guard didn't hear the steady drip, he would most certainly see the blood snaking out under the door.

Gritting his teeth, he pushed his thumb and forefinger as far into the wound as he could. He needed to get this right first time.

And he did.

His finger and thumb struck home.

YORKE FIDGETED IN HIS CHAIR. *Something wasn't right.*

Jake had still not updated him. Add to that, Severance's sudden need to go to the toilet.

He looked through Severance's cards again. One line jumped out at him.

Finality fast approaches.

Two realisations hit Yorke simultaneously, both with a significant physical impact.

The first realisation, which threw Yorke from his chair at the interview room door, was that all three of them, Sturridge, Chloe and Severance, had suffered a peculiar itch in his presence.

The second realisation, which sent Yorke sprinting down the corridor towards the toilet, was that when Severance offered his 'finality,' he was not referring to the outcome of the Salton situation in that storage unit. He was referring to the end of him.

And, of course, one and one made two. They shared everything. The itch was the doorway to their shared finality.

WHEN THE PRISON GUARD, Lucy Moss, opened the cubicle door, she almost threw up.

On the left side of Chloe Ward's belly button, her stomach was open. Blood bubbled out of the wound, flowed over her pubis and down her legs. Her head was slumped forward, and her long hair formed a curtain that covered her exposed chest. Moss could hear her struggling to breathe.

Had she been stabbed?

But how?

Moss turned full circle. There was no one else in the toilets with them. *But even if there had have been, how would they have got into the cubicle and stabbed Chloe? She had been standing right in front of the fucking cubicle door!*

Herself? Had Chloe stabbed herself? But, again how? There wouldn't have been a knife in those pocketless trousers? And why the fuck had she taken off her shirt?

'HELP! EMERGENCY! PRISONER DOWN!'

She turned and approached Chloe, knowing she had breached the growing puddle of blood, and lifted her prisoner's head. Chloe immediately vomited over Moss' chest.

Moss backed away as Chloe slipped from the toilet bowl into the pool of her own blood and sick, and began to convulse violently.

LIGHTNING FORKED across the sky and several more monstrous drops of rain thumped his forehead, but Jake didn't seek shelter; instead, he stared with horror into the storage facility, waiting for the tragedy to unfold.

Salton was starting to move his body around in the chair, and although his eyes were still closed, he was fast regaining consciousness.

He'd run out of ideas. Yes, he could chance everything. Sprint in, knock a superior officer aside, throw himself at Anthony Morris, hoping he could disarm him before the shears snapped shut.

But what kind of chance was that really?

Salton's eyes snapped open. Cue carnage.

Jake's phone rang. 'NO!' he shouted into the unit. He answered the phone. 'Hello?'

It was a girl's voice. 'Sir?'

'Briony?'

'Yes.'

He dropped the phone to his side. 'ANTHONY. IT'S YOUR DAUGHTER, SAFE AT HER FRIENDS!'

Chair-bound Salton was murmuring, and his eyes were widening.

'ANDREW DO NOT PULL YOUR HEAD BACK!' Jake shouted.

He couldn't go in with the phone as he'd lose reception, so he hit the speakerphone button. *'Tell your father you're safe, Briony, as loud as you can.'*

'DAD, I'M OKAY!'

Thunder rumbled. It sounded like the sky was being split in too. The garden shears hit the floor.

'What's happening?' Salton said, slurring.

Friars lowered the weapon and Salton burst into tears.

'Briony?' He came running out with his hand outstretched for the phone.

Jake handed it over, knelt against the wall between the units, and took some deep breaths. Then, the skies opened. The rain poured.

DURING HIS SPRINT from the interview room, Yorke had made a great deal of commotion, so he wasn't alone when he reached the toilets; although, he was first to fly through the door.

The guard, who stood outside the central cubicle, reeled back in shock when Yorke almost collided with him.

Yorke yanked the cubicle door open.

Severance sat on the toilet with his trousers and under-wear around his ankles, and his fingers buried in his thigh. Without looking up at Yorke, he plucked something from the wound and brought it towards his mouth.

Yorke sprang, clutched Severance's right wrist and slammed his hand into the cubicle wall. Something came loose from Severance's fingers, hit the ground, and rolled off.

After releasing his hand, Yorke backed out of the cubicle. 'Get hold of him and get him some medical attention.'

Obliging officers closed in on the cubicle.

Yorke swooped for the small plastic vile that Severance had dropped. His own clothes were stained with blood; he thought nothing of wiping it clean on his trouser leg. 'White powder. Some kind of poison. Cyanide, potentially. Doesn't look like much, but there could be over 100mg in here, and that would be enough to kill someone.'

He came out the toilets and latched onto two officers in

the corridor. 'I need you to run and contact the prisons where Chloe Ward and David Sturridge are being held. Tell them to suspect a suicide attempt.'

They both started to run, but Yorke knew it would be too late. Severance had looked at the clock on the wall before requesting the toilet. The three of them would have synchronised this suicide attempt. If testing did show it to be cyanide, and the dose was high enough, it could kill in three to five minutes following ingestion.

Tyler ran over, holding out his mobile phone, which he must have grabbed from the interview room. 'It's DS Pettman, sir. He's tried your phone, but you weren't answering.'

He took the phone call, and listened to Jake's good news, and sighed with relief.

As he ended the call, he watched Christian Severance being escorted out by two officers, each clutching an arm.

Severance's trousers and underwear were still around his ankles, inhibiting his movements, so he was being dragged by the officers. Blood was running down his leg from his thigh, but the bleed didn't look serious..

'Cover him up!' Yorke said, raising his voice. 'That is not how we behave in this station.'

Red-faced, one of the officers hoisted up Severance's underwear and trousers. Severance winced as it brushed against his open wound. The trouser leg started to glow red where the material met his thigh.

The officers grabbed his arms again. Yorke approached Severance until he stood in front of him.

'I just took a phone call from my officer at your storage unit.'

Severance looked up at Yorke. His eyes narrowed.

'They are both fine.'

Severance turned his head from side to side.

'You failed, Christian.'

Severance bared his teeth.

'Sir?'

Yorke turned. It was the officer he'd sent to make contact about Chloe and Sturridge. She gave him a sad expression and shook her head. He turned back. 'Your friends succeeded where you have failed. There will be no easy exit for you, Christian, I'm afraid. You told me before that you didn't believe that time was the greatest healer. I really, genuinely hope you are wrong about that because you will be spending a long, long time on suicide watch.'

Severance threw his head back, and started to wail. It was like no sound Yorke had heard before. An unearthly howl which seemed to burn him inside. He backed away as Severance started to fight the grips of the officers holding him.

He watched Severance being dragged away down the corridor, his cry fusing with the unbearable heat in the air, and making Yorke feel as if he'd just stepped into hell.

'Not so silent anymore, are you Christian?' Yorke muttered under his breath, and turned away.

19

I T WAS PAST nine o'clock and the rain was thrashing
down hard. Those brave enough to face the great storm
could be found occupying one of the many 14th century pubs
dotted around the city centre, while most were simply hiding
away at home with their loved ones.

DCI Michael Yorke wasn't doing either of those things
because he was busy banging on DC Wayne Bradley's door.

Bradley opened the door, wearing shorts and a string
vest. There was a cigarette hanging out of his mouth, and a
can of Red Bull in one hand.

Yorke pointed at the can. 'Isn't it a bit late for that?'

'Not like I have to be up in the morning, is it? I'd invite
you in, but I don't want you to wet my carpet.'

Yorke barged past Bradley into his hallway.

'Wow,' Bradley said, 'what happened to polite DCI
Yorke?'

Outside, the sky growled.

Yorke brushed his wet hair back to stop the rain running

into his eyes. 'I'm going to ask you once, and once only, where can I find William Proud?'

'Don't know what you're talking about.' Bradley closed the door.

'*Where is he?*'

Bradley turned around, smiling. 'You just asked me twice.'

'What?'

'You said you were going to ask me where he was once, and then you asked me again.'

Yorke moved in and Bradley grabbed his wrist. Yorke turned his hand over onto the bastard's own wrist and then applied pressure to his elbow with his other hand. Bradley went down onto his knees and the cigarette fell to the floor. Yorke kept the pressure up on his arm and slammed his foot down onto the burning cigarette.

'You are going to break my *fucking* arm,' Bradley said.

'You don't need it. Not like you have to be up in the morning.'

'Smartarse.'

'Let's remember who started it.'

'No more Mr nice guy, eh?'

'*William Proud?*'

'So, I shared this information with Harry, and it's probably cost me my job, and now you want me to share it again. What's my punishment next? Jail time?'

'At least you'll have your arm. Proud murdered my sister, so believe me when I say that I'm serious. Where is he?'

'Harry is pretty determined to finish him off for you, so why are you so desperate to get involved? Seems like an easy win.'

Yorke pressed on the elbow. Bradley groaned.

'Because, unlike you, and him, I'm a police officer. Now, where is Proud?'

'Ever drank Eagleshaw beer?'

'Yes.'

'Shite, isn't it? Proud got the daughter of a brewer pregnant ten years ago. Rufus Eagleshaw. Eagleshaw popped his clogs about five years ago and left the brewery to his daughter, Maria Eagleshaw. She employed some staff, but she managed to run it into the ground. Not sure if it was her fault or the shite beer.'

'Are you telling me that Proud is hiding out in a brewery?'

'Dunno. That's the information I gave Harry. Didn't hear back. If I do hear back from him, there's going to be a serious falling out.'

Yorke released Bradley and he stayed on his knees.

'You do know he's dying, don't you?' Yorke said.

Bradley turned his head to look up at him. 'Aren't we all?'

EAGLESHAW BREWERY WAS LOCATED over thirty minutes away. The journey was treacherous because the windscreen wipers were little match for the sudden downpour. Yorke was surprised when he made it to Amesbury, the town adjacent to Stonehenge, alive.

Throughout the journey, Yorke toyed with the idea of calling Harry. But would he answer? And even if he did, would he really want to have a phone conversation which could be monitored and recorded? Besides, keeping himself alive on a country road in this rainfall was taking enough of his attention.

Streaks of lightning burned the sky, and the thunder roared. His heart was pumping hard. He wondered what he would find when he got to the brewery. Would he be too late? Would Proud be dead, lying at Harry's feet? Or, could it be Harry lying at Proud's feet?

He had no idea, but he did *know* that he had to see this out to the bitter end. Like always. That was him all over. See it out to the bitter end and everything else be damned.

This made him think of Gardner and Danielle. They had both understood his relentless drive, his *need* to finish whatever he'd been motivated to start.

He saw Gardner and Danielle now, side by side, giving him their trademark *knowing* looks as Yorke, both younger and older, tried to pull the wool over their eyes. The football training and the promise he would be back for dinner; the French homework he'd done; his promise that he wasn't going to work late; and his claim that he hadn't touched a cigarette in months.

Gardener was like a sister to him. So, when he received a call from Barry on route, and discovered that she was back in surgery for another round, he hit the dashboard.

He hoped to God that surgery would be a success. Patricia and Gardner were two of the three most special people in his life and they had to remain with him.

The third, Danielle, was gone. He'd never get her back. Proud had seen to that.

Yorke wiped tears from his eyes. She had been like a mother to him: supporting him when he couldn't switch off his relentless engine; cheering him on during his football matches and runs; and bringing food to him when he was consumed by criminal history from the age of sixteen. His mother called this interest an obsession, Danielle had called it a passion.

He looked at the SatNav. In about ten minutes, he could be looking into the eyes of William Proud.

Fuck the rain, he thought, punching the accelerator, driving blind, *fate will get me to that bastard.*

YORKE HAD NOT SEEN another vehicle for a while. The sun had almost completely gone down, so when the forks of lightning came, they momentarily illuminated everything. Large, distant hills seemed to burst from the darkness with every strike.

Yorke turned down a long road that ran through a strip of trees and he could feel the mud and water spraying up from his wheels. He gritted his teeth. Getting stuck now would be a disaster.

Eagleshaw Brewery was housed in an old mill on the bends of the River Avon. Despite being an idyllic setting, which drew tourists and ramblers, it felt anything but idyllic at this late hour. You'd struggle to find a place which felt more isolated and alone.

Through the shimmer of rain, he immediately recognised the large, red-bricked brewery from a tour he went on many years ago, before it closed down. It was a narrow, four-floor building. The ingredients had been hoisted up to the top and the brewing process had worked its way downwards using gravity.

He killed his engine. Only one other vehicle was parked here. A silver Peugeot. Harry's?

Now, that he'd arrived, he appreciated how ridiculous

this all was. The only person who knew he was here was DC Bradley, and he'd not be checking on his safety anytime soon. And even if he survived this sorry situation, breaking and entering this building would end his career.

He thought of Danielle adjusting his tie and kissing his head at the school gates. Danielle with a burned face. Danielle lying dead beside an old stove.

His sister. His mother. His everything.

He gritted his teeth, got out of his car and fought the brutal rainfall on his march towards finality.

YORKE REMEMBERED a side entrance that visitors used when attending tours. The door was unlocked. After he rubbed water from his eyes, he looked around, finding the reception more or less how he remembered it. There was a bar area with three pumps lined up. One for their flagship ale, one for a lager and another for a seasonal brew. Here, tourists were able to sip on a freebie following observations of the brewing process. Bradley had been harsh. The brew had not been that bad.

The bar was heaped with dusty glasses, each sporting the Eagleshaw emblem of crossed hockey sticks. Some glasses had already fallen and smashed.

Yorke gave the bar area a wide berth and entered the ground floor of the brewery, where the packaging took place. The noise of the rain throttling the narrow mill was horrendous, and he could hear little else, making him extremely vulnerable to ambush. Additionally, there was no internal lighting. All Yorke had was the fading red twilight which crept in through the edges around doors and shutters. He had to be careful not to trip.

He manoeuvred around the kegs strewn on the floor, and past the huge doors which had allowed vans to drive in to collect the ale. For the tours, there had been a set of stairs running around the perimeter of the factory, but Yorke had no time to use these now. He took the route of the brewers up the ladder in the centre.

He thought he could hear loud voices upstairs from higher in the mill but couldn't be too sure over the turbulent sounds of the storm.

Out of breath from running and from scaling the ladder in the humidity, he paused on the second floor and leaned against a fermentation tank. The sudden reek was like a smelling salt, and when Yorke distinctly heard a 'FUCK YOU, PROUD!' from upstairs, he rode a sudden burst of adrenaline, and scaled the next ladder. Fighting the fatigue in his arms and legs from the rapid climb, he left the final floor, littered with vats for mashing grain and boiling hops and wort, and climbed up into the milling room.

The milling room was smaller than the other floors. It was also at the top of the building, so water was finding its way in through the aging roof. It streamed down the walls at the side, and large pools were gathered almost everywhere Yorke looked. He came off the ladder beside a large electric-powered milling machine for grain, and ran, weaving around some older and smaller hand-operated milling machines.

Beside the larger double door, where the ingredients were hoisted in during its operational days, Harry and another man were wrestling on the floor.

'STOP! POLICE!'

It had little effect. They continued to roll. Yorke moved closer and his breath caught in his throat.

They were grappling for a knife.

For God's sake, Harry, you couldn't even get this right.

'DROP THE KNIFE NOW, OR I WILL SHOOT!'

It seemed to work. With their hands locked around the weapon, they both looked up at Yorke...

It *was* William Proud. Older with a grey beard, and a shaven head, but William Proud nonetheless. Yorke felt his heart smashing into his ribcage.

Not now, Yorke thought, *no emotion. Be cold. In control.*

'There's no fucking gun,' Proud said.

Yorke reached to his side and scooped up a handful of grain from one of the smaller mill machines and launched it at the two men. Both reached up to protect their eyes, partly relinquishing their grip on the knife. Sensing the advantage, Yorke did it again. Each time he hurled the grain, he moved closer. Both men were sliding away from him now, shielding their eyes, with the knife sandwiched between them.

Yorke considered diving for it, but Proud turned onto his front, so the grain was no longer hitting him in the face. This gave his sister's killer the advantage he needed to pry the knife from Harry's hand.

'NO!' Yorke dived towards Harry, but he was too late.

Proud buried the blade into Harry's stomach. He then scurried away.

Harry was gasping. His hands were on the handle of the knife.

'Don't pull it out. Don't even move. I'll get help,' Yorke said. From the corner of his eye, he could see Proud clambering to his feet.

Harry gasped again. Blood was billowing out over his shirt. 'Just stop him =...'

Proud was running past. Yorke threw out his hand and brought the killer crashing to the ground.

Yorke rose from Harry and turned to stand over Proud. 'DO YOU KNOW WHO I AM?'

Proud turned onto his back and looked up at him. He had blood all over his face. 'Yes – the copper with a dead sister.'

'Stand up.'

'Why?'

'STAND UP!'

Proud rose to his feet, out-of-breath. He touched his forehead, and then looked at the blood on his fingers. 'Police brutality?'

Yorke stepped forward and punched him in the face. His head rebounded off a milling machine. He stood, clutching his face while Yorke circled him. 'You are a killer.'

'Wake up, pig.' Proud took his hands down and stared at Yorke. 'I'm just the blunt instrument.'

'What the hell are you talking about?' Yorke clenched his fists, preparing to go in again.

'The blunt instrument? I ask no questions. I do what I'm told. Get it?'

Yorke shook his head and kept coming. 'You're lying.'

'Look at your own, pig. There's a bent bastard shitting in the same toilet as you.'

'Who then? Tell me who?'

Taking a lesson from Yorke's earlier attack, Proud swooped a handful of grain from the milling machine and launched it. Yorke managed to close his eyes in time, but it allowed Proud the opportunity to turn and run towards the ladder.

Yorke gave chase and was relieved to see Proud slip through a puddle of water and tumble. By the time Yorke had reached him, he was back on his feet and held his palms out in surrender. 'Okay, you win. What do you want?'

'I want to know who this bent copper is.'

'What's it worth?'

Yorke took a step towards him. 'Your life?'

Proud took a step back with his palms still out. 'Immunity.'

'Tell me, and I'll get you whatever you want,' Yorke lied, taking another step.

'Okay, I'll tell you, but you need to back the fuck away from me.'

'TELL ME!' Yorke moved forward.

It was a mistake. Proud took another step back and disappeared down the ladder shaft.

'Shit, shit...' Yorke looked down the shaft at the crumpled mess. He climbed down and turned over his sister's killer. Proud's eyes were wide and unflinching.

He heard Harry's moans from upstairs. Leaving the body, he bolted back up the steps and sprinted back to his old friend, taking care not to slip in the puddle that had undone Proud.

He kneeled beside him. 'Why the hell did you come here, Harry?'

Harry grabbed Yorke's hand, widened his eyes, and spat out the words, 'For you ... for my friend.'

Yorke shook his head. 'You framed an innocent man, Harry.'

'I had no choice.'

'Everyone has a choice.'

'No ... You don't understand ... I was told ... I was given no choice ... They said that if I didn't do it...'

Harry's eyes were closed. Yorke slapped his face a few times, bringing him round. 'Stay with me, stay with me...'

'I did it for you ... If I didn't ... if I didn't...'

Yorke slapped him again. He was pale now and his eyelids fluttering. His shirt was drenched in blood. It was coming to an end.

'Don't trust them...' Harry said. 'They wanted Proud protected. If I didn't, they said they'd kill me ... and they'd kill you.'

'Who?'

Harry reached up and placed the palm of his hand on Yorke's face. He tried to speak, but his words sounded now like incomprehensible hisses. His eyes were locked onto Yorke.

His best friend's eyes.

And they stayed locked on after his life had departed.

Yorke kissed his friend's hand, rose to his feet, turned around and choked back tears.

20

THE RAINFALL HAD been sudden and intense but, as so often is the case with these summer storms, brief.

Yorke stood in the light rain watching the police cars assemble outside the mill. This didn't surprise him. Neither did the sudden appearance of Superintendent Joan Madden striding towards him. What did surprise him though was the presence of DC Parkinson in that small group of officers accompanying her.

Was Madden deliberately trying to antagonise him?

It was dark now, and several of the police lights flashed.

Madden was in her gym outfit. Yorke knew that pulling her away from the workouts she lived for wasn't going to stand him in good stead. At least Parkinson hung back with two other officers. The last thing he needed was him getting within spitting distance.

'Detective Chief Inspector, this was a road I warned you not to travel down.' She looked off into the distance and sighed.

'I know, ma'am.'

'But your reasons were personal?'

'Yes, ma'am, unfortunately, they were.'

'There will be costs, you know.'

'I'm fully aware of that, ma'am. There are always costs.'

She turned around and looked at the river Avon, shimmering under the beat of police lights.

'Always loved rivers, Michael. You know where you are at with a river. They always flow one way.'

'Yes ma'am.'

'What are we going to find in there, Michael?

'Harry Butler and William Proud.'

'Dead?'

'I'm afraid so.'

She sighed again. 'Best take a look. I trust you won't go anywhere?'

'You know I won't, ma'am.'

'Well done on today. You saved lives. *Again.*'

'It wasn't just me.'

'Goddamn it, Michael! You are my best.'

'Sorry, ma'am.'

'Don't move, you don't deserve to be hauled in.'

Madden waved a couple of officers over and they made their way to the brewery.

Parkinson remained with another couple of officers. He looked over and sneered. When Madden was out of ear shot, he shouted over. 'Always knew you liked beer, sir, but this is ridiculous.'

The group sniggered. Yorke turned his back. They had him vulnerable. They'd better hope it lasted.

He stared at the red-brick brewery, thinking about Harry.

His final words. His claim that he'd never actually betrayed their friendship. That he'd been protecting him.

Was this true?

And if it was true, it meant that he'd spent all these years rejecting one of his closest friends. Someone he'd admired and depended on. Someone he'd loved like a brother.

Both had implied corruption in the police force. Proud more explicitly: *bent copper.* Harry by saying that the police had wanted Proud protected. *Why?*

He thought of Proud's dead eyes staring up at him. The death of the man who'd torn Yorke's world apart. How did he feel about that?

The answer was that he didn't really know. For so long, he'd craved justice, and now that he had it, although not in the way that he'd ever envisaged, it didn't offer any peace.

Was that because it didn't feel over?

Bent copper ... they'd wanted Proud protected ...

Or was it because of the old cliché that justice would not bring someone back. Danielle, his sister, his mother, the only person who'd really loved him before Patricia, was never coming back.

His phone rang. He looked at the screen, it was Patricia's mother, Jeanette.

'Do not answer the phone, sir,' Parkinson said. He could not hide the glee in his voice at being able to order him around.

Yorke ignored him and answered the phone. 'Hello.'

'Michael?'

'Yes, Jeannette, it's me. Sorry, it's not a good time.'

'They've rushed Patricia to the hospital.'

'*Why?*'

'Blood, Michael. I'm sorry, she started—'

Yorke didn't hear the next part because the phone was snatched from his hand.

Yorke turned, stabbing his hand out to snatch it back, but Parkinson had already taken several steps back, wearing his now trademark smug grin. 'Sir, I asked you not to answer your phone.'

'Give me my phone back now, Parkinson!'

The officers around Parkinson took steps back.

'Looks a bit like my phone. The one you threw out the fucking window, sir. Might just hold on—'

Fists clenched, Yorke charged. Parkinson's smile fell away, but he was happy to meet Yorke head-on. With arms looped around each other, they crashed to the muddy ground.

Jeanette's words crashed through his head as he rolled with Parkinson.

Rushed ... hospital ... blood ...

He managed to work himself up Parkinson and straddled him.

What was happening to Patricia?

He slammed his fist into Parkinson's face.

Was she having a miscarriage?

He managed to drive his other fist home, before his arms were seized, and he was hoisted away.

Was her life in danger?

'LET ME GO!'

Two officers held him by the arms. He writhed, but they stood their ground.

'I ORDER YOU TO GET YOUR HANDS OFF ME!'

He watched Parkinson scurry backwards, clutching his nose. 'You broke my fucking nose.'

Yorke was taken to the ground by the two officers.

'CALL MY WIFE. PATRICIA. SHE'S IN TROUBLE.'

He was pinned to the floor. His arms were pulled behind his back. And he was cuffed.

EPILOGUE

YORKE RAN LIKE his life depended on it. He glanced at his sports watch and saw that he was clocking up six-minute miles. His lungs burned and his mouth was like sandpaper. He sucked on the tube running from his Camelbak, seeking out one friendly drop, having finished it off a mile back; and then cursed himself, again, for forgetting to refill it from yesterday's run.

It was the hottest part of the afternoon, during one of the hottest summers on record, he should probably call it a day.

He didn't.

As he ran, he thought of Danielle, Gardner, Patricia, Harry and Topham. He thought of them in no particular order, but cycled through them, again and again. For each person, he considered ways he could have avoided what came to pass.

If he had been less focused on himself, and his career, could he have been there for Danielle in those darkest months? The months when Tom Davies, and then, William Proud, became entangled in her life?

283

He pounded along Odstock Road. A driver honked. Seeing him sprint in record temperatures, spraying out a trail of sweat, either spoke to this driver of determination or - as was most likely the case - madness.

If he had been less distracted by Harry and his desperate need to atone, would he have been focused enough to spot the Robert Webster connection earlier? To get to the Conduit before he had Susie kill Topham's partner, Neil?

When he felt like he had nothing left, and his body told him, adamantly, to stop, he speeded up. A couple stood and stared at a man who now gulped for air like a drowning man breaking the surface.

And Harry? His best friend for so long. His enemy for many years. Innocent? He treated Harry like shit, when really, he'd had his back. And what had happened there? Was his sister's death really connected to the people he was working for?

He shot past another cluster of people, wondering if they would be able to see the tears in his eyes, or whether they would just assume he was sweating profusely.

If he had said 'no' to his job, if he had gone on his honeymoon with Patricia, would she be well now? Had the realisation of what she'd committed herself to finally struck home?

He stopped, placed his hands on a railing, and hunched over, gagging. Unbelievably, he held the vomit in, but it took him a while to catch his breath. Then, he looked up at the hospital.

Gardner.

If he'd stopped Chloe Ward in that school corridor, as he should have done, would Gardner be sitting at home right now?

Topham looked at the empty bottle of beer in his hand, put it on the coffee table, and went to the fridge to grab another. What he really wanted was Scotch, but he'd deliberately not bought any, opting for beer instead.

There was only one place a bottle of Scotch could take you.

After sitting down, he reached over and stroked the empty seat on the sofa. Then, he picked up the T-shirt that Neil always wore to bed. It read 'Pink Freud' and had a picture of the famous doctor himself, shaded pink.

A birthday present from Topham, and one he wore to bed most nights. He took the T-shirt to his mouth and breathed deeply, managing to catch his scent.

He picked up his phone and called Neil's personal number again.

'Hi this is Neil. I'm busy uncluttering either my mind or someone else's, so if you please leave a message.'

Topham hung up, drank his beer and cried.

Dr Martin Adams knew he shouldn't be here, not while him, and his entire project was under investigation, but he just needed to know that what they were saying was true.

Dr Paul Walsh and he went back a long way. He'd accommodate him for a few minutes. To observe of course. There could be no communication with his patient.

However, when Adams was led to the one-way window, to see her, he realised that communication would have been difficult, if not impossible anyway.

In light-blue scrubs, Susie Long sat by a window looking out over the hospital gardens. Her hair was tied back into a tight bun, and Adams observed, although he hoped that this was a trick of the light, that she was going grey. She simply sat there and stared, rocking back and forth so gently that it took a few seconds of scrutiny to pick up on it.

'The drugs?' Adams looked at Walsh.

'I'm afraid so.'

'I hate the drugs.'

'I know you do, Martin, but without them she is prone to moments of extreme mania. It's for everyone's safety.'

'And hers?'

'Yes, of course.'

'The bastard,' Adams said. 'What has he done to her?'

'He's reprogrammed her somehow.'

'Impossible in such a short space of time.'

'Yes, but there it is.'

Adams pulled his glasses off to clean them with his sleeve. 'And they are saying that he used HASD to do this?'

'A version of.'

'Bullshit!'

Walsh shrugged. 'As I said, there it is.'

Adams looked back at Susie, who had turned her head from the window to stare at the glass which they stood behind.

Her eyes were glazed, and she drooled.

'He used my research to do this,' Adams said. 'And now what? Where the fuck has he gone?'

Georgia Sharpe was under pressure.

She scoured the library shelves for a book that would bail her out. Preparing an essay on Margaret Floy Washburn, the first female psychologist to be granted a PhD in 1894, was no easy feat, especially with one day to go. Armed with books on animal behaviour, which covered Washburn's theories in depth, she headed over to a table.

Trying to push aside the turbulent experiences of the last week, experiences which had made her very late in preparing her essay, she started to research.

But it didn't take long before her mind returned to her boyfriend's infidelity and the best friend who'd betrayed her. No doubt, the images that flooded her mind were far more graphic than the actual reality – she hoped – but it offered no comfort. She started to cry.

'It was an era dominated by the study of rats,' a man said, suddenly standing at the opposite side of the table. 'So, she ripped up the rule book and observed over 100 species. Bees, elephants, snails, you name it. She *even* had an entire chapter on the amoeba.'

Georgia looked up at a burly, older man wearing a cap, shorts and a T-shirt.

'May I?' He said, pointing down at a chair.

She nodded and pointed at her tears. 'Sorry, it's been a tough week.'

'I can see. And you have an essay due in?'

'Yes, tomorrow.'

The man smiled. 'I'm Dr Franks. I do some part-time lecturing at the University, and I've got some time to kill. Need some help?'

'Are you sure?'

'Of course. Pen, my dear?'

'Here,' she said.

'Washburn was ground-breaking in that she suggested animal psyches contained mental structures similar to that of humans.'

Georgia made notes and then looked up. 'Which led her to claim that animal consciousness is not so different from human mental life.'

'Exactly,' Franks said. He reached up to his top lip. He opened his thumb and forefinger there as if he was stroking a moustache.

'Not so good for us vegetarians,' she said, smiling.

'Indeed,' he said. 'Now, before I go on, young lady, why don't you tell me what you already know? It is clearly more than I first anticipated!'

'Are you sure you have time?'

'Of course. This is what I love to do most. Help people. Think of me as a conduit young lady, use me to help guide forth that information...'

IT HAD BEEN one argument too many. And, two hours later, it had been one pint too many. So, on this Saturday afternoon, Jake staggered home through Salisbury.

Fortunately, his battery had packed in on his mobile thirty minutes before, ending the raging text war with Sheila while he'd guzzled Summer Lightning alone.

After the last pint, he'd come to his senses. Arguments with Sheila were common. Far too common, admittedly, but part of the norm now. Saturdays away from his beloved son, Frank, weren't. He'd grin and bear it, accept he was wrong, *even though he felt anything but wrong*, and finish the day off with his son, pending a strong cup of coffee.

But before he knew it, he was taking a different route home.

He wanted to tell himself that he'd not consciously made this decision, but he clearly had. Only moments ago, he'd been thinking about the first futile raid on Mayer's house, and how close it was to where he currently walked. Now, he was walking down the actual road, and it certainly wasn't to visit Mayer's empty house, which was currently sealed off with police tape.

When he found the house he was looking for, he considered turning back. He *knew* he didn't want to turn back, but that wasn't the point. He simply knew he *should* turn back.

After several minutes of fighting against the reckless nature of his drunken self, he decided to give it a miss, and started to turn, but then the front door opened. He turned back.

Caroline smiled. 'Have you come for that glass of water then?'

Jake nodded and headed down the path.

GARDNER WOKE to find Yorke holding her hand. He had his eyes closed.

She squeezed his hand. 'Oi! Is this what being out of work does to you? Turns you into a layabout?'

Yorke opened his eyes and smiled. 'Just catching a moment. Hit it quite hard out there today.'

'I can tell!'

Yorke leaned back in the chair and looked down at himself, clearly noticing his running vest and shorts were soaked. 'I must look some sight.'

Gardner laughed, coughed and then winced.

'You need me to get someone?' Yorke said.

'No, leave it. It's just the meds wearing off. They'll be round with some more after visiting hours. If I start asking for it, they'll think I'm not ready to leave.'

'And are you?'

Gardner looked around the hospital room. 'Not the Hilton, is it?'

'That's not what I asked.'

'I'm ready to leave.'

'To leave, and then *go* on sick leave?' Yorke raised an eyebrow.

'I don't think I'll have a choice, do you? Can't see me putting up with Jake's bad jokes with a minced lung? And you, what about you?'

'What about me?'

'How are you holding up?'

Yorke shrugged. 'Just thinking about all the fun, me and you are going to have while watching daytime television over the next couple of months.'

'Bollocks to that,' Gardner said. 'I'm going to write a book or something.'

'Steamy romance?'

'You really have hit it hard today, haven't you? Crime probably.'

'Bloody hell, you don't get enough of it day-to-day! Well, leave me out of this project, you don't want this miserable old bastard irritating your fanbase.'

'I don't know, Mike.' She grinned. 'You have your qualities.'

Yorke smiled back and she squeezed his hand.

'The Conduit?' Gardner said.

'Last time I spoke to Jake,' Yorke said, 'they were none the wiser. But we'll find him ... sorry ... they'll find him.'

'Enough of that! You've got bigger things to think about right now? Like Beatrice? You got more of those photos you promised me?'

'Well, I couldn't bring them out with me now, so I'll drive by and show you them tomorrow.'

'Won't be long now, will it?'

'She'll be out of the incubator in a couple of days.'

'And then you'll take her home to see that lovely new bedroom you've decorated for her?'

'Well ... first things first.'

Gardner flashed him a confused look.

'First, I'll be taking her on that that long walk from one side of the hospital to the other so she can meet her Auntie Emma.'

Yorke watched Gardner's eyes fill with tears, and then failed to hold back his own.

RISE OF THE RAYS

AN EXCLUSIVE EXTRACT OF THE NEXT DCI YORKE THRILLER

1918

THE PIGS WERE quiet this evening.

Unusually so.

The circling raven welcomed it. Not because this farm was its destination. Pigs weren't its thing. Instead, this breed of killer was targeting a neighbouring yard where it could feed on the eyes and tongues of new-born lambs. However, quiet pigs provided silence on its approach, and the raven enjoyed its advantage.

Below, on the pig farm, another breed of killer welcomed the silence.

This breed came in a pack. Six in total. Each of them driven by the same reason to kill. Not for food, like the bird above, but for vengeance.

It was past midnight and the pack weaved through the pig pens towards the rear of the farmhouse.

The pigs remained still.

These animals had been the most critical part of the

plan. The noise these beasts made, especially when disturbed in this manner, could raise the dead and would almost certainly bring out the mad farmer. He was rumoured to possess a Pattern 1913 Enfield rifle. Although they could probably have taken him with their Webley Pistols, souvenirs from the Royal Navy; they did not want to risk any loss of life.

So, despite these men's great loss, which was torturous, and nagged at them constantly for a rash response, they'd been patient. Over several clandestine meetings, they'd formulated a plan. The pigs had been drugged by a man who had been working on the farm for the past few months. It hadn't taken a king's ransom to convince him. The man had seen 'depraved acts,' referred to his employer as a 'vile individual,' and had considered it his 'solemn duty as a god-fearing man' to assist in the plot against him.

One soldier pointed overhead at the raven. It circled and drew dark veins on the full moon.

'Bad luck,' one whispered.

'In twos or threes, maybe. There's just one,' another hissed.

'Even so, whose bad luck? I think the luck of the bastard farmer has just run out.'

The pack of wronged soldiers came in their uniforms. They were proud of their achievements. They'd fought for King and Country. *Won* for King and Country.

The least they could expect was a welcome return. One full of happiness and love.

Into the arms of their families. Except...

There was a problem. The pig farmer had taken their children.

***

2015

PAUL SAW THAT there was no reception on his mobile phone and shivered.

But really? What had he expected? The middle-of-nowhere had always been very good at cutting off contact from the outside world.

Acknowledging his foolish actions, he glanced back at his mother's vehicle; illegally driven here because he was only sixteen and had no driving licence. He'd parked it alongside several gnarled trees.

A branch curled out the largest tree like a finger beckoning to him. He struggled to tear his eyes from it. It was a significant branch on a significant tree. Dripping with history.

This was why he came here. For history. *His* history.

He turned back to the farmyard. It was a cold night, but not a wet one, and the skies were clear. A large black bird rose and fell above him, etching inky black lines into the full moon.

He began his journey into the eighty-eight-acre farm questioning the wisdom of this impulsive trip. The grass came up to his knees, and shrubbery clawed at him, but despite the explosion of life that nature brought, the place itself felt long dead.

Fences that used to house the pigs lay broken and smashed. Barns looked decrepit, and the farm house that he now drew nearer to looked skeletal. Parts of the roof had fallen away, and ivy had torn through the walls.

Maybe that was all he needed? Knowledge that the place had fallen. That it was all over. That the Rays were no more?

So, why was he still going? Why had he not turned for the car?

Probably, because it wasn't strictly true, was it? The Rays were still here.

He was a Ray.

Not his mother. No. She'd had a lot of misfortune in her life, but that wasn't part of it; she'd only married into the diseased line and adopted the name. So, he was, potentially, the last of the Rays – depending on whether his aunt, Lacey Ray, was still alive. *And*, he thought, *it would probably be better if she wasn't.*

As he neared the farmhouse, he started to sweat despite the cold. The weight in his left hand was becoming a real burden.

He stopped metres from the farmhouse, he closed his eyes and pictured that young nurse broken and bloody on the pathway, riddled with pellets. He turned and looked at the old barn to his left. The murderer, Thomas Ray, had been found dead and mutilated in there years later.

He wasn't at all surprised that this place had been a thorn in the council's side for so long now. This place would never be bought. These may be less religious and superstitious times, but the things that happened here? Could anyone really deny the existence of evil?

He took a deep breath and looked up at the circling black bird.

Now the last of the Rays was back. Back in *this* blood-drenched hell hole.

He marched down the pathway lugging the plastic fuel can.

***

1918

THE PACK OF wronged soldiers made their move.

Frank, the older of the soldiers, and most natural leader among them, grabbed the farmer while he slept.

***

Pre-order *Rise of the Rays* today on AMAZON

ALSO BY WES MARKIN

A LESSON IN CRIME

A DCI Michael Yorke Thriller

Your student years should be the most carefree years of your life.

Not for Michael Yorke.

When a student party ends in violent murder, Michael Yorke begins to realise he harbours a fascination with crime which goes way beyond the norm.

Driven to discover the truth behind a series of murders which shocks the university community, Yorke turns his back on those closest to him: his girlfriend, Charlotte, and his best friend, Brandon.

With bloody and disastrous consequences

A super-fast one-hour thrill ride, which will define the relentless and compassionate police officer who stars in One Last Prayer for the Rays

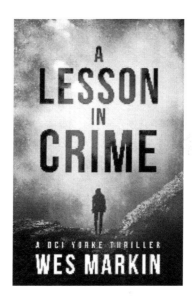

Sign-up here to receive the book for FREE!

https://mailchi.mp/0666fd5c1323/wesmarkin

Plus, get lots more exclusive content for a deeper look into Yorke's world.

ALSO BY WES MARKIN

ONE LAST PRAYER FOR THE RAYS

"An explosive and visceral debut with the most terrifying of killers. Wes Markin is a new name to watch out for in crime fiction, and I can't wait to see more of Detective Yorke." *– Bestselling Crime Author Stephen Booth*

School should be the safest place in the world. Not this winter.

DCI Michael Yorke faces his most harrowing case yet.

When 12-year-old Paul disappears from school, Yorke's only clue is a pool of animal blood. Fearing the worst, he turns toward the most obvious suspect, recently released local murderer, Thomas Ray.

But as the snow in Salisbury worsens, Ray's mutilated body is discovered, and Yorke is left with no choice but to journey into the sinister heart of a demented family that has plagued the community for generations. Can he save the boy? Or will the evil he discovers change him forever?

The shocking and exhilarating new crime thriller will have you turning the pages late into the night.

"A pool of blood, an abduction, swirling blizzards, a haunting mystery, yes, Wes Markin's One Last Prayer for the Rays has all the makings of an absorbing thriller. I recommend that you give it a go." *– Alan Gibbons, Bestselling Author*

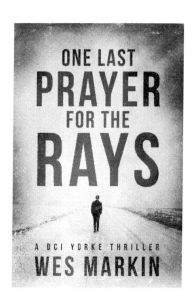

Click **HERE** to get your FREE copy now

https://mailchi.mp/0666fd5c1323/wesmarkin

ALSO BY WES MARKIN

THE REPENTING SERPENT

A DCI Michael Yorke Thriller

A vicious serial killer slithers from the darkness, determined to resurrect the ways of a long-dead civilisation.

When the ex-wife of one of DCI Michael Yorke's closest allies is left mutilated and murdered, Yorke and his team embark on their greatest test yet. A deeply personal case that will push them to their very limits.

And as Yorke's team are pulled further into the dark, the killer circles, preparing to strike again.

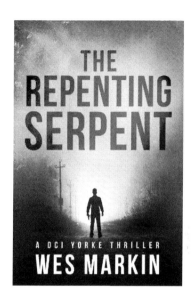

**The Repenting Serpent is a true edge-of-the-seat,
nail-biting page turner**.

Buy it now HERE

ACKNOWLEDGMENTS

As always, massive thanks must go to Jake Lynn. An unstoppable machine, who knows an unbelievable amount. Whenever I'm flagging, he keeps me going with words of motivation. Thanks again to Debbie at *The Cover Collection*, who really has found a unique style for the Yorke covers. Thank you to all my Beta Readers who took the time to read early drafts and offer valuable feedback. Huge appreciation goes to Jenny Cook and Jo Fletcher for their savage – but necessary – final edits. Thank you to the magnificent Eileen and Ian for their endless support during these busy times. Also, thank you to my little people, Bea and Hugo, who keep me laughing throughout the whole process.

Lastly, thank you to every reader, and every wonderful blogger, who continue to read my fiction. I hope *Severance* entertained, and I hope you are all as excited about *Rise of the Rays* as I am...

ABOUT THE AUTHOR

Wes Markin is a hyperactive English teacher, who loves
writing crime fiction with a twist of the macabre.
Born in 1978, Wes grew up in Manchester, UK. After
graduating from Leeds University, he spent fifteen years as a
teacher of English, and has taught in Thailand, Malaysia and
China. Now as a teacher, writer, husband and father, he is
currently living in Harrogate, UK.

STAY IN TOUCH

To keep up-to-date with new publications, tours and promotions, or if you are interested in being a beta reader for future novels, or having the opportunity to enjoy pre-release copies please follow me:

Website: https://wesmarkinbooks.weebly.com/
Twitter: @MarkinWes
Facebook: @WesMarkinAuthor

REVIEW

Without a huge marketing budget, it is difficult for indie authors to compete with the big publishing houses, no matter how worthy our books are. But what we do have is an army of loyal fans and readers, and it is with your help we can continue writing and publishing books for you to read. So, if you enjoyed reading **_The Silence of Severance_** please take a few moments to leave a review or rating on Amazon or Goodreads.

Printed in Great Britain
by Amazon